WHEN THEY WERE BAD

Maria Hoey

For my sister, Deborah, who is stronger and more beautiful than she knows.

CHAPTER 1

Monday 13th February

Detective Sergeant Tina Bassett was having a bad day, and it wasn't quite 10am. It had begun with the sting of cystitis and continued with shampoo in her eye. Then came the phone call, followed by a dash to the hospital through heavy rain and heavier traffic. It was just too much, Tina decided, for a Monday. The sort of grim Monday only an Irish February can produce, freezing rain falling on a world that seemed shrunken beneath a glum sky. And then the final insult; an overheard remark as a gust of wind propelled her through the doors of the station's front office. She was not looking where she was going, too busy shaking rain from her hair. Too busy growling into her phone that no, ten thirty this morning did not suit for an appointment with her GP. She had a team meeting in five minutes that would go on until at least eleven. But yes, she supposed tomorrow afternoon would have to do. Great, thought Tina, ending the call, so a whole day of perpetual peeing to look forward to, that and resisting the urge to scratch her crotch. Plus, her eye was still smarting. Next thing she had cannoned into two uniforms and trod on one of their feet, she wasn't sure whose. She was on the verge of apologising, but they were already halfway through the door. That was when one of them made the remark, which another burst of wind carried back to her like a slap about the ears.

"What's eating the hound this morning?"

The answering laugh came back too, and Tina blinked as she always did. Not in surprise, the stupid nickname didn't come as news to her, half the station had them. But that didn't stop the dart of paranoia every time she overheard it used.

"It's because of your surname. You do know that, right?"

So said her best friend Carol, when, tired, emotional, and drunk one night, Tina had confided her worst suspicions. But she and Carol had been friends since their first day at school as five-year olds, so she would say that, wouldn't she? Seeing the doubt in Tina's eyes, Carol had her head in disbelief.

"Oh, come on Tina, you cannot seriously believe it's because you actually look like a dog?"

And of course, she didn't, not really. But that hadn't stopped her googling images of basset hounds all the same. Nice dogs in fairness to them – those big soulful brown eyes, the dark red markings on the long droopy ears. Nice dogs, but you didn't want to look like one.

Tina had light brown eyes, but you couldn't call them big. She had dark red hair too. Nice hair, people always said so. *Nice hair, shame about the face*. Peter Ward, who had lived on the same road as Tina, had said that to her when she was fourteen. But Peter Ward had had a limited imagination, all his insults were mere variations on a theme – *nice legs, shame about the face, nice boobs, shame about the ...*

Bassets are single-minded, and once having caught an interesting scent, may try to follow it, no matter how much danger it poses to them. Which actually pretty much summed up Tina's attitude to the job. In fact, it was probably one of the reasons she'd made Detective Sergeant two years ago at the age of thirty-two. *The Basset Hound is a short, relatively heavy dog, in fact they are essentially big dogs on short legs. The dog's hindquarters are very full and round.* Which, Tina had to admit, was what she was essentially - a short girl with a big arse. Just as well the force had replaced the height requirement with a physical competence test. *Adapts well to apartment living.* Actually, Tina would much prefer to own a house, with a garden. But small chance of that with Dublin property prices at escape velocity levels. *Tolerates being alone.* Sure, she tolerated it. She didn't like it a whole lot, but she tolerated it. *Potential for weight gain...*

Tina had stopped reading at that point. She was known as the Hound on account of her surname. Of course, she was, just as DI Coleman was Mustard, Detective Garda Con Kearney was Chilli and DS Alan Patterson, because there wasn't anything he wouldn't eat, was known as the Gannett. And then there was Tina's partner, Detective Garda JP O'Rourke whom the lads had christened Marbles, because he spoke like he had a mouth full of them. Not that it stopped anyone, including Tina from liking JP. Yes, Carol was right, she told herself.

"It's because of your surname and the way you do your job," Carol had assured her. "And to be honest, in your line of work, I'd have thought being known as a hound was a bit of a compliment."

But right now, on this miserable morning, after where she'd just been, it didn't feel like a compliment. It wasn't even as though it had been her first time seeing someone who'd recently attempted to slit their wrists. But it was the first time with someone she had come to know, someone she had made a promise to, made a very stupid promise to.

Orla Reid had downed a bottle of vodka before slicing into her wrists, not horizontally, but vertically like she'd really meant it. Any wishful thoughts Tina had been harbouring about it being 'a cry for help' had evaporated as soon as Orla, met Tina's eyes over the edge of the white hospital sheet.

"I couldn't even do this right," she had whispered. Her tone held neither self-pity nor despair it seemed to Tina. Like her eyes, there was simply an emptiness there.

Just for a moment, Tina had thought about telling Orla that she shouldn't feel too bad on that account. Few people actually managed to slit their wrists 'right', ending up just as Orla had, in a hospital bed, arms stitched up and bandaged. People didn't seem to realise that there was a lot of stuff you had to get through, if you wanted to kill yourself in that particular manner. Stuff like fat cells and tendons and muscles. A lot of people didn't even get as far as Orla, who had actually passed out. That alone would have taken at least ten minutes; Tina imagined it would have been a long ten minutes. Orla's heart rate would have slowed, as would her blood loss. Slowed enough in Orla's case that the wounds would have begun to clot. If her sister hadn't arrived at the family home when she did, hadn't tapped on the bathroom door to check on her, Orla might have died. But she could just as easily have woken up with a bad headache and a case of the cold sweats and started vomiting her guts up. However, Debbie had arrived and as a result, Orla was still here, face grey, eyes empty.

And that morning she had turned those eyes on Tina, pleading, "Please don't ask me why I did it."

"I wasn't going to," Tina had lied.

"Why not, everyone else has. They all want to know why. But why should I have to explain? They know what he did to me."

"Perhaps it's just their way of trying to help you," said Tina. "Maybe they're trying to understand what you were feeling when you…when you did this. And it's only because they care about…"

"No, they're angry with me," Orla cut across her.

"I don't think they're angry with you, Orla, I think…"

"Oh, but they are! And yes, they probably do care about me, but that doesn't stop them being angry with me too. It will be seven months tomorrow; did you know that?"

Tina shook her head.

"Well, it will. Seven months to the day since they read out that verdict. I'm supposed to be getting better, that's what they think, but then I go and do this. And now they don't know what to do with me, and that makes them angry with me."

Tina said nothing, mostly because she was thinking that to some degree, Orla was right.

"And I would get better if I could," Orla sounded like a forlorn child. "I would, but I don't know how."

"You just need to give it time, Orla," Tina muttered the platitude, at a loss for anything better to say.

“That’s what everyone else keeps saying too,” Orla’s eyes reproached Tina.

“But I don’t believe that. It’s like when you were little, and something was keeping you from getting to sleep. Your Mam would say - don’t worry, it will all seem better in the morning. I wish that were true now. But every morning it’s the same. I wake up and I feel exactly the way I did when I went to sleep. And I can’t bear it anymore. I just can’t bear feeling this way.”

*

***

Perhaps you know this already, but there is a part of the brain called the dorsal striatum, which is stimulated by the mere anticipation of exacting revenge. OK, technically it is stimulated by the anticipation of any pleasure, but still, I find that fascinating.

Someone – I don't know who - called revenge 'a wild justice' and I must admit I can see where he or she was coming from. Because the law does not deal in revenge, it dispenses what is termed justice and, for the convicted, punishment. But what then of those times when we discover we cannot rely on the law? What when it falls short, or fails to deliver at all? We exclaim, we protest, we rage against the system, or - we take matters into our own hands. Which is when things get visceral, get biblical. We are in retaliation territory. We are talking eye-for-an-eye, tooth-for-a-tooth. We are quite literally outside the law. We are in the wild, wild west now.

*

CHAPTER 2

Monday 13 February

And it was those eyes that Tina could not seem to get out of her mind, as she hurried to her desk in the corner of the big, shared office that was the detectives' room. The smallest desk in the room, in spite of the fact that JP had joined the team almost a month after her. Not to mention she outranked him. And why? Because he was a man and needed the extra space for manspreading? Or could it have anything to do with the fact that JP's Da just happened to be James O'Rourke, one time Attorney General? And to add insult to injury, Tina's desk was right next to the ancient oak coat stand, which today stank of wet wool and damp leather. Plus, there wasn't even room on the stupid thing for her own damp coat. Flinging it over the back of her chair, Tina hunted frantically through the avalanche of papers on her desk, for the files she needed. A glance across the partition at JP's desk showed it in its usual irritatingly pristine order. His chair was conspicuously empty though, reminding Tina that she was late for the morning team meeting. JP would have arrived on time no doubt, would be sitting comfortably right now, sipping a coffee. Not for the first time, she reflected that if it wasn't for the fact that she liked the guy so much, she'd positively hate JP O'Rourke.

*

Coleman pointedly stopped speaking the moment Tina hurtled through the swing doors to the briefing room. As a result, she had to make her way in the resulting silence, to the only empty chair available. It was the one next to JP, she could see him gesturing her toward it with a tilt of his head, for which she rewarded him with a scowl. As she made to slip in next to him, she tripped over the Gannet's unfeasibly big feet. Her files dropped from her hand, the contents tumbling to the floor. Immediately, JP was on his knees to retrieve them.

"I can manage, myself," Tina hissed at him, but JP carried on gathering up the scattered papers. But in spite of her irritation at the man on his knees before her, Tina's brain still managed to register how impossibly wonderfully good he looked today. He reminded her of a photograph she had seen of a young Che Guevara, the same dark eyes and glossy dark hair. And God, his hair smelled good today too - must be that that seaweed and citrus shampoo…

Christ, if he knew she'd had a snoop through his bathroom cupboards, on the hunt for signs of a regular female presence… Irrationally, the memory only increased Tina's irritability. The last thing on earth she needed was this idiotic pash for her partner.

"I said I can manage," she hissed again, yanking the papers from his hand.

In the meantime, Coleman had picked up where he'd left off but somehow Tina found her thoughts wandering back to earlier that morning and the overheated hospital room. To Orla Reid's parting words. "How can this be right?" she demanded, a sudden energy in her previously listless voice.

"He lied and I told the truth, but everyone believes him and call me a liar. He raped me, but he got off scot free. How the hell can that be right?"

*

Somebody was having a fit of coughing and Tina's focus returned to Coleman. He had moved on to a report on the impounded packages of heroin and cocaine brought in overnight by a couple of members of the Drug Unit. For a while, Tina concentrated her whole attention, but again her thoughts insisted on straying. This time she found herself thinking of the first time she had met Orla Reid. It had been three years ago, Tina's second to last day in uniform. She had gone with Garda Sean Dolan, to take Orla's statement, Orla having requested it be taken in her own home. The door to the apartment had been opened by Orla's flatmate, a girl called Ursula, who had led them to the small living room where Orla huddled in a corner of the sofa, a red blanket swathing her slight form. That was the first thing Tina noticed about Orla, how tiny she was. Doll-like, in fact, with her elfin features beneath a cloud of dark brown hair. Humungous eyes - light blue but with lashes so thickly dark they looked almost smutty against the pallor of her skin. In comparison, tall, ruddy-complexioned Ursula with her springing strawberry hair seemed almost oversized. Ursula, her eyes on Orla, offered to leave them alone, but Orla had given one swift shake of her head.

Immediately Ursula crossed the room and positioned herself at the far edge of the sofa, primed and ready, thought Tina, like a watchdog. It was not the first time Tina had taken the statement of an alleged rape victim, and aside from it not being taken at the station, the procedure was the same. By prior agreement, Tina had done most of the questioning and couldn't help but notice that when Dolan put in the odd question, Orla had replied with her eyes on Tina. She'd noticed too that Orla repeatedly covered her mouth with her hand and wondered if it was on account of her teeth. Orla had tiny little teeth, very white but just ever so slightly protuberant. Tina thought they added to her attractiveness, perhaps Orla saw them as a flaw. Beautiful women always found fault with themselves; it was a source of never-ending wonder to Tina. Orla's statement finished; they had then taken another from Ursula, being the person in whom Orla had first confided the alleged assault. Tina had then advised Orla to attend the nearest Sexual Assault Treatment Unit, knowing however that with eight days having elapsed since the alleged attack, the chances of there being much in the way of forensic evidence to be gathered was pretty minimal. Tina did not say as much to Orla, but Dolan had clearly been thinking the same thing.

"Why did you wait so long before reporting this?" he suddenly demanded.

In fairness, it was a perfectly valid question, one which, were the case to go to court, would certainly be asked there. The trouble was a certain something in Dolan's tone, some nuance in that single word this. Tina saw the effect it had had on both women. Ursula frowned at Dolan, while Orla's hand went to mouth once more. And Tina found herself considering that after all, the habit might have nothing to do with the girl's dislike of her teeth, and more a protective instinct.

"Why do you think?" Ursula had fired reproachfully at Dolan. "She was traumatised, she still is."

And Orla, her voice dull, said listlessly, "It doesn't matter Urse, I told you no one would believe me."

*

Realising she had zoned out again, Tina pulled herself back to the present. Coleman had moved on to the recovery of the body of a young woman at first light that morning, from the base of the cliffs at Howth Head. Uniform had cordoned off the area and preserved the scene for SOCO. The Garda Technical Bureau were checking for any signs of suspicious activity.

"Obviously, we'll await the outcome of the PM before determining the course of the investigation," said Coleman. "But in the meantime, DS Bassett, Detective O'Rourke, I'd like you to set the ball rolling. Talk to the dead lassie's family. It seems it was the brother who reported her missing, so the bad news has already been broken to the parents."

"Right, sir" Tina and JP chimed in perfect unison, which annoyed Tina almost as much as Coleman's habit of referring to every woman under the age of fifty as a lassie.

This was turning into a right pig of a morning - cystitis, her smarting eye, Orla - and now bloody Coleman sticking them on what might well prove to be a suicide case. And there I go again, she reproached herself, thinking about Orla Reid. What the hell was wrong with her? She had done her job. An investigation file had been carefully compiled and forwarded to the DPP. The decision had been made that there was a case to be answered. It had duly gone to court. What more could she have done? Tina knew what Sean Dolan would say.

"Nothing more. Our job is to get them to court, that's it, that's all."

Which was technically true of course, except that she had made that stupid promise to Orla. She had looked her in the eye. "I promise you Orla," she had said. "The bastard won't get away with it."

Except that the bastard had gotten away with it.

*

***

I read somewhere that it is very often the behaviour of a murderer, as opposed to any physical evidence, which arouses the suspicion of crime investigators. That does not surprise me. I think a lot of murderers are quite stupid, because let's face it, a lot of people are quite stupid. But when it comes to murderers, often they are caught simply because there was just too little preparation and no contingency planning.

One has to consider so many things, time and place and opportunity. Things like hair and skin and fibres and sweat, all that sort of thing, after all everybody knows these days that every contact leaves a trace. So yes, planning, let alone committing a murder, is actually quite stressful, unless you happen to be a sociopath. I am not a sociopath.

***

CHAPTER 3

Monday 13 Feb

The big black gates, glittery with rainy cobwebs, were shut against them - against the entire world most likely, given the circumstances, Tina reflected. There was a security keypad to one side, and while JP got out to buzz for admission, Tina stayed in the car swigging at the carton of cranberry juice she'd picked up to help fend off the worst symptoms of her UTI. The gates parted slowly, and JP slid in next to her. The car moved forward and under a tunnel of tree branches, naked except for a smattering of last year's faded leaves. Between the branches the house could be seen, gleaming whitely.

JP gave a little appreciative whistle, "How the other half live."

Tina threw him a look; in her world he was the other half. No children's home for J.P O'Rourke. Though in fairness, most people would say that Tina had been lucky there too. Lucky in that, out of her three years in the home, she had only a scatter of memories and none of them of a particularly scarring nature. And then there had been Phyllis and Gerry, her adoptive parents. All the same, there was her kind of luck and then there was JP's kind, and sometimes she couldn't help wishing...

Then again, she conceded, remembering why they were here - there was also the Brady's kind of luck. All the big houses in the world couldn't save them from this pain. Tina let her mind run over the details of the case. Nicole Brady, thirty-seven years old, PR executive, single, running enthusiast, had failed to keep a lunch appointment with her brother. When she'd neither showed up nor phoned in the course of the afternoon, he had alerted the Gardai. As she'd been due to take a run on the Hill of Howth, a search had been instigated of the lower cliff walk where Nicole habitually ran. But with the fading light and deteriorating weather conditions, the search had been suspended overnight and it was not until the following morning that a Garda helicopter had spotted Nicole's body, one hundred metres down the cliff face. A winchman had had to be lowered to recover the remains, which were initially taken to the coast guard station at Howth Pier and then on to the County Morgue. Post-Mortem results were not yet in, but Tech had found no signs of suspicious activity and none of the usual signs of a struggle. Which meant that, pending the PM results, they were looking at a tragic accident or, equally tragically for all concerned, a possible suicide. Tina hoped for the family's sake, it would not be the latter. As they crunched their way across the gravel drive, Tina threw a disgusted glance at JP who was hunched so far inside his jacket, his head was in danger of disappearing. Admittedly, although the rain had stopped, the air was positively frigid, but she had yet to meet anyone who hated the cold as much as JP did. Wuss, she thought, and would have said it aloud, only she knew he'd be only looking for a chance to start moaning, and weather-talk always put her on edge.

It was because of Phyllis and Gerry of course. After every falling out, each of which could last for a week or more, they'd stop speaking to one another unless when absolutely essential. Tina could still remember those mealtimes, the silence broken only by the chink of cutlery against china, and the sound of masticating. Someone, she later decided, must have told them not to shout in front of her. But she'd so much have preferred it if they'd roared and shouted, sworn even, or thrown the dishes at one another's heads. Anything but that pent up anger, that unspoken resentment like a presence in the room, an unseen fourth at the kitchen table. Even now, she didn't need to close her eyes to be able to picture Phyllis' tight smile and Gerry's set gaze fixed on the world beyond the kitchen window. But nothing had been as bad as that endless inane weather talk Gerry had used in an attempt to break the tortuous silence. For Tina's sake, she now realised. *Look at that, the nights are drawing in already, or - isn't that a grand stretch in the evening no, or - it looked like rain, it smelled like snow, it's raining cats and dogs out there…*

And to please him, Tina would smile, in spite of the knot in her tummy, because whatever she did, she must never, ever, give them any reason to send her back. Because they could, anytime they liked, they could just send her right back. That was what it meant to be adopted. If she misbehaved, or if Phyllis or Gerry died. If they got separated, the way the people who lived across the road had, or just got fed up with her, they could send her back to the home where they had found her. A boy at school had told her so, after she had thumped him for hitting a boy smaller than himself. He had told her and taken great pleasure in doing so, thinking of course that it was news to her. But it wasn't. She had heard Gerry and Phyllis talking about her that night…

"Jaysus, it's freezing bulldo..." JP began.

"Don't even start, JP. Don't even bleedin' start." Tina snapped as she lifted the brass knocker and rapped it sharply against the Brady's door.

*

Nicole's parents received them – there was no other word for it - in a large and gracious room, which Tina was fairly certain they referred to as the drawing room. They were seated together in the middle of a big pale blue sofa, and, as the door opened on them, and just before they rose to their feet, Tina had a mental image of them islanded on a sea of grief, clinging together like shipwreck survivors. She told herself to get a grip. The truth was, she wasn't quite over the shock of the Brady's front door being opened to them by the SC who had defended the man accused of raping Orla Reid. She'd had no inkling that the Keith Brady who had gone searching for his missing sister on the hill of Howth was self-same Keith Brady of the courtroom. And to be honest, she had hardly recognised the man who'd welcomed them into his parent's home. That obese, puffed up arrogant little performer who'd postured and pontificated through the weeks of the trial was barely discernible. Clearly Nicole's brother had been badly shaken by her death, all the arrogance replaced now by a sort of quiet helplessness.

"Please sit down, won't you?" Mrs Brady, having been introduced to the two detectives, waved Tina toward a powder blue and gold brocade chair.

Tina eyed it uncertainly – surely it had to be some priceless antique and not actually intended for sitting on. Lowering herself gingerly, she avoided touching the pale gold armrests. She'd only just put away a jam doughnut and there was bound to be sticky traces on her paws. Meanwhile Mrs Brady was urging tea on them and suddenly Tina was overwhelmed by an urge to pee. Don't think about it, she commanded herself.

With Mrs Brady out of the room, JP and Keith Brady engaged in an attempt at small talk, but Mr Brady sat in silence. Tina took the opportunity to take her mind off the demands of her bladder by surreptitiously studying 'the fat barrister'. She had had to admit that he'd done his job well; the defendant had been acquitted of all charges – not guilty. For the second time that day, Tina asked herself why she was so hung up on this one case anyway. Everyone knew there was little chance of getting justice in sexual assault or rape cases. Even without the illegal social media breaches which, during this trial, had ended up with both accused and accuser being named on Facebook and Twitter, there was always a good chance that the defendant would end up as the one vilified in the witness stand. And still Tina had made that stupid bloody promise. Mrs Brady returned with the tea and for a few minutes there was no sound in the big room other than the gentle ticking of a clock and the rattle of china. Tina, still on the edge of her chair, gazed in dismay at the flowery cup in its matching saucer perched perilously on her knee. She picked it up by its impossibly slender handle; it felt slippery, as though the slightest flexing of her finger would shatter it into pieces. Bringing it to her lips, she caught sight, over the wafer-thin rim, of JP. He was eyeing her with an expression on his face which told her he knew exactly how deep in hell she was. Sticking out the baby finger of the hand which held his own cup, he proceeded to sip his tea in a show of mock gentility. Tina frowned and looked away quickly, at the same time making to replace her cup in the saucer. The result was a loud clack as china struck china.

"Shit!" The word came out like a shot resounding round the quiet room.

Tina looked up in apologetic agony, in time to catch Mr Brady Snr's flinch which unnerved her so much the hand holding the saucer shook, setting the cup wobbling in its saucer.

"Bugger!" Tina made a grab for the cup and only just saved it from falling to the floor. A strangled sound came from JP.

Tina daggered him with a look. "I'm sorry," she muttered.

It was Mrs Brady who replied. "It doesn't matter. It really doesn't matter at all."

The expression in her eyes, distanced and glazed by grief, reminded Tina why they were there. She reached out, placed the cup and saucer down with deliberate care on the nearest table and settling herself firmly back into the chair, said, "Let's begin then, shall we, Detective O'Rourke?"

*

CHAPTER 4

Monday 13 February

JP turned his attention first to Nicole's brother. "Mr Brady…"

"Keith, please…"

"Keith, thank you. So let me first say that we realise you've already given your statement. But perhaps you wouldn't mind bringing us again through the sequence of events on the day your sister, Nicole lost her life?"

Brady sat forward in his chair, "Of course, no problem."

He began with the day before Nicole died, and her text to him that morning confirming their arrangement to meet for lunch at 1.30 on Sunday. A standing arrangement, Brady explained, something they did every second Sunday, if at all possible. On that particular Sunday, Brady had arrived at the restaurant in Howth just before 1.30. When, by 1.45, Nicole had still not arrived, he hadn't been particularly concerned, punctuality not having been his sister's strong point.

"Then when Nicole still hadn't shown up by two o'clock, I texted her, asking how far away she was. I was supposed to be meeting a friend at 3.15 that afternoon. When she didn't reply, I tried calling her, but her phone went to voicemail. I was a tad worried by then, I have to admit. Nicole would usually text if she was running that late. But I gave it another ten minutes before I tried her phone again. That went to voicemail too, so I left a message to say I was heading round to her place. And that's what I did."

"Your sister's place was where?"

JP glance up from his notebook. A new one, Tina noted, another natty little Moleskin number, she thought sourly. A proper grown-up notebook, not like the rolled up, coffee stained, jam-smeared school exercise book in her own jacket pocket. God, she needed to pee. She forced her attention back to Nicole's brother.

"Nicole has…I mean she had an apartment at the Marina in Malahide. But she wasn't there. I tried the bell a few times, rang her again too. Then I let myself in. I have a key, Nicole asked me to keep one for emergencies. But…," Brady glanced at his parents, "she wasn't there…"

JP allowed a short pause before he went on, "Did Nicole always run alone?"

"Not always, but I'd say usually, yes."

"And the route she took that day," Tina interjected.

"The lower cliff walk I think they call it. From your initial statement, it appears this was a route your sister had run many times?"

Brady nodded his agreement, "Yes, it was a favourite spot of hers. She liked the challenge. It's pretty rough in places, but she knew it really well. That's what makes it so hard to understand how anything like this could have happened."

"Had she ever suffered any mishaps before while running along that route?" asked JP.

"She slipped once and sprained her ankle. But, as she said herself, that could have happened just as easily if she'd been running on a pathway".

"I see," said JP. "And would you say you were close to your sister, Keith?"

"Very close," Brady replied without hesitation, and Tina noticed how both his parents nodded their own silent confirmation.

"Then you'd have known if she'd had anything on her mind, anything troubling her perhaps?"

Keith Brady shook his head, "No there was nothing, I'm sure there wasn't. She was enjoying her job and was happy with her life."

"Mr Brady, Mrs Brady?" JP looked to the couple.

"Were either of you aware of anything that might have been troubling your daughter?"

Mr Brady shook his head. Mrs Brady who had been fingering the material of her skirt looked up.

"Nicole was happy again," she said quietly. "That's what makes this so very, very hard to bear." Her voice broke and she began to cry quietly.

Without a word, her husband got up and helped his wife to her feet. JP and Keith Brady rose too, leaving Tina uncomfortably the only person still seated, but if she stood up, she was afraid the pressure on her bladder would prove unbearable. She stayed where she was and watched as the man led the woman from the room, their son waddling ahead of them to hold the door open for them. With his parents out of the room, Brady turned back to the two detectives.

"It's hit them hard," he said. "It's hit us all hard."

"Of course," JP agreed.

Tina said, "What did your mother mean just now, when she said that Nicole was happy again?" Brady sat down again.

"Look," he said, "obviously I know what you were getting at just now. But if you're thinking my sister might have taken her own life, then you couldn't be more wrong. If this had happened two years ago, that possibility might have crossed my mind. Though even then I'd have struggled to believe that Nicole would ever take her own life.

"But two years ago, it might have been a possibility," Tina persisted. "Why was that?" "Because two years ago, my sister was engaged to be married," said Keith.

"The bastard decided to call it off a couple of weeks before the wedding. Nicole, needless to say was devastated and humiliated and all the rest of it. She took it very hard and became very ill. To be honest, we were all very worried about her."

"But things had gotten better since then?"

"A whole lot better, thankfully. She came home from London, where she'd been living, got a new job that she's being enjoying, bought her own place. And there was a guy she's been seeing. My parents don't actually know anything about that yet. They were extremely upset when the wedding fell through, so Nicole decided to keep this under the radar for a while. But she's been seeing Colin Christie for about four months now and she seems really happy with him. I mean…"

Brady's pudgy hand passed over his face, and he shook his head with an air of helplessness. "Christ how do you get used to everything suddenly being in the past tense?"

The answer, thought Tina, was that you probably didn't.

"Anyway," Keith continued, "I met Colin, and I liked him. He seems like a good guy."

"We will need to speak to Mr Christie," said JP. "I assume he's been informed of your sister's death?"

Brady shook his head, "The poor bastard knows nothing about it. He's in Dubai on business, and I have no way of getting in touch with him. Like I say, I did meet him, but I don't have a number for him."

"We can take care of that," said Tina. "Your sister's phone has been recovered. Chances are that Mr Christie's details will be stored in the contacts."

Her phone vibrated in her pocket, and she pulled it out, scanned the brief text message and stuffed it quickly back in.

"Right well I think we can wrap things up for now. Thanks for your cooperation, Mr Brady."

*

"So that's that then," said JP, as they trudged back to the car. "Young woman in the first flush of new love. Boyfriend out of the country when the incident occurred, though we'll need to check that. But no sign of suspicious activity at the scene. So, unless the PM turns up something, I'd say we were looking at accidental death."

"The preliminary results are already in," said Tina. "I asked the lads to let me know the bottom line soon as." She read aloud from her phone. "No signs that would indicate a struggle. No sign of any blunt force trauma to the head."

"So, we're looking at an open verdict then," JP observed. "I can't see the coroner bringing it in as anything else."

"No, I suppose not," Tina said absent-mindedly.

JP shot her a glance. "What, you don't like it?"

"What? No, I'm just thinking, is all."

The truth was that she couldn't have explained to herself, let alone JP, just what it was exactly about the whole thing that she didn't like. But there was something, and because of it, she already had the feeling she wouldn't rest until she had taken herself up onto the Hill of Howth and stood at the spot from where Nicole Brady had fallen to her death on the rocks below.

She said, "Now let's get the hell out of here, I need a loo before I burst!"

*

CHAPTER 5

Thursday 16th February

So here we are again, thought Anna Fox. The A Team all together again. At least in a manner of speaking. Her eyes moved along the row of people on the far side of Nicole's open grave. From Jennifer O'Keeffe to Rachel Quinn, on to Bethany Doyle and finally to Megan McGrath before coming back to the woman who stood next to Jennifer, linking her arm. Paula Murphy as was, now Paula Murphy-O'Keeffe, Jennifer's sister-in-law. For a moment, Anna's eyes strayed to Paula's husband, Jennifer's brother. He was standing next to Paula, but their bodies did not touch. It was many years since Anna had seen Paula. With her fluffy blond hair, pink scarf and lipstick to match, she seemed like an only marginally older version of her girly teenage self. No wonder Paula had never been part of the A Team, that pink lipstick would never have passed muster.

And suddenly Anna was assailed by a memory - the six of them hurrying behind the gym as the school bell rang for home time, in a rush to put on their black cherry lipstick with the aid of Nicole's compact mirror. On the heels of that memory came another – Nicole's face as she must have looked the last time Anna had spoken to her - beautiful as always but frowning in her perplexity. That, Anna remembered, was the day those photos arrived, followed by the phone calls. Rachel first, sounding breathless, as she always did when she was bothered, or something had upset her, and unable to conceal her relief to hear that Anna too had received a photo.

"In this morning's post," she had told Rachel, climbing out of her car. "Have you any idea what it's all about?"

And Rachel, clearly a little thrown, “Oh, I was hoping you’d know?”

“Me? I haven’t a clue.”

Rachel had begun speculating – perhaps it had something to do with the plan to re-take the school group photo? But Anna had had to confess she knew nothing about that either.

“But you must have seen it, Anna,” Rachel mildly reproachful now. “It was on Facebook. We’re all supposed to get together, the whole class, with everyone standing in the same position as in the original photo. I’m sure you were tagged.”

“Well, if I did see it, I must have pretended I hadn’t. Who’s genius idea was this anyway?”

“Liz Wade, remember her? At least, I think it must have been her. She posted the photo to Facebook in the first place. Anyway, whoever suggested it, Liz nearly shat herself with the excitement.” Rachel gurgled with laughter.

“And yes, it’s a stupid idea, I agree. As Jennifer said, if we’d wanted to see one another again we wouldn’t have waited nearly twenty years to do it, would we? But never mind all that, Anna, what do you make of these photos? I mean, look at the state of my face, it looks as if it’s actually been scratched out!”

“Hang on a second, Rachel.” Anna, her phone trapped between ear and shoulder, scrabbled for her house keys in the depths of her bag.

Opening the door, she let herself into her apartment, shrugging off her coat as she made for the kitchen-cum-dining room. Switching on the light, she threw her coat across a chair back, then crossed to the breakfast bar and picked up the photo she’d earlier left propped against the fruit bowl. It was a poor copy, clearly produced on a home-printer using photo paper. Anna had tried and failed to recall the day it was taken. Outdoors clearly, and shot from above the subjects’ heads, all of whom were squinting into the sunlight. One or two of the girls had raised a hand to shade their eyes and looked like they had been caught mid-salute. She had studied Rachel’s image, the mass of dark hair, the wide and lovely smile.

"Nope," she had said into the phone. "Your face looks perfectly fine to me. It's my face that's been hacked about."

"What are you talking about? I'm looking at it right now and your face is just fine. It's my face that been all scratched out."

Silently, Anna had studied what remained of her own image in the photograph. Impossible to tell how she had looked that day, the place where her head should have been just a series of jagged white gashes as though someone had taken a knife or a pin or the edge of a coin, some sharp object anyway, and quite literally defaced it and Anna too.

"Then it seems as if we each got a specially personalised copy, doesn't it?" she'd told Rachel. "Yeah but…," Rachel's voice had faltered. "I mean why would Liz do something like this?"

Anna had slipped onto one of the bar stools, slid her feet from her shoes and let them clatter to the tiled floor.

"But do we even know for sure that it was Liz who sent them?"

"OK, no, we don't," Rachel had agreed with obvious reluctance. "But who else would it be? It was Liz who posted that photo to Facebook in the first place. But this, this is just weird. Do you not think it's weird, Anna?"

"I suppose it could just be somebody's idea of a joke." Even to her own ears Anna had sounded unconvincing.

"But it's not funny," Rachel had protested.

"Did I say I was laughing?"

*

And then a couple of hours later, Nicole had called with a similar verdict.

"It's not funny, Anna. I mean who sends people photos of themselves with their faces ripped up like that? You know Jennifer and Bethany and Megan all got one too?"

"No, I didn't know that. I've only spoken to you and Rachel. What do the others make of it?" "They think it's weird, same as I do. Jennifer said Liz Wade always was a weirdo, and I agree. Imagine doing that to someone's face."

She means her own face, Anna had thought, and smiled to think of Nicole's outrage at the violence done to her image. Then for the third time that day, Anna had picked up the photograph. She had to admit that those ragged edges where her face should have been, definitely spoke of some violence or passion.

As if to underline her thoughts, Nicole had said plaintively, "I don't like it, Anna. Looking at my face like that gives me a bad feeling. It's as if someone has it in for me or something."

"Well, I'm not exactly thrilled about it myself," Anna had told her. "But why would anyone have it in for you, Nicole?"

"I don't know, but that's the way it makes me feel. It's so…" Nicole had fished about for a suitable adjective.

"Juvenile? Silly?" Anna had offered

"Mean," Nicole had replied. "Mean and nasty and unsettling. I mean, doesn't it bother you that someone would go to the effort of doing something like this?"

Anna had considered this. Mean and nasty, yes, she would have to agree.

"Still, try not to lose sleep over it," she offered, "it's not worth it."

"Mmm, I suppose you're right."

Nicole had sounded unconvinced, and Anna had spent another few minutes attempting to put her mind at ease. But, as she hung up on the call, it was clear that the other woman was still disturbed by the whole thing. And now, five days later Nicole was in her grave.

*

CHAPTER 6

Thursday 16th February

Anna's gaze returned to Paula's sister-in-law, Jennifer O'Keeffe was undeniably still a strikingly attractive woman. The blue/black hair was no longer worn poker straight as in her teens but fell in beachy waves below her shoulders. She was as slim as ever, slimmer if anything; Anna took in the pronounced hollows beneath the perfect cheekbones, the slight puffiness and dark circles under the long slanting blue eyes, which make-up had not quite managed to conceal.

As if suddenly conscious of being scrutinised, Jennifer glanced up and caught Anna's eyes upon her. It was a long time since she'd felt the force of that cool unblinking stare, and Anna was the first to break contact. Her eyes went back to Jennifer's brother. Lorcan O'Keeffe had always been considered good-looking, most would say he still was. Objectively, Anna supposed they were right; she just never happened to admire the type. Lorcan was very tall and broad-shouldered, fleshier now, but still showing signs of that rugby poster boy swagger he'd adopted, before a nerve injury to his right leg had put an end to his career and dreams. Unlike his sister, Lorcan's eyes were light brown, his hair, once strawberry-blonde was streaked now with a blend of honey and caramel highlights, carefully styled to hide a little thinning on top. Anna wondered how much he spent on it. She wondered too, if when Lorcan got angry, those ugly dark red patches still appeared on either cheek, as they had when he was seventeen. And then he too, suddenly raised his head and Anna once again averted her gaze.

*

After the funeral, Anna stood about with Rachel – Rachel who'd been the one to phone Anna with the news.

"Anna? Oh God! Have you heard?"

"Heard what, Rachel? You sound upset. What's happened?"

"Oh Anna, it's Nicole. She's dead, Anna, Nicole is dead. I just can't believe it."

And Anna, shocked into silence at those stark words, eventually opened her mouth but only to utter that inane phrase people invariably use in such circumstances.

"But she can't be dead."

"I know. But she is. She's dead Anna."

"But how, what happened?"

"I don't know. She was out running. She must have slipped or something. They found her bo…they found her down on the rocks in Howth. Oh God, Anna, I can't even bear to think about it."

Anna, knowing how close Rachel had remained to Nicole over the years, said quickly,

"Don't think about it, Rachel. Chances are, if she slipped and fell, it was all over in a matter of seconds. Nicole probably wouldn't have felt much at all." Even as she said it, Anna knew she was talking out of the side of her ear. What did she know of what or how Nicole would have felt? Was that final plummet really all over in a whirling flash, or did time slow to a seeming eternity? Was there time for surprise, fear, terror, regret…?

"Do you think so, Anna?" Rachel's voice showed her eagerness to grasp the comfort Anna was offering.

"Oh, I really hope you're right. But it still really upsets me to think of her down there on the rocks all alone all night. They didn't find her until this morning. She was supposed to be meeting Keith for lunch yesterday, and when she didn't turn up or text, he went round to her apartment. Then he drove out to Howth because he knew she'd been planning a run in the morning before they met."

"So, it was Keith who found her?" asked Anna.

"No, Keith couldn't find her. He got really worried, so he called the guards, and they sent a search party out to look for her. They had to call it off when it got dark, and they only found her this morning. It makes me feel sick just thinking about it. Oh God, Anna, I just can't believe she's gone. Nicole has gone and we'll never see her again. Never."

In truth, Anna could hardly believe it herself.

*

Anna was passing a tissue to a hopelessly sobbing Rachel when Nicole's brother, Keith came up behind her and touched her shoulder. She had turned to find him smiling sadly up into her face. The first thing that struck her was the fact that the only remaining resemblance to his dead sister were the soft blue eyes, and even they seemed in danger of being swallowed up by the dough that was his face. Keith enveloped her in a hug, thanking her in his rich deep-toned voice, for coming to say goodbye to Nicole. It, at least, had not diminished with time.

"You'll come back to the house of course," it was less a request than an assumption, and Anna accepted it as such.

"Of course," said Anna. "How could I not."

Later, as her car moved beneath the canopy of tall old trees, she was struck by the thought that these were the same trees under which the six of them had passed on all those school day evenings, weekend afternoons and long, freedom-filled summer days. The same trees, she reflected, just taller and older. Face-to-face with Nicole's parents, she reflected that they too were older but, unlike the trees, seemed shrunken, diminished. Mrs Brady's face wore its habitual gentle smile, as, on her own insistence, she stood just inside the drawing room doors next to her husband, to greet their guests individually. But her gaze, Anna noticed, kept straying off into the distance, as if she could hear something no one else could. Nicole's father, a quiet gentle man, in the true sense of the term, and one whom Anna had always liked, had cried at the graveside while Nicole's coffin was lowered. His tears had fallen openly, and he'd made no effort to stem them; Anna had found herself wishing he would. At the same time, she liked him the more for honouring his lost daughter with his unashamed grief.

Keith Brady introduced her, "It's Anna, Mum. You remember Anna? And look, here's Rachel and Bethany and Megan and Jennifer of course."

"Of course, I remember Anna," Mrs Brady said in her gentle way. "You're very welcome, Anna, thank you for coming."

She reached out, taking both of Anna's hands and held them between her own cold thin fingers, fingers that made Anna think of the bones of little birds. "You were all such great friends of Nicole, such very great friends."

Mr Brady hugged Anna, just as Keith had. "Can you believe it," he spoke into her ear, his voice a terrible ragged whisper. "Can you believe we've lost our beautiful girl?"

Then Anna was introduced to Colin Christie, whom the Brady's were introducing as Nicole's boyfriend. He looked stunned and somewhat uncomfortable, but then, as Anna knew, Nicole had only been seeing him for a matter of months. Nicole had described him to Anna as "a total ride", and Anna thought him attractive in a clean cut, blonde sort of way. With the introductions done, everyone stood about in the big, beautiful, room, and drank and ate catered food from silver trays, passed about by teenage girls and boys in blindingly white shirts and black skirts or trousers. Then somehow, at some point, the five of them, each with a glass in hand, gravitated to one quiet corner of the room where they formed an unconscious circle. At first the talk was of how beautiful the flowers were and did anyone know who the caterers were. Then Bethany said wasn't Mrs Brady bearing up unbelievably well and Megan began sniffing.

"Oh, for God's sake, don't you start too," Jennifer snapped. "Rachel's been at it all morning."

"I'm sorry, I can't help it," Megan whined, tears spilling from her big blue vapid-looking eyes.

Anna who had not seen Megan since they were teenagers, looked at her curiously. The long blonde locks, of which she had been so vain, had been cut into a sharp chin-length bob. Her boobs were still enormous, and she'd put on a bit of weight everywhere else too.

"Leave her alone, Jennifer," said Bethany. "Why wouldn't she cry? Nicole has been our friend since forever, and now that she's gone, it feels like the end of something."

Anna, who had never heard Bethany speak that way to Jennifer, turned to look at her. Of them all, Bethany had changed the most, she thought. Not so much in appearance, although the freckles she had so despised were less obvious now and her mane of auburn hair was piled high on her head and twisted into a messy bun instead of hanging loose as in her schooldays. The difference Anna decided, lay in the expression in the hazel eyes and in the energy that seemed to emanate from her. Even the telling off she had just given Jennifer had lacked the edge she remembered in the old Bethany. Something had softened her Anna decided.

"It's because she's happy, of course," Rachel said when Anna commented on the change, after Bethany had wandered off to speak to someone she'd spotted in the crowd. Jennifer made a sound in the back of her throat, which Anna assumed was intended to denote scorn.

"Yes, she is, Jennifer," insisted Rachel. "Come on, admit it. You only have to look at her to know she's happy-out."

"That's not happy, that's brainwashed," said Jennifer.

"Did I hear she got married recently?" asked Anna.

"Yeah, she got married," Jennifer's tone was contemptuous. "To a hippy-dippy tree-hugging dyke, whose sixty if she's a day and looks like a scarecrow."

Rachel looked to protest at Jennifer but giggled at the same time. Some things never change, thought Anna. "I take it you don't approve of the bride, then?" she asked.

"It's a joke." Jennifer sneered. "Bethany meets this Dee person, who's more than twenty years older than her. Next thing we know, she's moving into the woman's hobbit house and giving up her job to grow onions and turnips and I don't know what else. I mean she's taken up spinning now for God's sake! Bethany, spinning, did you ever?"

"What's so bad about spinning?" Megan protested. "I do a spinning class twice a week and let me tell you it's a lot harder than it looks." Jennifer rolled her eyes.

"Not that kind of spinning, Megan," said Rachel. "Dee has an actual spinning wheel. She's giving Bethany lessons. And Dee's not sixty, Jennifer, she's fifty-three. Not that age matters when you love somebody. Besides, I think it's quite romantic."

"You would," said Jennifer. "But what's romantic about growing turnips and making your own pickles? Not to mention that she has Bethany harping on about polytunnels and cold composting."

"Well, I like Dee," said Rachel, her tone one of mild obstinacy.

"And I'm telling you, she has Bethany brainwashed," Jennifer's voice was rising. "She's a completely different person since they met. I mean she didn't even invite any of us to their so-called wedding. Even Bethany's Dad doesn't speak to her since she ran off and got married without telling him and Ross."

"Ssh! She's coming back" Megan warned. They changed the subject. But afterwards, Anna would reflect that Bethany had been right when she'd said that it was the end of something. But wrong too, because really it was just the beginning.

*

CHAPTER 7

Friday 24th February

The day the hit and run case landed, had begun with a follow-up visit by Tina to Orla Reid. This time she called to Orla's family home, a three-bed semi-detached in what had once been a local authority housing estate in Santry. The Reid's were typical of the majority of the families who lived there; quiet, hardworking people who had bought their houses from the Council and wanted better for their kids than they had had themselves. Tina had been to the house a number of times before, Orla having moved back home shortly after her ordeal. The door was opened to her today by Karen Reid. Orla's mother was a widow, a slight, stringy-looking woman from whom Orla had clearly inherited her dark hair and blue eyes.

In the past Karen had greeted Tina with warmth, pressed her into accepting cups of tea, asked her advice and sought her opinion, thanked her even, for her concern for Orla. Today there was neither thanks nor tea and precious little welcome.

"Oh, it's you," said Karen, no shadow of a smile on show. "Orla's not so good today. I'm not sure she's up to talking to you."

"I'm sorry she's not well," said Tina. "I did drop her a text to say I'd come by. She didn't say I shouldn't."

Orla hadn't said she should either, the text having gone unanswered. But Tina had stood her ground and eventually Karen stepped aside to let her pass.

"She's up in her room."

"Is it alright if I go up?" Karen nodded silently, but as Tina made her way upstairs, she called after her.

"I suppose you know she's given up the lease on her flat and is moving home for good?"

Tina hadn't known. The last time she had seen Orla had been that day in the hospital. Since then, she'd been aware of a reluctance to face the girl again. She wondered if Karen Reid suspected as much and knew this was a duty call, she'd been putting off. Oh well, she was here now. She knocked gently on Orla's bedroom door.

"Orla? It's Tina, Tina Bassett, is it alright if I come in?"

There was no reply, and after a moment she tapped once more.

"Orla, it's Tina. Can you hear me?" A sudden fist of fear punched Tina in the gut. She rapped sharply on the door.

"Orla, I'm going to come in now, is that OK?" Again, there was no reply, and she turned the handle. Orla was sitting upright on the bed, her face turned toward the window. She didn't look away as Tina closed the door quietly behind her. For a moment she was so relieved she stayed there, just inside the door, conscious now that she had not been invited into this room, and even more conscious that she was not welcome.

"Hi Orla," she said, eventually. "I just came to see how you were doing. Your Mam said you weren't feeling too good?"

Still Orla said nothing. Tina, feeling at a loss, gazed about her, trying to think of what best to say or do. The room, she knew, had been Orla's all her life before she left home to share a flat with Ursula. To Tina, it still had the appearance of a young girl's room too – pink and white walls, white curtains and furniture. The bed took up most of the available space and it dwarfed Orla, making her look, if that were possible, even tinier than she had in the hospital room.

"Why did you let me do it?" The question when it came, took Tina by surprise, not because she hadn't been expecting it – she'd been expecting it for a long time really, just not right this minute. She met Orla's eyes, which were fixed on her now. She felt shocked at the change in the girl, who had lost weight, and looked almost haggard. But that wasn't it, Tina thought. There was some new quality in Orla's expression. That lost bewildered look was still there, but there was something else too, something that gave her an older, harder appearance. She's angry, thought Tina, she's angry with me. She found herself wondering what had taken Orla so long.

"I asked you why," Orla repeated.

"Why did you let me go ahead with that court case, when you must have known I had no chance. Isn't that the reason so few women come forward? Why would they, why would anyone? Why put themselves through that hell, and for what? It took almost three years for the case to come to trial, and I was sick to my stomach every single day of that time, just thinking of having to stand up in front of him. And in the end, all that happened was that fat little barrister making me out to be a dirty little slag."

Tina opened her mouth to protest but Orla beat her to it. "Don't you even dare try to deny it," she said.

"You were there, you heard him. He might have used fancy words but everyone in that room knew exactly what he was saying. He was saying that I was dirt. He was saying that I was a dirty little slag who drank too much, and slept around and dressed like a tart, and only got what was coming to her."

"But you know that wasn't true, Orla. And I know it wasn't…"

"What do you know?" Orla reared up, got to her feet and stood before Tina, hands on her hips. "Nothing, you know nothing! It didn't happen to you, it happened to me. It wasn't you up there being called those things, it was me, me! And that was your fault. Do you hear me, I blame, you!"

"I know you do, Orla," Tina made a move toward her, but Orla's arms came up to ward her off. The sleeves of her jumper fell back revealing the taped wrists and stopping Tina in her tracks.

"But why should it matter how many drinks I had that night," Orla demanded. "Or how many guys I slept with? So, I let him buy me drinks. I thought he was good looking, mature. And I was tired of immature boys with nothing to say for themselves. And yeah, I let him kiss me in the taxi…"

Orla shuddered as though she was remembering a nightmare, which she was of course, Tina knew only too well.

"Orla, please," Tina pleaded, " you don't have to justify yourself like this…."

"…and yeah, I let him into the flat, but only because he kept going on and on at me about how badly he needed a cup of black coffee. But that was all it was supposed to be. I didn't want what he did to me. I told him no. I kept on telling him no. I said it over and over and over and over…"

"I know you did, Orla, I know you did." This time Tina's words registered, a look of naked hostility came over Orla's face.

"Didn't I just tell you, you know nothing?" she sneered. "You come around here like you're my friend or something. But you're not my friend. You're a cop, and you don't give a damn about me. So, stop pretending you do. Just get out, OK? Get out and don't ever come back here again."

"That's not true Orla, I do care…"

"I said get out," Orla was yelling now. "Do you hear me? Get out, get out get out!"

The door behind Tina burst open and Karen Reid sped past her. She pulled her daughter into her arms and over the top of her head she glared at Tina. "What the hell have you been saying to her?"

"Make her go, Mam," Orla sobbed into her mother's hair. "Tell her to go, I want her to go."

"You heard her," Karen told Tina. "Now do us all a favour and leave us the hell alone."

*

CHAPTER 8

Friday 24th February

Driving away from Orla's home, Tina made no conscious decision to drive to Howth. But that was where she ended up, and for the second time in less than a fortnight she found herself pulling into the car park where Nicole Brady had left her car on the last day of her life. Tina's first visit here had grown out of an urge to see for herself the place from which Nicole had fallen to her death. Today she had no clear purpose in mind as she set off at a brisk pace against a gnawingly cold wind, along the uphill track which had been Nicole's habitual running route. The track was narrow, taking her over rugged terrain which looped clockwise around Howth Head. To her right, and much too close for comfort, was the cliff edge, below which the sea crashed on the rocks.

As she walked, Tina, eaten up with guilt about Orla Reid, found herself thinking about Nicole's brother. Not the grieving and shaken Keith Brady she had encountered at his parent's house, but Keith Brady, the fat barrister. Because a great deal of what Orla had said was true. In the course of the trial, Orla had been skilfully degraded, vilified and finally discredited, as Brady painted a picture of heras a promiscuous party girl with, as he had put it, "a penchant for knocking back drinks."

And all because, she, Tina Bassett, who should have known better, had pushed her to go ahead with the case. Sure, Orla had been warned that the defence would seek to undermine her credibility, but nothing could have prepared her for what she had been subjected to. Because the truth was, that to all intents and purposes, it was not Lorcan O'Keeffe who had been on trial, but Orla herself. At a bend in the track, Tina paused to catch her breath next to a sign which posed the question - *Need to Talk?*

Beneath was a number for the Samaritans. Had Nicole Brady needed to talk, Tina wondered. On the surface it would seem not - a new relationship, a new job, her own apartment, not to mention a supportive family and no shortage of friends. On the surface at any rate, it appeared as though life for Nicole Brady had been hunky-dory. And the coroner, finding nothing to suggest the death was in any way suspicious had certified it as due to musculoskeletal injuries consistent with a fall from a height. Only the lack of witnesses to what exactly had occurred had led to an open verdict being returned. So that, it seemed, was that. Tina moved on again, until she came to a spot where dead and dying flowers lay under rain and mud-spattered cellophane. It was impossible to be absolutely certain, but the experts had decreed that this, based on where the body had landed on the rocks below, was most likely the place from which Nicole had fallen. There was evidence to back up the theory – a lifelong friend of Nicole's, Bethany Doyle, who had accompanied Nicole on her hill-top runs on a number of occasions had confirmed that Nicole was in the habit of pausing here. According to Bethany, she had actually once begged Nicole not to stand so close to the cliff edge. To back up her statement, Bethany had given the officer taking it, the name of another friend who had gone running with Nicole even more frequently than she herself. This was Anna Fox, a local dental surgeon. Curious to speak in person with someone who had run the actual route with Nicole, Tina had gone with JP to take Anna's statement at her Sutton home.

Having buzzed them into the lobby, Anna Fox met them at her apartment door, then led them through to a large and airy living room where she waved them to a pristine cream sofa. Tina looked about her appreciatively at the high white ceilings, pale walls, cream carpets and drapes. The only splashes of colour in the room came from the matching glass troughs of hyacinths on either end of the high white mantlepiece, and some vivid green scatter cushions on sofa and chairs.

Tina tried to imagine herself living in such a room and almost grinned to think of the mess she'd have made inside a week of that cream suite and carpet. Taking the lead this time, she began the interview with Bethany Doyle's comment that Anna had been in the habit of accompanying Nicole on the cliff path.

"It's true that I went running with Nicole a few times," Anna confirmed. "Four, maybe five times, but I gave it up. Nicole was far fitter than I am, I'm afraid."

"OK. But would you be able to tell us if Nicole's runs followed any particular pattern? For instance, did you notice if she was in the habit of stopping in any one spot?"

Anna frowned, "I think so, I think it was the same place she stopped each time."

"And was it the same place as the one it's believed she fell from?"

"That I don't know," said Anna.

"You don't know if it's the same place?"

"I don't know where it's believed Nicole fell from," said Anna.

So, none of those floral tributes to Nicole had come from Anna then. Studying the woman against the backdrop of the beautiful and elegant room, Tina concluded that her first impression had been spot on. A cool customer she had decided when she'd rang her to arrange the interview. Anna had shown no sign of surprise at being phoned by a Detective Sergeant, and no desire to speculate as to why. Most people did; quite a lot of people expressed, or in some way betrayed, signs of actual alarm. Of course, Tina reminded herself, Anna would have known about Nicole's death by then.

Glancing at JP, she saw that his gaze was fixed on Anna too. There was no doubt that she was an extremely attractive woman, and she was quite certain that JP was thinking exactly that. Mid-thirties, Tina decided, beautiful skin. Amazing teeth, unsurprisingly, thought Tina, considering her profession. Real eyebrows too, composed of actual human hair, which in Tina's experience, was fairly uncommon these days. Shoulder-length hair, the colour and sheen of a hazelnut shell, large golden-brown eyes in a perfect oval face. Tall too, and slim, with long legs. Not fair, some people get it all. *Oh, for feck sake, Tina, build a bridge and get over it!*

"OK," she said aloud and more sharply than she had intended. "But perhaps you could give us some insight into Nicole's state of mind in recent weeks?"

"I'm afraid I can't help you much there either," Anna smiled regretfully. "You see Nicole and I lost track after we left school, and only really caught up with one another again quite recently. So, I actually know very little about the nitty-gritty of her life as an adult."

"How recently?"

"How recently did we catch up with one another? I'm not sure exactly, but I'd say it was around two months ago, something like that. And even then, it was purely coincidence when Nicole turned up at the same yoga class I take."

"OK. But you stayed in touch after that? Well, clearly you did, if you went running together a number of times. Did you see her in any other contexts?"

"Well yes, Nicole suggested we meet for coffee, and so we did that a few times. And we met for lunch once, and for a drink one evening after yoga, too. I think that was pretty much it really."

"And presumably you talked to one another at these coffees and drinks and lunches?"

"Yes, we talked," Anna sounded mildly irked. "What point are you making DS Barrett?"

"I suppose I'm making the point that you may know more about Nicole's life than you realise," Tina smiled. "So, what did you talk about?"

"Oh Lord," Anna shook her head, "everything, nothing." She got up and moved to the French windows and adjusted the silk drapes.

"Yoga, Nicole's hair extensions, the calorific content of a single peanut. Nothing deep and meaningful if that's what you mean, Nicole wasn't that sort of person."

"Not a lot in common then, would I be right in thinking?"

Anna turned from the curtains and met Tina's eye, "I strike you as deep and meaningful do I, DS Bassett?"

Tina failed to hide a smile. "All the same, you must have picked up some clues as to how Nicole was feeling in herself. For instance, would you say that she seemed happy, content with her life? Or did she appear to you to be sad, dissatisfied, worried? Just your gut feeling – was Nicole in a good place in her life or not?"

"My gut feeling?" Anna folded her arms across her body and raised her eyes to the ceiling as she considered this.

Watching her, Tina's eyes fell on a silver framed photograph on the dresser next to the window. It was a black and white head and shoulders shot of a young girl whom Tina recognised as the teenaged Anna. She was wearing her hair in youthful plaits but apart from that, Tina saw little difference between Anna at fifteen or sixteen and Anna as she was now. What difference there was, lay in the expression of the lovely eyes. Those of the girl held a softness which had not survived the intervening years. Glancing at the grown woman again, she realised that Anna was watching her, an expression in her eyes which Tina could not quite fathom. Then in a moment it was gone, and Tina belatedly realised that she had missed what Anna had been saying.

"Sorry," she apologised quickly, "I didn't quite…"

"I was saying, that to me Nicole seemed content with her life. She was full of some guy she was seeing, she seemed to think he might finally be 'the one'."

Anna ghosted a smile, "And who knows, maybe he would have been, given the chance."

*

CHAPTER 9

Friday 24th February

"I wouldn't mind my dentist looking like that," said JP, as soon as they were outside.

"I bet you wouldn't." Tina tried to keep the bitterness from her tone. No surprises to discover that the Anna Fox types of this world would be his type.

"All the same," JP mused, "what do you think makes people decide to be a dentist? Do they just wake up one morning and say – God, I love teeth! I want to spend the rest of my life staring into people's mouths."

"Why does anybody decide to become anything," Tina snapped. "And I don't imagine the pay is too shabby."

JP's eyebrows rose, the way they did, when for no apparent reason, Tina had suddenly taken his head off.

Back in the car, Tina said. "I've seen her somewhere before, Anna Fox."

"Yeah?"

"Somewhere to do with work, I think. I just can't put my finger on where exactly. No matter, it will probably come to me."

*

Up on the cliffs now, the sun had made a sudden appearance, but the wind was stronger than ever. Above her head, gulls wheeled and cried.

Like Bethany Doyle, Tina was not overly fond of heights, and on her first visit here, she'd gone down on her knees and crawled to the edge of the cliff in order to peer over at the drop to the sea below. Today, she satisfied herself by standing well back and viewing only what could be seen from that safer distance. Certainly, the views were spectacular here, in the distance she could see Bray, Killiney, Dalkey. All very lovely, Tina told herself, but what the hell was she doing here? As a head clearing exercise after the upsetting confrontation with Orla, it had its uses, but if there had been anything to learn up here about Nicole Brady's death, she'd have learned it on her first visit to the place from where Nicole had fallen.

And what exactly was she hoping to find anyway? Put simply, she knew that what was bothering her came down to a single question. Did healthy young people just fall off cliffs? Well yes, actually, and surprisingly often in fact. Each summer tourists seemed to fall off the bloody Cliffs of Moher with monotonous regularity. But, and this was the thing, Nicole Brady had been running this route for a long time. Added to which she had been in the habit of pausing at this very spot. Which meant, that on the day she died, Nicole had been doing nothing more than she had always done. So, given all of that, why, Tina asked herself once again, on this particular occasion had she not arrived back safely at her car?

Because something different had happened that particular day, it must have done. Granted, the something different might be nothing more than that, Nicole, fearless of heights, had taken one step too many closer to the edge. So close that just one slip, one sudden gust of wind would unbalance her and send her hurtling through the air. The trouble of course was that no one had seen her fall. The appeal to the public for information had produced just one elderly man, who believed he had seen Nicole up on the hill that day. A young female jogger was how he had described her, with a long blonde ponytail and wearing a purple beanie hat, which matched the description of the one Nicole had been wearing that day. Asked if he had noticed anyone else on the cliff path, he said he thought he'd seen another jogger dressed in a black track suit with a hooded jacket but couldn't be absolutely certain if it had been a young man or a woman. He thought a man had passed him on the hill too, although he could not be quite certain that it was even on the same day.

With a small shiver, Tina realised that while she'd been standing there brooding, the sun had gone in again. Ominously dark clouds had also appeared out of seemingly nowhere and were galumphing across the sky. Time to get off the hill she decided, and turning her back on the sea, she pulled the collar of her jacket tighter about her chin and set off down the pathway.

*

"You OK?" JP who had been swivelling in his chair, stopped as Tina came hurrying into the Detectives' Room, and eyed her over the top of his screen.

"I'm fine," said Tina. "What have I missed?"

"Mustard wants us on this fatal hit-and-run."

"OK. Do we have an ID on the victim yet?"

"Bethany Doyle," JP read from his screen. "Went out last evening to pick up a pizza she'd ordered earlier and was struck on her way back to her car, by a speeding vehicle which failed to stop."

"Bethany Doyle, did you say?"

"Yup, Bethany Doyle, thirty-seven years of age, worked as a Graphic Designer. Lived with her..."

"Not the same Bethany Doyle who was interviewed about the Nicole Brady thing?"

JP frowned, eyes on the screen once more, then gave a soft whistle.

"One and the same. I have to admit I didn't make the connection. What made you..."

Possibly the fact that I was just standing on the Hill of Howth thinking about her, less than half an hour ago, thought Tina. Aloud she said, "Dunno, the name just stuck in my head, I guess. So, what have we got?"

*

***

Avenge is an old-fashioned word, but I make no apologies for using it. It was the word that came to me from the beginning. Not revenge but avenge. I am not sure I had ever really fully appreciated the fine distinction in meaning between those two things before. Revenge it seems, applies to vindicating oneself, evening up the score for personal satisfaction, that sort of thing. To avenge, on the other hand, more often suggests the punishing of another, when one is intent on serving the ends of justice, or of vindicating someone other than oneself. Someone other than oneself – that sounds good, doesn't it? But I cannot lie, this is about me too. It always is to some extent.

***

CHAPTER 10

Friday 24th February

"So, what do we have from this eyewitness?" asked Tina. They were on their way to interview Bethany Doyle's wife, Dee Hall.

JP glanced at his notebook. "Her name is Mrs Evelyn Thorpe. Her house is next to the car park where Bethany left her car to go pick up the pizzas. Mrs T had taken her dog out for a short walk while the rain had eased up."

"Hallelujah for dog owners," Tina sang. "Where would we be without them?"

"It started raining heavily while they were out, and she was back at her gate when Brutus stopped for a sniff…"

"Brutus! What is he a Rottweiler?"

JP grinned. "Mini dachshund. So, while Brutus was sniffing, Mrs Thorpe says she heard an engine revving, then a car came speeding out of nowhere – her words – and ploughed into a woman who was crossing the road. The car didn't stop or even slow down, just sped away."

"Was she able to give us anything on the car?"

"Just that it was dark-coloured, black possibly navy blue and travelling northbound. Couldn't say if the driver was male or female. She was pretty shook up of course, so we'll be asking her to go over her statement again on the off-chance she remembers anything more."

"But she actually said she heard the engine revving before the car came into sight?"

JP consulted his notebook. "Her actual words were, 'I heard the sound of an engine revving. I looked up and saw a car come speeding out of nowhere. It ploughed into a poor woman who was on the road. It didn't stop, didn't even slow down. It just kept on going.'"

"Right. And what about CCTV?"

"Some of the businesses on the main street have cameras, they're being checked. And Napoli, that's the pizzeria, have Bethany coming in and going out again. There's CCTV in the carpark, but I'm not sure we'll get anything from the spot where the actual impact happened, still, we live in hope."

*

The village's main street was little more than a straggle of shops, a post office, a couple of pubs, chipper, Chinese take-away, and the pizzeria Bethany Doyle had visited minutes before her death. According to JP, people came from miles around to buy their pizzas at Napoli.

"What's so special about it?" Tina demanded, her nose pressed up against the window of the Pizzeria.

They had left the car in the car park where Bethany Doyle had parked on the night she died, then walked back to the place where she had met her death, marked now with a few floral tributes. From here they made their way to the far end of the street and Napoli, which according to a sign on the door was closed and not due to reopen until 5.30 that evening.

"It looks like a little hole in the wall sort of place to me," Tina complained. "There are only four tables as far as I can see. And why is it closed at lunchtime?"

She was starving and had been looking forward to a pizza.

"Probably because they don't need to open," said JP. "That's how good it is. Come on, with any luck this Dee Hall will give us a cup of a tea and a sandwich."

*

At first it seemed no-one was home, and they stood in the tiny porch of the tiny cottage for some time before the door opened slowly on a woman who surveyed them silently from eyes devoid of expression.

"Ms Hall," Tina enquired. "Ms Dee Hall?"

She was thinking that this couldn't be Bethany Doyle's wife. Bethany had been thirty-seven years old; this woman looked old enough to be Bethany's mother. When the woman continued to stare in silence, Tina tried again.

"I'm Detective Sergeant Martina Bassett, and this is Detective Garda O'Rourke. Is Ms Dee Hall at home, we're here to talk to her about Bethany."

"I'm Dee Hall," the woman's voice was deep, but toneless. "Bethany is dead. Come in if you must."

With a glance at one another, Tina and JP followed Dee along a narrow hallway and into a miniscule sitting room. The curtains had been only partially drawn, but the lights had not been switched on, so the room was dim. Tina's eye was immediately drawn to a spinning wheel standing next to the single window. Dee made straight for one of a pair of rocking chairs on either side of a wood-burning stove which emitted neither light nor warmth and began rocking gently to and fro. The temperature was Baltic, so much so that Tina expected JP to start blowing on his fingers at any second. She gave it a minute or two, then with no invitation to sit down forthcoming, took matters into her own hands and dropped down on the low settee. After a moment's hesitation, JP sat down next to her. Dee looked at him dully.

"Forgive my lack of manners, and I should have offered you something to drink. Water or juice or…." her voice dwindled away as though the endless possibilities had exhausted her mental facilities.

Both detectives hurriedly declined, and Dee closed her eyes once more. Tina and JP exchanged glances, and for a moment they sat in silence just watching the rocking woman. Dee was a tall, solidly built woman, with long, messy hair straggling to well below her waist. It was steel grey in colour but showing streaks here and there of its original red-gold. Her face was naked of makeup, the striking translucent blue eyes showing no sign of recent weeping. She was bizarrely dressed in a shapeless jumper of vertical purple and green stripes, which clashed spectacularly with her baggy rainbow patchwork trousers. Her feet, in spite of the chill of the cottage were shod in orange flip-flops. She looked, thought Tina, like a caricature of an aging hippie; one who had got dressed in the dark. She glanced at JP again and nodded at him to kick off the interview, otherwise they might be here all day and night.

"Ms Hall, Dee, may I call you Dee?" JP began. Dee's eyes remained closed, but her head inclined almost imperceptibly.

"Thank you, Dee, and first, let me offer you our sincere condolences on the loss of your wife, Bethany. Please believe that we appreciate how difficult a time this is for you, and how the very last thing you might want…"

"You want to know about last night?" Dee's tone was gruff. "Fine then. Well, it was Friday, so it was pizza night."

"Right. And pizza night – this was a regular thing, was it?"

"Every Friday. I phoned in the order and Bethany went to collect it."

"Was that usual, collecting the pizza? You didn't ever have it delivered?"

"Napoli don't deliver. Nuisance, but Bethany said it was worth it. She wasn't wrong, but I don't suppose I'll ever eat it again now."

For a moment there was silence in the room except for the creaking of the rocking chair. Tina caught herself thinking, I used to say the same about Chilli Con Carne. Gerry had suffered his fatal heart-attack while eating his dinner. He had fallen forward across the table and the food had adhered to the front of his blue V-neck jumper. It was the first time Tina had seen anybody die, and for a long time afterwards, death and Chilli con Carne had been indelibly linked in her mind.

"OK," said JP, after a moment. "So, Bethany would go and collect the pizza every Friday evening? Was it always Bethany who went?"

"Always Bethany. I don't drive, never took to it."

"Then am I right in thinking you're a one car household?"

"Just the one. Bethany's car". The rocking stopped and Dee's eyes opened. "I suppose it's still where she left it?"

"That's being looked after," JP reassured her. "The car will be returned to you as soon as possible, we'll see to that."

Dee closed her eyes and the rocking resumed. "Don't want the car. Want Bethany, alive and smiling, the way she was last time I saw her. See to that can you?"

As another silence fell, Dee opened her eyes once more and looked directly at JP. She said, her voice suddenly gentle, "Sorry. Know you're only trying to do your job. You were asking about pizza night. Yes, it was always Bethany who collected the food. Fiori di Zucca for me. Capriccioso for Bethany. Always the same. Only thing that changed was the dip. Bethany had to have a dip to dunk her pizza crust. Sometimes garlic, sometimes blue cheese. Last night it was blue cheese…"

God, I'm starving, thought Tina, then forgot her stomach as Dee's voice broke and she began to cry. The sounds she made were hoarse, rasping and guttural. And listening to those sounds Tina knew with certainty that this was the first time since learning of her loss, that Dee had permitted herself the release and relief of tears. Let her cry, Tina told herself. It was good and it was necessary. The weeping stopped as suddenly as it began. Dee pulled a cotton hanky from her trouser pocket, wiped her eyes and shook herself like a dog shaking off raindrops.

"Sorry about that," she said briskly. "Uncomfortable for you but made me feel better. Still, want to help you find whoever did this to her. So, fire away with your questions, young man."

"If you're sure you feel up to it," said JP. Dee who had resumed her rocking, eyes open now, nodded her head.

"Good, so we know that Bethany went out to collect the pizzas and parked in the car park next to the church. Is that where she'd usually park?"

"Always," said Dee. "Parking not permitted on the main street, not without a permit. Bethany always drives… drove to the car park, then walked back. Had to cross the road to get to Napoli." The wonderful blue eyes opened suddenly, fixed on JP.

"The police told me the car didn't stop. Ran her down and left her there. Who does a thing like that?" There was of course no answer to that. In the ensuing silence, Dee leaned forward suddenly. "When can I have her back?"

JP and Tina exchanged glances again. "That's difficult to say exactly," JP's tone was extra gentle. "You see, under the circumstances there will have to be a post-mortem."

Dee sank back in the chair and resumed rocking. "Understood. But things need to be done, plans have to be made. Her family want to know."

"Of course, I understand. And as Bethany's legal next-of-kin, you will be kept informed of everything, and Bethany's… Bethany will be released to you as soon as possible."

Dee bowed her head in acknowledgement, then looked up with a sudden grin. "He hates me, you know. Bethany's old man. Didn't come to the wedding. Doesn't believe in it, he said, doesn't believe in homosexuality! Sorry, doing it again, dragging you into my personal woes instead of letting you do your work."

"Not at all," a flustered looking JP assured her. "Please don't feel that you're hindering us in any way. You've been more than helpful." He looked a question at Tina, and she got to her feet.

"Yes, that's enough for now," she agreed. "We'll let you get some rest. We can let ourselves out."

But Dee insisted on getting up. Following her along the narrow hallway again, JP asked, "Have you…is there someone we could call to come and sit with you?"

Dee glanced back, "Thank you. Thoughtful. Nobody I want, except Bethany. Self-sufficient, always was. Need to learn to be alone again. No time like the present to begin."

Outside the air seeming warmer than in the frigid room, Tina turned to Dee. "Am I right in thinking that Bethany had suffered a recent loss herself? A close friend, wasn't it?"

"Nicole Brady," said Dee. "Accident. Terrible business. Same age as Bethany, went to school together. Bethany went to the funeral. Next funeral will be hers. Makes no sense. You'll catch them, won't you? Catch whoever did this to my Bethany?"

An image of Orla Reid's reproachful face rose before Tina's eyes. "All I can promise is that we'll do our best," she said firmly.

*

"Would you prefer to be buried or cremated?" asked JP, as they were heading back toward the village once more. Tina took her eyes off the road to stare at him bemusedly.

"I'd prefer not to be dead, if it's all the same to you."

"But you will be some day," JP assured her cheerfully. "Personally, I can never quite make up my mind between the two."

Tina rolled her eyes but considered the question. "Cremation," she said. "Then stick the ashes in the ground and plant a tree on top." She glanced at JP again. "You should opt for cremation too. If they buried you, you'd be moaning from the grave about the cold."

"I don't moan about the cold, I comment on it. By the way, you just drove past the chipper, I thought you were starving. Then again, when aren't you starving? You remind me of one of those killer shrews that have to eat every three hours or die."

"You know you basically just called me a rodent?" said Tina. "And anyway, I want to take another look at the scene of the hit-and-run first."

*

Standing at the footpath's edge, Tina surveyed the road.

"What's on your mind?" asked JP.

"Habits. How people are creatures of them. Take Bethany Doyle, we know from Dee that Bethany always ordered the exact same pizza from Napoli every Friday night, and always parked in the same place. And I'd be prepared to bet that she always crossed it at more or less the same place, wouldn't you?"

"Yeah, chances are she did cross the road at the same place more or less, but what of it?"

"Well, your witness, Mrs T and her dog, Caesar, was it?"

"Close, but no cigar. Brutus."

"OK, well she heard the sudden revving of an engine, right? Then a car comes out of nowhere and ploughs into poor Bethany. What I want to know, is where did the car from? I mean presumably Bethany checked nothing was coming before she stepped off the pavement into the road…" Tina turned to JP. "We need to have someone go over her statement with her again. Get her to focus on the moment she heard the revving of an engine. See if she can remember where exactly Bethany was at the time – still on the pavement, just about to step off the pavement or already on the road."

"Sure, I'll get onto it, but you have to remember it was a filthy night with heavy rain, and Bethany was wearing a parka with a fur-trimmed hood. The CCTV footage from Napoli shows her pulling the hood up as she was leaving. Plus, she was balancing those pizza boxes. All of that might well have affected her hearing and vision for the worse. What's to say that she didn't just step out on to the road at the wrong minute, as the car speeded up?"

"Or what's to say that the car speeded up, just as she stepped onto the road?" asked Tina. "OK, don't look at me like that, JP."

"No but hang on, Tina, are you really suggesting that this wasn't just a hit-and-run, that Bethany Doyle was the target?"

"I'm not suggesting anything, I'm just imagining a scenario," said Tina. "Now let's go get some grub, my stomach thinks my throat's been cut."

*

CHAPTER 11

Saturday 25th February

"This can't be happening," said Rachel.

"I know," Paula shook her blonde head. "It's all like some awful nightmare. It just doesn't seem possible."

"First Nicole and now Bethany," Megan chimed in, her vapid blue gaze fixed on the bubbles in her champagne flute, as though they held her spellbound. Anna, whose glass held nothing more than sparkling water, said nothing. Once again, a death had brought them all together again, this time to Jennifer's exquisite living room. Jennifer had insisted they come back with her, after their group condolences visit to Dee's tiny cottage.

"For a much-needed drink", she had said.

Anna suspected that Dee's raw grief had made an impression, even on Jennifer. In spite of having clearly been drinking before they set off, she had not uttered even one catty remark during the entire visit. Then again, it had been impossible not to be touched by the quality of the widow's devastation, which probably explained why no one, Anna included, had refused what was more an order than a suggestion. Not for a drink, she had told Jennifer pointedly, as she was driving, but just to keep them company. She agreed to meet them at Jennifer's and Jennifer, Megan and Paula set off in Rachel's car.

Anna was glad of the chance to be alone for a while, Dee's grief had been difficult to witness. She took her time and by the time she arrived, the champagne had already been opened and Rachel who was on sparkling water was sipping it from a champagne flute. Presumably because, as Jennifer, who was definitely three sheets to the wind now, informed Anna loudly, "I'm absolutely insisting that everyone, even the boring ones are having bubbles today."

"That's you and me told," Anna smiled wryly at Rachel. There was no answering smile. Rachel appeared shell-shocked, and Anna reminded herself how fond of Bethany she had always been.
Anna was re-called to the present by Jennifer's loud and strident tone.

"Will everyone please stop saying it's impossible, that it can't be happening. It's shit, but it's happening. It's all shit, life is shit. So, let's have some more bubbles! Bubbles make everything more bearable."

Picking up the empty bottle from the table, Jennifer strode from the room, a little unsteadily in her high heels. For a moment there was silence in the room, then Megan and Paula began whispering. Rachel seemed locked in her thoughts, so Anna left her to it. Jennifer returned, carrying a bottle of champagne in each hand. She had changed out of the black trousers and black tailored jacket she had worn to visit Dee and was now sporting a cobalt blue bikini under a matching short kaftan which hung open. The stilettos had been replaced by a pair of white platform heeled fit-flops and her hair had been pulled into a topknot.

"Guys, guys," she called, waving both bottles over her head. "I've decided enough doom and gloom. Now come on, let's all pile into the hot tub!"

"Oh, here we go!" Anna heard Rachel mutter under her breath. Aloud she said, "Count me out, Jennifer. I have to get home to…"

"No, you don't, you don't have to do anything," Jennifer insisted.

"Then I want to get home," said Rachel. "It's been a horrible day and anyway, I said I'd be back to …"

"Oh whatever," Jennifer cut her short. "Come on Paula, come on Megan, you'll both get in with me, won't you?"

"I haven't got a swimsuit," said Paula, weakly.

"Me neither," Megan made it sound like she had erred in not packing one when visiting a recent widow.

"So? I can loan you both one," Jennifer sang blithely. "Anna, what about you, I can loan you one too?"

"I don't think so," Anna smiled but shook her head. "It's February, and it's freezing out there."

"Eh duh," Jennifer blinked at such lunacy. "I said HOT tub. What does it matter what the weather is like? We can drink champagne and look at the stars. The stars look better with bubbles. Everything looks better with bubbles."

Jennifer's eyes narrowed, "You know, Anna, I can remember when you used to be up for a bit of fun. And it's not like you have to run off home like perfect little Mummy bear, there."

The jibe was clearly aimed at Rachel at much as Anna. Rachel put her glass down and got to her feet and Anna saw her chance and got up too.

"I actually do have to head," she said. "As Rachel says, it's been a difficult day. But another time maybe."

"Fine then, go! Come on you two," Jennifer turned to Paula and Megan. "Let's get upstairs and find you all some suits. Though your tits are three times the size of mine, Megan, but maybe you can squeeze into one of Stacey's."

Laughing, she sailed from the room, followed by Megan. Paula followed more slowly. Turning she said in an undertone to Rachel, "I'll see if I can talk her out of it."

Rachel looked at Anna. "She always does this when she's upset, or when she's pissed. I keep telling her she shouldn't be in that hot tub when she's been drinking. But at least she won't be on her own this time. You coming? I really do have to go, Finn has a thing to go to and I need to take over with the kids."

*

CHAPTER 12

Saturday 25th February

Outside in the frosty air, their feet crunching on gravel, Anna turned to Rachel.

"Am I imagining it or is Jennifer going heavy on the booze these days. Or is it just on account of Nicole and Bethany?"

"No, it's not just about that," Rachel sighed and shivered "Tell you what, let's sit in my car to chat, I'm freezing."

"Good idea, if you're sure you don't have to rush away."

"I can spare five minutes."

"That's better," Rachel turned on the heating in the car. "So, as I was saying, it's not just because of what's happened. Jennifer's been drinking far too much ever since Jason left her for another woman."

"But that was a few years ago now, wasn't it?"

"It's more than four," said Rachel.

"Jason left shortly after Stacy's fifteenth birthday, she's coming up to nineteen now. They're actually divorced now. Jason remarried, pretty much as soon as the ink was dry on the divorce paper and of course that just made Jennifer's drinking even worse. I mean, the divorce really set her back, but him getting married like that so soon after, practically drove her batshit crazy. She just couldn't believe it could happen to her. She's not even particularly good-looking, this other woman, this Yvonne. And that's not just Jennifer being bitchy. I've seen her myself, she's really ordinary looking. Plus, she's five years older than Jennifer just to rub salt into the wound. I don't think I've ever seen Jen so angry and hurt and bitter."

"Yes, I can imagine it was hard to swallow for someone like Jennifer," said Anna.

"Though in fairness to Jason," Rachel went on, "he didn't fight her over the divorce. Jennifer kept the house and the kids of course and she got an eye-watering settlement into the bargain. I mean it's not like Jason couldn't afford it or anything, but to be honest, I think it only made Jennifer even angrier that he didn't put up a fight. Because that way she could have fought back and won, if you know what I mean."

"Jennifer always did like to win," said Anna.

Rachel glanced at her quickly, then sighed. "Yes, I suppose she did. And there's this thing with the kids now. At first, Jennifer refused to let Jason see them. She tried to turn them against him. But now, they're older and they're choosing to spend more and more time with their dad, which means they're spending time with Yvonne too. I think they actually quite like her, and that's killing Jennifer. Not that I can really blame them. I mean, Jennifer must be a bit of nightmare to live with, with her drinking so much now. You can see why they would want to spend more and more time with their dad. It's just a mess."

For a moment, they sat in silence, just staring at the outline of the handsome big house in the growing darkness.

"But never mind Jennifer," said Rachel suddenly. "How are you doing really, Anna? You must miss your dad very much?"

"I do, of course I do," said Anna. "Though in a sense I feel like I lost him a long time before he actually died. But anyway, I'd better go and let you get home to your boys." She reached for the door handle, but Rachel stopped her.

"Anna? I can't stop thinking about those photographs, the ones with our faces all scratched out."

Taken by surprise, Anna turned back. "What made you think about that now?"

"I don't know, I just keep wondering, and I know you thought it was just somebody's idea of a stupid joke?"

"I still do. What else could it be?"

"I don't know. But Nicole… well Nicole thought they were sent to us out of spite. She said it gave her a nasty feeling seeing her face scratched out that way. She said it made her feel that someone wished her ill or something, like they wanted to harm her even."

"Well, I knew those photos upset her," said Anna. "But to be honest, I put it down to shock at the possibility that anyone might not like her."

Rachel smiled thinly, "Yes, Nicole was like that, wasn't she? All the same, Anna, when you think about it, harm did come to Nicole. I mean she had that accident and now…well now she's dead. And so is Bethany, and I just can't help wondering, that's all."

"Come on, Rachel," Anna chided gently. "You're not seriously telling me you believe that defacing a photograph of somebody can actually do that person harm? Like some kind of voodoo, or something. Granted it was a nasty sort of thing to do, but even so, don't you think you're taking it a bit much to heart?"

"You think I'm being silly, don't you?"

Anna smiled, "Maybe just a tad. But I also think it's understandable. You've lost two close friends and you're feeling shocked and sad."

Seeing the glitter of tears in Rachel's eyes, she leaned in, put her arms about her and held her while she cried.

*

***

Am I better off for what I have done? Is the world a better place?

Was it as I imagined it would be? Effective, dispassionate? Do I have the temperament for an avenger? Has it changed me, will it change me?

These and other questions I don't have time for. Onward.

***

CHAPTER 13

Sunday 26th February

Anna woke to the trilling of her phone. "Anna? Anna, I think I did something really stupid last night."

Anna sighed, took a deep breath. "OK, what did you do, Rachel?"

"It was those photographs. I just couldn't stop thinking about them."

Anna sat up, pushing off the duvet. "What about the photographs?"

"It was because of Jack, he woke up crying for me and I suddenly thought - imagine if he woke like that wanting me and needing me, and I wasn't there for him. And I'd had a few glasses of wine, and I got really upset about Nicole and Bethany. And the more I thought about it, the more I…"

"Rachel, could you just get to the point, sweetheart?"

"I rang the police," it came out in a rush. "I rang the police, and I told them about the photographs."

Anna got out of bed and walked to the window, pulled the curtains on a grey day.

"You told them what about the photographs?"

"You know, that we'd got them, been sent them, and how our faces had been scratched out and how upsetting it had been. And the guard asked me if we any idea who'd sent them and….well I told them how I'd got it into my head that it might have something to do with the A-Team."

"The A-Team?" Anna couldn't hide her surprise. "What on earth made you think the photos had anything to do with the A Team?"

"I don't know," said Rachel slowly. "It just came into my head last night. I mean, all six of us got them, and no-one else did."

"You don't know that Rachel," said Anna.

"No, but that's just it, I do, Anna. Because before I called the guards, I rang Paula and just asked her out straight if she'd had one. She hadn't a clue what I was talking about. So, then I decided to ring around a few other people, you know some of the girls from our class that I've kept in touch with."

"And what, you just rang a bunch of people and asked them if they'd been sent photos with their faces scratched out? Are you serious, Rachel?"

"No, no I didn't say anything about the faces. I made out I was calling about the reunion and the plan to re-take the photo. Then I just asked if they'd got their copy of the photograph. And you know what, Anna, none of them had. I'm telling you, it was just us six who got them. And that was when I started thinking about what happened to Nicole and Bethany again, and I got myself into a state and…"

"And rang the police," Anna finished.

"Yes. But then this morning I felt really stupid about it. But it's too late now because they're sending someone round to talk to us."

"To us?"

"To me and you, and Jennifer and Megan. Some detective rang me back this morning and started asking me a lot of questions. I tried to tell her that I'd just overreacted, but she said she thought it was best if she interviewed us anyway. All together, Anna, she wants to talk to us all together. And Jennifer is going to go ape shit when I tell her. And you're probably annoyed with me now, too…."

"I'm not annoyed with you Rachel," Anna told her quietly. "You did what you felt you should do." She was speaking the truth, but she was fairly sure that Jennifer would not receive the news with the same equanimity.

“Honestly? And you don’t think I’m mad or stupid?”

“No, I don’t think you’re either mad or stupid. So, where are we supposed to meet this Detective? What’s her name?”

“Detective Sergeant Martina Bassett, but she says to call her Tina. And I don’t know where we’re meeting her yet. She said I had to talk to you all first and let her know where best suited everyone. But she wants it to be today.”

“Today? It’s Sunday, she’s not wasting any time, is she?” Anna thought for a moment. “OK, well, look Rachel, it can’t be helped. So just try to calm down, then call Jennifer and the others. And keep me posted.”

“I will, thanks Anna.”

*

In the kitchen, Anna took the photo from the dresser drawer where, having decided to hold onto it, she’d put it away. She gazed at the place where her own face should have been. Then one by one she picked out the other girls who had made up the A-Team, Nicole, Bethany, Rachel, Jennifer, and Megan. Six girls who were now women, two of them were dead. Thinking about that, she carried the photograph with her as she went back to her bedroom. No doubt, Detective Tina Bassett would want to see it for herself.

*

CHAPTER 14

Sunday 26th February

Tina looked up from the photograph she had been studying, letting her gaze move over the four women assembled before her.

"And it was a copy of this photograph you each got sent through the post," she asked.

Three heads nodded, the fourth, that of Jennifer O'Keeffe remained bent over her right hand, the nails of which she appeared to be inspecting with great interest.

"So, is there anything you can tell me about the photo," said Tina. "When was it taken? Does it have any particular significance to you all, that sort of thing?"

"Not to me it doesn't," said Jennifer O'Keeffe sourly, her gaze still on her fingernails.

Tina eyed the woman in whose home the interview was taking place. It was a beautiful home, she had to admit, built on an incline just off the coast road on the outskirts of Malahide, so that it commanded views of the sea. "Remind me to ask her for her architect's number before we go," Tina had ordered JP, as the car pulled up before it.

And inside the house was equally as impressive. The décor was ultra-modern, and light flooded through the big windows of the living room in which they now sat. Tina had recognised their reluctant hostess the moment the woman unsmilingly opened the door to them. Unsurprisingly, considering that Jennifer O'Keeffe had sat in the courtroom through every day of her brother Lorcan's trial for the rape of Orla Reid. From the outset, Jennifer had made it very clear that the interview was happening against her wishes and was in her opinion, a waste of her time. That it was taking place at her home, it was also made clear, was purely due to Jennifer having flatly refused to be put to the inconvenience of it taking place elsewhere. Still, at least there was coffee, Tina comforted herself; very good and very hot black coffee. No biscuits though, which while a pity did not particularly surprise Tina. Jennifer O'Keeffe struck her as someone who might conceivably gone her entire lifetime unaware of the existence of biscuits. Unnaturally skinny, was Tina's verdict, what Phyllis would have called bony. But undoubtedly very attractive, if looking a tad green about the gills. Been on the sauce, Tina guessed, which come to think of it, probably also accounted for the coffee.

Aloud she said, "Surely it has some significance to at least one of you?"

"Why don't you ask Liz Wade about it. She's the one who sent it to us."

"We don't know that Jennifer," said Anna, and Tina turned to her enquiringly.

"It was Liz Wade who posted the picture on Facebook," Anna explained.

"She was a classmate of ours. And now she's involved in organising a class reunion and some plan to retake the photo. That's why we thought it was possible that Liz might have been the one who sent the copies."

"Liz is in the photo," said Rachel, getting to her feet. "I'll show you." She went and stood behind Tina's chair and pointed over her shoulder. "That's Liz in the back row, third from the right."

Tina studied the image of a tall, somewhat heavy looking girl with frizzy hair and glasses, who was smiling a toothy and enthusiastic smile for the camera.

"Actually, she's Liz Warren now," Rachel added. "She got married."

"Hard though it is to believe," Jennifer sneered, and Megan, the blonde with the enormous boobs giggled.

Like a silly teenager, thought Tina. "I take it you're not a fan of the lady, then?"

Jennifer shrugged her thin shoulders. "I have no opinion on her, one way or another. She's just someone who went to the same school as us, that's all."

"Were any of you particular friends of Liz Wade?" Tina glanced from one to the other of the four women but was met with silence.

Rachel spoke eventually, "Liz wasn't really one of us. One of our crowd, I mean."

"But you think it may be her who sent these photos? Has anyone actually tackled her about it?"

The women looked at one another a little blankly. "Well, no," said Rachel, still standing behind Tina's chair.

"Not me," said Anna. "I personally never saw any reason to suspect it was her in the first place."

Megan just shook her head and widened her vapid looking blue eyes, as though startled at the idea she might have taken such an action.

"Jennifer?" Tina turned to their hostess, who curled her lip.

"I wouldn't give her the satisfaction. Besides, I never see the woman, let alone speak to her."

"OK then," said Tina. "So, going back to the photograph itself, you must have some idea when it was taken? Last day of school, the day you finished the Leaving Cert? Something like that?"

"Well, it definitely wasn't taken the year we left school," said Rachel. "We all look way too young for it to be then. No, I think it must have been taken a couple of years earlier than that."

"So roughly when, would you guess?"

Once again, Rachel leaned in to inspect the photograph. "I'd say it was taken before we started transition year. There are a couple of girls in it who wouldn't still have been in our class if it were any later. Girls who went straight into fifth year and didn't go to transition year with us. So that would make it sometime in 1995, I think. Am I right, Anna?"

"Sounds about right," Anna agreed.

"And the more I think about it," Rachel went on, "the more sense it makes that a group photo would have been taken then, as the last time we would be all together as a class. I imagine it was taken before we broke up for the summer."

"And any idea who took it?" asked Tina. There was a collective shaking of heads.

"One of the teachers, probably," Rachel offered. "I seem to remember one of them taking a group shot from a first-floor window."

"Right, so let me get this straight, the photo was recently posted on Facebook as part of a school reunion thing is that it?"

"Well actually," said Rachel, "the photo came first. Liz posted it to Facebook, and it was after people saw it and started commenting on it, that the idea for doing a re-take came up. And then a group was formed - the Class of '98. That's the year we did our Leaving Certificate. Even though, as I said, there are girls in the photo who did it a year earlier and..." Rachel broke off as Jennifer suddenly stretched her arms above her head and yawned theatrically.

"Is it just me," she drawled, "or is anyone else bored to absolute bloody tears by this nonsense over some old photograph? Surely the police have more important things to do with their time. And quite frankly, if they don't, I do."

Tina opened her mouth to reply but JP beat her to it.

“It may have slipped your mind, Ms O’Keeffe,” he said dryly, “but it was your friend, Rachel here, who drew our attention to the photographs in the first place. In her own words, she found them upsetting and unsettling. As, she gave us to understand, did your late friend, Nicole Brady.”

“That’s rubbish,” said Jennifer. “The only reason Nicole got upset was because someone had the nerve to have a go at a photo of her precious face. But she got over herself. And as for Rachel, the only reason she called you last night was because she got pissed and spooked herself silly. She’s already wishing she’d said nothing. And as for the idea of these stupid photos having anything to do with what happened to Nicole or Bethany – that’s pure nonsense too. Nicole fell off a cliff. Bethany got run over by some drunk too terrified to stop, as likely as not.”

There was an uncomfortable silence for a moment, then Tina picked up where she had left off. “OK then, I believe we’d established when the original photograph was most likely taken. And we know that a copy was posted to Facebook, you suspect by your old classmate, Liz Wade. Nobody can be certain who was responsible for the individual defaced copies you each received in the post. Is there any actual reason to suspect that might have been Liz Wade too?”

“Rachel?” Tina prompted, when no-one else looked set to speak. “Can you think of any reason why Liz would do such a thing?”

“No,” Rachel shook her head, “I mean, not really. Except well…I suppose we were a bit mean to her.”

“Who’s we exactly?” asked Tina.

“Well, you know, all of us really, everyone who was part of the A-Team gang."

“This is the gang you were all a part of while you were at school?”

Jennifer exploded, “Oh, for God’s sake. I actually do not believe it. Are we really going to…? OK fine. Fine!”

Getting to her feet, she marched across the room to where JP sat, arms extended before her and stuck her upturned wrists under his nose.

“The games up,” she announced. “I confess! Now take me away, officer.”

*

CHAPTER 15

Sunday 26th February

"What exactly are you confessing to, Jennifer?" asked Tina mildly. Anna studied her toes in obvious embarrassment, while Rachel frowned, and Megan giggled in seeming helplessness.

"To a bit of teasing," said Jennifer. "Possibly even - shock horror - a bit of name-calling. To being mean in fact. Isn't that what we're being accused of here? I mean, for God's sake, we were teenagers!"

"Is that how you saw it, Rachel?" Tina asked quietly.

"I suppose so," Rachel's tone lacked conviction. "I suppose it was just teenage stuff."

"But was it harmless?" said Anna, and all heads turned toward her.

"You didn't think so?" asked Tina.

Anna shrugged, "I think that's probably for others to decide, the people we teased, for instance, the people we bullied."

"Now just hold on a minute here," said Jennifer. "I don't know how the rest of you remember it, but I for one categorically deny there was any bullying involved. We called one another names and took the piss out of people. But nobody got hurt, I don't care what anyone says."

She flounced back to the sofa and threw herself down once more. Again, Tina turned to Anna.

"What about you, Anna, do you believe anyone got hurt?"

“I believe feelings got hurt,” said Anna. “Actually, I know for a fact they did.”

“You’re thinking about Claire, aren’t you?” said Rachel.

Anna, clearly taken aback, blinked, then shook her head, “Actually, I was thinking about Liz. All that business about letting her think she could be one of us, a part of the A Team, when we had no intention of ever letting her in. All that initiation stuff we made her do”

“Oh God,” Rachel sounded dismayed. “I’d sort of forgotten about that. That really was very mean…”

“Oh, for God’s sake, here we go again,” Jennifer groaned.

Tina looked from Rachel to Anna. “Would anybody care to share? Anna?”

Anna shrugged, “It’s like I said, Liz wanted to be one of us and we knew it. Liz was one of those people who just couldn’t hide it. And so, some of us,” Anna looked pointedly in Jennifer’s direction, “had the idea of getting a bit of fun out of it. So, we invented an initiation process, you know, tests Liz had to pass, tasks she had to complete if she wanted to become a member of the A Team.”

“What kind of tests and tasks?” asked JP.

“Well, it started with small things, Liz had to bring in things for us, biscuits, cakes, sweets, that kind of thing. And then it moved on to other things, cigarettes…”

“Drink,” piped up Rachel, looking pleased at the sudden memory. “Remember she came in with a half empty bottle of sherry and we made fun of her about it?”

“Yes, drink,” Anna agreed, “and after that, it was money, so we could buy our own drink and cigarettes.”

“And we made her do our homework,” offered Megan. “Our Irish homework mostly, because Liz was brilliant at Irish, so we made her write our essays and that awful Irish poetry stuff.”

“Nobody *made* her do anything,” Jennifer corrected. “Anything she did, she did because she wanted to do it.”

“Yes, technically that’s true,” Anna agreed. “But we let her believe that it was all adding up to becoming a member of the A Team.”

“I see,” said Tina, and she thought she actually did see. She had known girls like Liz Wade in school; girls who wanted more than anything to be one of the popular gang. She hadn’t wanted it herself, mostly, if she were honest, because she had never been able to fool herself that she could be. But also, because she had seen what it did to those girls who wanted it too much.

“So, besides giving you food and cigarettes and alcohol and money,” Tina continued, “what else was involved in this initiation process?”

“She had to do stuff, just silly stuff in the beginning, like standing up in the middle of class and flapping her arms and making chicken noises. Another time we made her hide in a cupboard.

“Oh, I remember that” Megan chirped with seeming delight. “It was in Biology class. We told Liz to grunt and groan and rattle the door. And Jennifer made everyone in the class pretend they couldn't hear anything. Poor old Mr O’Dea took half the class to figure out where the noises were coming from.”

“So, all pretty innocuous schoolgirl stuff so far then?” said Tina. “Would I be right in thinking things got a little more serious?”

“You could say that” said Anna wryly. “Liz had to stop doing her homework, and of course she got into trouble for that. Then we made her say stuff to people, nasty stuff, I mean. That didn’t come naturally to her, Liz wasn’t that sort of person.”

“She did it all the same though, didn’t she?” Jennifer’s voice was hard.

“Then we made her eat raw kidney,” Anna went on. “We told her we’d all had to do it.”

“And she actually did it too,” Megan’s tone blended wonder with disgust. “She was gagging and crying, but she did it. But then she threw up.”

“You don’t say,” said Tina icily. “Is there more?”

“We made her pierce her ears with a stapler,” Anna continued.” We all had multiple piercings in our ears, it was a thing in the A Team. So, we lied to Liz, told her we'd all done the piercings ourselves, using a stapler."

"And she believed that?" JP sounded horrified.

"I don't know if she believed it or not,” said Anna. “Maybe she just wanted to be one of us badly enough, but either ways, she agreed to do it. We borrowed a stapler from Nicole’s Dad’s study, the old-fashioned metal kind, with a real heft to it. Poor old Liz went white when she saw it. But again, fair play to her, she went through with it. Well at least on one ear, then she saw the blood and fainted.”

“It was awful,” said Rachel. “We did it in the park and we had to put Liz lying down on a bench. Jennifer had to slap her hard across the face a few times, to bring her round. And afterwards Liz got into a load of trouble at home over it. And her ear got infected…”

“I can’t think why,” said Tina. “Anything more?”

“We made her come to school one day, with no knickers on,” said Anna. “We convinced her we’d all be doing it on the same day, all the A Team, I mean.”

“She hardly fell for that?” Tina was incredulous.

“Oh, but she did. We worked up to it, you see, started with socks. We all had to wear particular colour socks to school. It was against the rules to wear anything but the uniform socks, so Liz risked getting into trouble. Then it was eyeshadow, we convinced her we’d all wear it to school one day, and we did that too. So then when we told her we’d all turn up for school knickerless, Liz believed us. She still didn’t want to do it, but we convinced her it was the final stage of the initiation process. We told that if she did this, she’d be one of us, one of the A Team.”

“So, let me guess,” said Tina. “This time it’s just Liz who turns up at school with no knickers on. And I’m assuming that wasn’t the end of the prank?”

"No, it didn't end there," said Anna. "The idea of course, was for as many people as possible to find out, but one in particular. We had this priest – a sort of Father Trendy type. Fr Bobby was his name, he was young and good looking in a floppy haired kind of way. He gave guitar lessons to the transition year students. Liz had the absolute hots for him, actually a lot of the girls did. So anyway, we chose a time we knew Fr Bobby would be coming out of the prefab building, they used for guitar lessons. Then we set it up so that Liz had to walk right in front of him. One of us, I can't remember who, tripped her up and sent her flying and someone else whipped up her skirt so everyone, including Fr Bobby, got a close-up of her bare ass."

"Oh God," Rachel groaned, "we really actually did that. Poor Liz."

"Yes, we did," said Anna. "And of course, Liz was mortified. And then she realised that we had no intention of ever letting her be part of the A Team."

"How did that go down?" asked Tina.

"She was angry, threatened to tell on us. But who and what was she going to tell? She'd gone to school with no knickers on – her mother would have killed her if she'd heard; she was the prim and proper sort. So really all poor Liz could do was to threaten to get her own back on us, tell us that we better watch out, that sort of thing."

"And did she get her own back?"

"No, it was all just talk really. Not that you could blame her. I don't suppose it was much fun going through school being called Liz-No-Knickers-Wade. And yes, before you ask, it was us who came up with that name too."

"Who could blame her indeed," said Tina. "So, was that it, or is there more?"

Anna shook her head, "No, that was it, as far as Liz was concerned."

"Meaning that there might be other people out there bearing grudges?"

"I suppose it's possible," said Anna, "but no-one in particular comes to mind."

"Right then, I think we'll leave it there for now," said Tina. "If you all just place your copy of the photo and the envelope it came in, if you have it, in the evidence bags Detective O'Rourke will provide, we can go and let you get on with your day. You've brought them along as we asked, I hope? As was explained, it's purely for elimination purposes."

"I haven't got the envelope, but I've already given my photo to Detective O'Rourke," Rachel smiled across the room at JP. Megan too, Tina noticed, favoured him with a smile from under her false eyelashes, as she slipped the photo, also minus its envelope, into the bag he held open for her. There was no smile for him from Anna however, nor from Jennifer who had no photo to hand over either. "I tore it up, why would I keep a photo of me headless in a hideous tartan skirt?" she demanded imperiously. There was, Tina decided, no answer to that.

"It may be necessary to test the photos for fingerprints," JP explained. "Purely for elimination purposes of course. And if that is the case, we'll need to arrange to have your fingerprints taken. Once that's done, the photographs will be returned to you, should you wish to have them. Can I ask each of you, who other than yourself handled the photo?"

"I showed mine to my husband," Rachel admitted. "And I… I showed it to Nicole, and she showed me hers"

"Just my Mum," said Megan."

"Nobody but me," Anna confirmed. Tina wrapped things up then and left JP to do the thank yous, while she escaped into the fresh if bitter air.

*

“What a coven of teenage bitches!” JP said with feeling as he joined her.

“Mmm,” Tina agreed, but her mind was elsewhere. She had a niggling sense of having missed something. Or was it some question she had left unasked? But for the life of her she had no idea what it was. Never mind, she told herself, as she drove off, if it was important, it would come back to her.

*

CHAPTER 16

Monday 27th February

At just after eleven the following morning, Tina and JP pulled into the narrow little street in Drumcondra where Liz Wade, now Warren, lived in one of a row of identical, small, red-bricked terraced houses facing the railway tracks. Liz answered the door to them, a tall, broad-shouldered woman with a shiny flushed face, a lot of fuzzy hair of indeterminate colour and eyes which blinked at them repeatedly from behind a pair of pink-rimmed oversized glasses.

"Oh, you're here!" she said. She stuck her head round the door and peered first right, then left.

"Did you find a place to park OK? It can be a bit of nightmare around here."

"Yes, we were lucky enough to find a spot," said JP. With a glance in Tina's direction he added, "Do you drive yourself, Ms…?"

"I prefer Mrs Warren," Liz smiled, displaying a mouthful of tombstone teeth. "I know it's considered old-fashioned to call yourself Mrs nowadays, but I just prefer it and so does Ray. Ray is my husband."

This last was said with unmistakable satisfaction bordering on pride. What does she want, a medal for being married, thought Tina sourly? "Detective O'Rourke was asking if you drive, Ms Warren?" she said impatiently.

"Oh, please call me Liz, yes I drive. But we're a one car family and my husband has it today. He wanted to be here for me today, but he runs his own business, an electrician. I told him there was no need, but he worries about me, my husband does."

She led them through a narrow hallway to a kitchen-cum dining room. Please sit down, won't you?" She indicated a well-scrubbed pine table which had been set with jug, matching sugar bowl and four white china mugs, each, Tina noted with something akin to awe, resting on matching saucers.

"You'll have tea." It was not a question, and they sat down at the table, while Liz busied herself making it. Real tea leaves and an actual teapot, Tina noted with no surprise.

"You say your husband is self-employed," she said. "I hope we haven't kept you from your own job?"

"Oh no, I'm off, today." Liz came toward them with the teapot in one hand and a large plate in the other. "I'm a nurse, so you know, I work shifts. Will you have some chocolate chip biscuits? I know we're all supposed to say cookies nowadays, but I don't make cookies, I make biscuits."

Tina accepted a biscuit and had to concede that it was good. JP clearly agreed, demolishing four in quick succession. Liz beaming with gratification pressed him to take more, eyes running him over from head to toe in unabashed appreciation. JP, grinning like an eejit, gave in and helped himself to more biscuits.

"Perhaps when everyone has had enough biscuits, we can get on with the reason we're here?" said Tina sourly.

Liz blinked from behind the hideous glasses. "Of course, you said on the phone you wanted to ask me some questions about poor Nicole and poor Bethany. So sad and so very shocking. But both accidents and I don't quite see…"

"Yes, as you say, both incidents are being treated as accidents," Tina conceded. "But as we explained to you, we're making enquiries of people who knew the dead women, family, friends…would you have considered yourself a friend of Nicole Brady and or Bethany Doyle?"

Liz, who had just picked up a biscuit, stared at it and frowned. "Would I?" she seemed to consider the question. "You know, I don't think that I could really say I considered them friends. Not anymore, I didn't."

"And while you were all at school together, would you say you'd been friends then?"

"Oh well," Liz gave a small shrug, "you know how it is when you're teenagers, all hanging about together in one big gang." She took a bite from the biscuit in her hand and smiled at Tina as she chewed.

"So, you're saying that back then you were part of the same gang as Bethany and Nicole, that would be the A-Team, I think?" said Tina.

The smile vanished from Liz's face, the chewing stopped, at the same time the blinking became almost maniacal. "What? No, that's not what I mean. I mean that's not what I said. I have no memory of any A-Team, no memory at all."

"You don't?" Tina showed surprise. "Only we've been given to understand otherwise, that a group of that name included girls you went to school with, among them the now sadly deceased Nicole Brady and Bethany Doyle. Other members were…"

Tina pretended to consult her notes. "Rachel Quinn, Anna Fox, Jennifer O'Keeffe, Megan …"

"I didn't say I don't remember the girls," Liz's tone was sulky.

Tina glanced up, smiled, "Then you do? Excellent."

"Yes, I remember them. "But like I just told you, we're not friends. I see Rachel Quinn around sometimes, and Anna Fox is a dentist, not that I go near her, I have my own dentist and he's absolutely lovely. And I never see Megan or Jennifer O'Keeffe. Though I did hear that Jennifer's husband left her for another woman. An older woman too, which just goes to show… not that I'd wish that on anyone of course, because I wouldn't."

"Of course," said Tina, who had enjoyed the little show of spite at Jennifer O'Keeffe's expense. "Then if you remember the girls, I imagine you remember the gang or group of which they were members, surely?"

"Well, but it was all so long ago, a lifetime it seems like," Liz protested. "I haven't thought about all that silly nonsense in years."

"By silly nonsense," said Tina, "you mean the A-Team, is that right?"

"I had no part in any of that," said Liz, her tone cold now. "Never wanted to, if you must know."

"Really? You're saying that you never were or wanted to be, a part of the A-Team?" Tina sounded frankly incredulous.

"Why would I? They were nothing but a bunch of immature girls who thought it was clever to sit at the back of the class and pull faces and make fun of people."

"Then you do remember the A-Team after all," said Tina. "And isn't it true that in fact at one time you wanted quite badly to be a part of it. That in fact you took part in a series of initiations challenges for that very reason?"

"What have those girls been saying about me?" Liz, her face on fire now, demanded. "Because whatever it is, it's lies, just lies. And if I'd known that you would come here asking me… questioning me and bringing back memories…"

As the other woman fell silent, Tina said quietly, "I'm sorry if our line of questioning has brought back painful or humiliating memories or if…"

Liz, whose fingers had been worrying the fabric of her top, jumped to her feet, the blinking frenetic now.

"Humiliating memories?" she echoed. "What do I have to be humiliated about? What have those girls been saying about me? I'll have you know that I happen to believe that if you know your own worth, then nothing anybody says or does can make you feel humiliated."

Where did she pick that one up, Tina wondered, Facebook or some counsellor she'd told her Father Trendy story to? Liz turned her back on the detectives.

"I don't even know why you're here, bothering me like this," she said. Everyone knows that what happened was an accident. Two awful terrible accidents, but what any of it has to do with me, I just don't understand."

"We are here, Liz," said JP in his gentlest tone, "simply as part of a line of routine questioning, nothing more. Do you think you might sit down again and then we can ask our questions and leave you in peace?"

As though he had cast a magic spell, Liz wheeled about and went back to her chair.

"Of course," she said, with a smile for JP. "I understand. Please ask me any questions you need to."

"Excellent" said Tina briskly. "In that case could you please tell us where you were and what you were doing on the morning of 12th February and on the evening of the 24th?"

Liz's mouth gaped. "You want to know where I was. But why? You only ask people that question if you suspect them of doing something wrong. But surely you don't think that I…that I….?"

"Not at all," JP assured her hurriedly. "Please believe me, these questions are purely routine, and for the purposes of eliminating you from our enquiries."

"Eliminating me, I see. Well in that case…," Liz got up again, went to the large dresser, opened a drawer and came back to the table with an A4 desk diary. From this she quickly established that on the day Nicole Brady went missing, Liz had been at home with her husband.

"It was a Sunday," she informed them. "We stayed at home until three o'clock in the afternoon, when we walked together to our local pub for a carvery and to listen to some live music. That's what we do any Sunday I'm not on duty."

And on the night that Bethany Doyle had been mown down, Liz it seemed had been working.
"My shift finished at 9.30pm and I was driven home by a colleague. I'm sure you can get verification of that if you feel it's necessary."

"Great," said Tina. "Thank you for that. And just one last thing we need to ask you. Can you tell me if you've seen this photo recently? I'll hold onto it, but if you could just take a look."

Tina held up the photo and Liz leaned in to peer at it. "Well yes, I've seen it recently. I found it, I mean I found a copy of it recently when I was doing a clear-out. It's our class from school. I shared a copy of it on Facebook."

"Do you still have that copy?" asked Tina.

"Yes, yes I have it somewhere. Do you want me to go find it?"

"If you wouldn't mind."

Liz was already on her feet. "I won't be a minute."

As her footsteps thumped on the stairs, JP leaned in and helped himself to two more biscuits. Tina scowled at him, but helped herself to another one, too.

Liz came back with the photograph. "It's actually turned into a plan for a school reunion, me posting a copy to Facebook. Plus, we're going to have the photo re-taken, everyone standing in the exact same place as in the original."

She was plainly delighted by what she had started. Tina took the photograph and studied the now familiar group of squinting schoolgirls. "So other than sharing it to Facebook, did you copy the photograph in any other ways?

"How do you mean?"

"Did you make any physical copies, for instance?"

"No, I didn't need to, I just took a copy of the photo on my phone and shared it to Facebook."

"And you didn't send copies of the photo to anyone, say any of the girls who are in the photograph?"

"Send it to them, you mean email it or something?" Liz appeared genuinely puzzled.

"No, I just put it on Facebook and tagged a few people and they tagged other people and it sort of snowballed from there and now there's going to be…."

"A reunion, yes lovely," Tina impatient now at what was beginning to seem like a waste of time, was on her feet. "Well thank you, you've been very helpful, I don't think we need to take up any more of your time just now."

Making for the door she paused and turned on her heel. "One last thing, what car do you and your husband drive?"

Liz blinked, "Car? A Ford Focus. Why…?"

"Colour?" "Black but why…."

"Well thanks again, if we need to talk to you further, we'll be in touch."

*

CHAPTER 17

Monday 27th February

"You made a sudden get-away," said JP. "And that stuff about the car she drives, you don't seriously have that woman in the frame for knocking off two of her ex-classmates, do you? Because I have to tell you, I can't see it, myself."

"Why? Because she fed you homemade biscuits? You do know it's possible to be a domestic goddess and still be a psycho killer, don't you?"

"Granted," JP grinned. "But I'd be willing to say that's not the case with this particular domestic Goddess. Though I can see how she might conceivably be behind those photographs. The poor woman is clearly still emotionally scarred by what those girls put her through. But I can't see why she'd have waited this long to do something so petty."

"Except it wouldn't be petty," said Tina, "not if it's a precursor to something much more serious, would it? And as to why it took until now for her to do it, let's say she came across that class photo and posts it to Facebook. It's not hard to see how that might have stirred up old memories and resentments she'd manged to push to the back of her mind. Get herself all riled up, then has the idea of running off some extras copies of the photo, carving out the faces of her tormentors and posting each of them a nice little present. I can see how that might have happened, can't you?"

“I’ve already said I can see how she might have flipped and sent those hacked up photos,” said JP. “What I can’t see is Liz being responsible for what you’re suggesting.”

Tina sighed, “You mean, Liz pushing Nicole Brady off a cliff and running Bethany Doyle down in the street? No probably not.”

“But you still do think that someone deliberately ran down Bethany Doyle?”

“Did I say that? No, I didn’t,” Tina protested.

“You pretty much said you thought it possible the car was lying in wait for her.”

“I still do think it’s possible,” Tina conceded. “I mean we know now from the Napoli CCTV tape that no car matching the description of the one that killed Bethany drove past the pizzeria in the relevant timeframe. So, it must have been parked somewhere between the Napoli and the car park.”

“Yes, but it still doesn’t follow that it was lying in wait for the specific purpose of taking her out.”

“I know, I know. It’s just that something feels wrong to me about all of this.”

“I know it does,” JP looked at her, head on one side, “but all the same…”

“It’s not enough,” Tina finished for him. “This thing with the photos and those girls bullying Liz, it’s not enough. I know myself that it’s not. Plus, it’s all so long ago. And that thing about them tricking Liz into going to school with no knickers on – if that happened nowadays, her bare arse would have been shared to social media before Fr Trendy had the chance to bless himself at the shock of it all. As it was, the only witnesses were the ones who were actually there when she was sent sprawling and had her skirt whipped up.”

“You mean that by present day standards, it all seems quite tame? I doubt Liz would agree. It was as cruel then as it would be now.”

“I agree,” said Tina. “And I’m not trying to minimise the impact it might have had on Liz. But again, is it enough to suddenly, after all this time spark a vendetta in a happily married woman of thirty-something?”

Tina sighed again. She could also feel the beginning of a headache at the base of her neck. Reaching back, she tugged at the elastic band that held her hair firmly back from her face during work hours. Sighing with relief as it came loose, she raked her fingers through it, leaned back against the seat rest and closed her eyes in appreciation of the physical relief. When she opened them, she caught JP watching her, a smile on his lips.

“What?” Tina quickly sat forward and checked her face in the rear-view mirror. “Have I got biscuit crumbs on my face or something?”

“No. I was just thinking what great hair you have. You should wear it down more often.”

The compliment took Tina by surprise. Dismayed, she felt a wave of heat starting at her temples. To counteract this, she opened her mouth, then heard herself say in a coy tone she did not recognise, “Oh, shut up!”

Horrified now and desperate to remedy things, she landed a great thump on JP’s upper arm. For a moment there was complete silence as they stared at one another, JP’s face showing a comical mix of surprise and confusion. In the end it was him who spoke first.

“Ouch”! he said. He began rubbing the place where the punch had landed in a pretence of being in pain. Gratefully, Tina caught the bone he had thrown her.

“Southside wimp!” she said.

“Northside scumbag!” JP flung back.

It was their go-to insult, and they smiled at one another, relieved, if still a little uncertain. Then JP’s phone rang, and Tina started the engine, and everything felt normal again.

"Anything?" asked Tina, as JP finished the call.

"They didn't find any fingerprints on the photographs, other than those of the four women who received them, and the people they'd confirm handled them."

"Do you not think that's a bit odd," said Tina. "Does it not sort of point to the sender having gone out of his or her way to make sure they left no trace of themselves on the photos? I mean, assuming this was just some kind of practical joke, why would they bother?"

"Perhaps because he or she was worried they'd get into trouble? That what has happened would happen – someone not seeing the funny side and coming to us about it."

"I suppose you're right," Tina sounded doubtful.

JP glanced across at her, "But you don't believe I'm right, though, do you?"

"Sometimes you're right."

"Sometimes?"

"Occasionally. Infrequently. Rarely, almost never…"

*

CHAPTER 18

Monday 27th February

They stopped for lunch in a small café in Drumcondra and ate their soup and sandwiches in the window seat, watching the world go past the rain-spattered glass. As they were leaving, the doorway was blocked by two hugging women.

As they broke apart, Tina heard one of them say, "I'd better run, but I'll see you on Friday, Claire."

Tina put a hand to her head. "That was it," she said.

"That was what?"

"Nothing. I just remembered what it was I overlooked that time at Jennifer O'Keeffe's place." "Which was?"

"Tell you later, right now we need to go have another little chat with Rachel Quinn."

*

"Excuse the mess," said Rachel, as the two detectives preceded her into the big living room. Looking about her, it struck Tina that as a rule when people made this request, it was merely a social convention, and nine times out of ten there was no real mess to excuse. But right now, she found it hard to remember the last time she'd seen such an untidy room. Toys and books and wooden blocks littered the floor. The sofa held more toys as well as a pile of unfolded washing. Tina had to remove two plastic swords from an armchair before she could sit down, and JP picked up a ragged stuffed giraffe and a sippy cup from his chair.

Rachel smiled apologetically, “I know, it looks like a pack of rabid badgers have just torn through it, doesn’t it? Is that a terrible thing to say about your own kids, but it feels like that some days.”

Tina couldn’t help laughing. “How many children have you got?”

“Three, two boys and a girl, and all under the age of six.” Rachel pulled a face which quickly shifted back to a smile.

“Though I know to look at this place you’d think there were actually six of them. That’s them there.”

Tina and JP looked at the wall Rachel was indicating, which had been given over to a gallery of family photographs. Smiling babies, squinting tots against backdrops of beaches and playgrounds, a beaming Rachel and a tall dark grinning man surrounded by their children.

The word joyful came into Tina’s mind and for no earthly reason she had a sudden mental image of Phyllis’s living room and the photograph of herself taken on the day she made her First Communion. It perched on one edge of the mantlepiece, next to the row of brass ducks, with centre stage given over to a Tipperary Crystal carriage clock and a matching pair of china figurines. In the photograph Tina’s hair was bound up in a French plait which did not suit her, her dress an ankle-length puffy affair, all the rage at the time. The expression on her face was inscrutable, but joyful it was not. Shaking herself mentally, Tina brought her attention back to Rachel Quinn. She looked tired, unsurprising in the mother of three young children. But that did not account for the sadness in her eyes, the visible strain in her face.

“We’ll try not to keep you too long,” Tina told her. “No doubt you have your hands full.”

“Oh, don’t worry about that,” Rachel smiled properly this time. “My sister’s just taken them swimming and she’s keeping them until it’s time for bed, to give me a break. I haven't been sleeping very well lately. So anyway, can I get you something to drink, tea or coffee...?"

Tina spoke for both of them, "Thanks, but we've just had lunch. So, if you don't mind, we'll come straight to the point."

"Sure, what was it you wanted to talk to me about?" Rachel shoved the pile of washing aside and sank down next to it on the sofa.

"Who is Claire?" asked Tina. Seeing Rachel's obvious puzzlement, she clarified.

"When we spoke to you all together at Jennifer's home, you mentioned someone called Claire. It was in the context of someone who might have had a reason to dislike the members of the A-Team. Who's Claire?"

"Oh, you mean that Claire!" Rachel's face cleared. "Claire Fox, she was Anna's sister."

"Was? Did something happen to her?"

Rachel nodded, "Claire died," she said quietly.

Tina fought to keep a pulse of excitement under control. "OK, and how did she die?"

"It was an accident." Rachael leaned forward and picked up a stuffed elephant from the floor at her feet. "A road traffic accident. It was awful, she was only twenty-one. Their father had to go over and bring her home, so she could be buried here."

"Had to go over where?"

"To England. Claire died in London, she was living there at the time. Actually, she left school without even doing her Leaving Cert and the next thing we knew she'd gone to London. I think she got an office job or something. And next we heard she'd died. It was all so sad, for Anna and her father. Their mother was dead by then, she died of cancer when Anna and Claire were still teenagers. Anna's all on her own now, her father died not very long ago. He'd been sick for a long time, he suffered from early onset dementia. So awful for him, and for Anna too."

"Yes, it must have been," said Tina absently. Damn and double damn, wherever she had imagined this might be going, this wasn't it.

"But I think the biggest blow was losing Claire," Rachel went on. "With them being twins and all."

"Anna and Claire were twins?"

"Identical twins, actually," Rachel let the elephant drop into her lap. "So, it was a terrible shock for Anna."

"I can imagine," said Tina mechanically. "So then if they were twins, I suppose they'd have been in the same class. Is Claire one of the girls in the group photo?"

Rachel shook her head, "No, Claire isn't in the photo. They were in the same year alright, but not the same class. But I don't see why…?"

Tina ignored the hanging question. A thought had occurred to her – Anna a dental surgeon, Claire in an office job straight out of school. "They were in different classes – was that because…wasn't Claire as bright as Anna?" she asked.

"No, no, nothing like that," Rachel shook her head firmly. "Claire was just as bright as Anna, but in different ways. She was brilliant at English and history, that kind of thing. Anna was brilliant at maths and science.

"And the A-Team, was Claire a part of that?"

Rachel fingered the soft toy, "No, Claire wasn't in the A Team."

"Really?" Tina was certain she hadn't imagined the hint of discomfort in the other woman's tone. "Identical twins and all that, you'd think they'd have been really close?"

"I didn't mean that they weren't close. They just liked different things, that's all. Claire was a lot different to Anna. Quieter."

“So, what you’re saying is that a gang like the A-Team wouldn’t have appealed to Claire, is that it?” asked Tina.

“Yes. I mean no, I don’t think Claire ever really wanted to be in the A Team.”

“Is that why the rest of you picked on her, bullied her?”

Rachel’s eyes widened, “I never said we did that…”

“Didn’t you?” Tina raised her eyebrows. “Granted, maybe not in so many words. But last time we spoke, I couldn’t help but notice that when Anna raised the subject of the A-Team being responsible for hurting people’s feelings, you immediately assumed it was Claire Anna had in mind.”

“Did I say that - I don’t remember.”

“Come on Rachel, we both know that’s not true.”

“Well, if I did say it, I only meant that I think Anna feels a bit guilty sometimes. Over Claire, I mean.”

“What has Anna to feel guilty about over Claire, Rachel? Was Claire one of the girls the A Team targeted?”

“Look, OK,” Rachel abandoned the elephant. “Maybe we were a bit mean to Claire. But nothing serious, not like Liz. The way we behaved to Liz, that was unforgivable. And I don’t even know why… what I’m trying to say is, I’m not that person anymore.”

You’re telling the wrong person, thought Tina. Aloud she added in a neutral tone, “OK, but back to Claire – how bad did the bullying get?”

“Well, mostly it was just a bit of teasing,” said Rachel. “Jennifer knew, well she just knew she couldn’t push Anna too far when it came to Claire. So, it was just things like making fun of the clothes Claire wore, the bands she liked or the way she always wore her hair in plaits, that sort of thing.”

Something stirred in Tina’s memory, “Claire wore her hair in plaits?”

"Yes, I don't know why, she had beautiful hair, just like Anna's. Jennifer made a big deal out of the plaits, that, and other stuff. Mostly I think it was just to get at Anna. She'd say something mean to Claire then look at Anna, like she was defying her to say something, daring her to tell her to shut up. Stand up for Claire or something."

"And would she? Would Anna stand up for Claire?"

Rachel shook her head, "No she didn't. And I think that's the part that hurt Claire the most. I'm fairly sure Anna wanted to stand up for her, she just couldn't bring herself to give Jennifer the satisfaction. There was always this sort of tension between those two, between Anna and Jennifer. And now that Claire has gone, I suppose it makes Anna feel guilty that she chose the A-Team over her sister."

"And that was it?" said Tina, "A bit of teasing and low-level bullying?"

"Yes. That was it. Look why are you even asking me all these questions?" Rachel demanded.

"I mean, what has Claire Fox got to do with anything?"

Sweet feck all, by the look of it, thought Tina ruefully. Aloud she said, "I know it must seem that way, but if you could just bear with me a little longer, Rachel, there's just a couple more questions."

But Rachel had clearly had enough. "Look, I'm sorry but I'm wrecked, I just can't answer any more questions," she said, the colour rising in her pale face. "If you want to know more about Claire, it's Anna you need to speak to, not me. Though why you would, is beyond me to be honest."

*

Outside once more, JP turned to Tina. "What was all that about? Why all the questions about Anna Fox's sister? Claire died in London, in a road traffic accident. She was twenty-one at the time. It's all wrong for our timeline, Tina."

"I know it is," Tina admitted.

Back in the driver's seat, she stared ahead reflectively. "Remember that time we went to Anna Fox's apartment? I don't know if you noticed, but there was a photograph in a silver frame on the dresser thing next to the window."

"I can't say I did, what of it?"

"It was a photo of a teenage girl. At the time I assumed it was Anna, it looked just like her, only younger. But now I don't think it was Anna, now I'm almost certain it was a photo of Anna's twin, Claire. You heard Rachel just now, Jennifer & Co used to tease Claire because she wore her hair in plaits – the girl in the photo on Anna's dresser had her hair in plaits."

"So, what if it was Claire? What's strange about someone keeping a photograph of their dead twin sister on display?"

Tina reached for her seatbelt, started the engine. "There's nothing strange about it. But what was strange was Anna's reaction when she saw me looking at the photo. I could see it had thrown her. At the time I didn't tie it in with the photo though. It wasn't until Rachel mentioned Anna and Claire being identical twins that I made the connection, that, and hearing how Claire always used to wear her hair in plaits."

She shot a glance at JP, "And before you accuse me of imagining things, I'll tell you something else. The last time I saw that exact reaction from Anna, was when we were all in Jennifer O'Keeffe's living room. Rachel had just mentioned a name. It took Anna by surprise. She covered it up well enough, but not before I caught the look on her face. It was the same look I saw there when she caught me examining that photograph of Claire."

*

CHAPTER 19

Monday 6th March

"Anna Fox's car was run off the road."

"What? Fuck!" Tina let go of the towel she had draped about her still damp body, and it fell to the bedroom floor. JP's call had come as she was stepping out of the shower, and she'd raced to the bedroom to pick up her mobile before it rang off.

"Is she hurt, she's not…?"

"She suffered a bit of an injury to her neck, but mostly she seems to be just shaken up. Though by the sounds of it, she's lucky to be alive."

"Where did this happen?" Tina picked up her towel and tried to wrap it about herself once more, she was shivering now.

"She was driving home, along the coast road from Malahide to Portmarnock. A car came up behind her, rammed her car, then had a go at her from the side and eventually forced her off the road. She ended up going over the embankment there, a bit further and she'd have ended up on the rocks below or in the water."

"Christ! And I'm guessing we're not just talking road rage here?"

"Doesn't sound that way. There's no CCTV on the particular stretch of road, but we have an actual witness. Another driver coming from the opposite direction, saw her as she actually went off the road and up onto the embankment. He stopped to see if she was OK and stuck around to give a statement to the lads in the squad car who took the call."

"Well, that's something," said Tina." "Look JP, I'm just out of the shower and I need to get dressed. Then we need to go talk to Anna Fox. Where is she now, still at the hospital?"

"No, she's been discharged, she's back home apparently. And it's your day off, or had you forgotten?"

"No, I hadn't forgotten. So, will you come by and pick me up or should I meet you at Anna Fox's apartment?"

"I'll come get you. Oh, and Tina, I spoke to the dog woman, Mrs Thorpe? She's as positive as she can be that when she heard the sound of an engine revving, Bethany was already on the road. She said it was the sound that made her look up from the dog, and then the car itself appeared to come out of nowhere."

"OK, thanks JP," said Tina. "I'll be ready and waiting in ten."

In fact she was ready and waiting for fifteen minutes before JP pulled up outside. As she ran to his car, a pale winter sunshine burst through the clouds and opening the passenger door, she was met with another burst - Katrina and the Waves belting out *Walking on Sunshine*. JP turned to her, all dark sunglasses and shining white teeth. "For feck sake, can you turn that down?" Tina growled. "And you do know it'll be raining again in five minutes?"

"And a very good morning to you too," said JP, leaning forward and turning the volume down.

"Right, yeah, good morning," Tina buckled up. "Just couldn't hear myself think with that racket. So, fill me in. I don't suppose Anna Fox was able to ID the driver of the other car by any miracle?"

"No such luck. She couldn't even say for sure if it was a male or a female behind the wheel."

"And what about this witness? You say he was driving in the opposite direction to Anna. Was he able to give us anything more?"

"His name's Anthony Fitzpatrick, calls himself Ant. Seems he was driving home after a night delivering take-aways."

"Bit late to be delivering food, wasn't it?"

"Apparently, he and the other drivers had a game of poker after they'd finished up for the night, a regular thing for them on a Thursday night. He was no help with regard to the other driver but is fairly certain the car was a black Ford Focus, though he admits he was more concerned with getting to the spot where Anna Fox's car left the road. Seems he thought whoever was in it was a goner."

"OK. So, what was Anna doing out driving at that hour of the morning, anyway?"

"That I don't know," said JP. "Right then, let's go ask the lady herself then, shall we?"

*

Anna opened the door to her apartment bare-foot and wearing a long Chinese-style kimono in a pattern of white and striking cobalt blue. She was also wearing a neck brace and there was a strip of plaster on her right cheek. She led them to the living-room where, judging by the drawn curtains and the rumpled blanket on the sofa she had been, if not sleeping, then at least resting. "I'm sorry if we're disturbing you," Tina told her. "I understand you've been through a traumatic time of it last night. Do you feel up to answering some questions?"

"Fine. But you do know that I already gave a statement to the police last night, don't you?"

"We do, and I know it's a nuisance having to go over it all again, but if you feel up to it…"

"And if I say no, you'll only come back, right?" said Anna.

Without waiting for a reply, she crossed to the window and pulled back the curtains setting the wooden rings rattling on their pole. As she turned to face them, the flood of pale lemon winter sunshine showed her make-up free face clearly. Tina saw how pale she was, noted the blue-black circles beneath the eyes and, as Anna raised a hand to brush away a fall of hair, another strip of plaster on the back of her hand. "Are you in much discomfort," she asked.

"You mean this and these?" Anna raised a hand and touched her fingers to the neck brace, then to the strip of plaster on her face. "My neck is a bit stiff, but the collar is just precautionary really. The cuts I'm told, are only superficial, so mostly it's just some aches and pains. Now, if only I could switch off my mind. But that's always the difficult part, right?"

The words were spoken lightly, but Tina sensed a weariness and something else. This was not the usual cool Anna Fox – she was clearly really rattled. JP obviously saw it too. "We won't keep you a moment longer than absolutely necessary," he said gently. "Then you can go back to getting some..."

But Anna cut across him curly. "Look, I'm fine. Now can we please just get this over with? Again."

Tina tried not to grin openly. Nope, JP's charms really didn't cut any ice with this one. "Right," she said, "well then perhaps you could take it from when you first noticed the vehicle in question."

"OK. Well, I was driving home along the coast road between Malahide and Portmarnock. I was about..."

"Driving home from an evening out, was it?" Tina interrupted.

"Actually no, it was a conference, a dental conference I'd been attending in Belfast. I was supposed to stay on another night, but at the last minute I decided to come back. It was late but I figured the roads would be empty and I'd make good time. And I did. And as I was saying, I was on the coast road between Malahide and Portmarnock when I first noticed the car behind me."

"What time was this?"

"Just after three-thirty."

"You can be positive about the time?"

"Yes, I can, because I remember I'd checked the clock on the dashboard as I passed the Grand Hotel in Malahide, and it was coming up to three-thirty then."

"OK. So, you were approaching the Martello tower?"

"Yes. The car may have been behind me for a while, I can't be sure. I was busy concentrating on the road ahead. The rain was almost torrential, and visibility was very poor. I only really took notice of the car when it came up right behind me. It was travelling fast, and I remember thinking how stupid that was on a night like that. Then suddenly it was alongside me, overtaking me as I thought. But it was much too close to me. It annoyed me, because it wasn't as though there was any traffic approaching from the other direction. And then it veered even closer to my car and struck it. At first, I thought it was accidental, that the wind had buffeted it or something, but I'd got a bit of a shock and I moved to the left and sounded the horn. But it came at me again and that was when I realised that it wasn't an accident, that whoever it was, was doing it on purpose."

"So, what did you do then?"

"I sounded the horn again and then I speeded up a bit, but the other car did the same. It came alongside me again, so I veered to the left to try to avoid it, but he struck my car again, only harder this time and…"

"He?" Tina interrupted sharply.

"Actually, I don't know why I said that, because I couldn't tell whether it was a man or a woman."

"But you say the car was close enough to strike your own repeatedly on the driver's side? Yet you couldn't make out if it the driver was a man or a woman?"

"No, I couldn't," Anna was unapologetic. "It was dark, and it was raining very heavily. And I can't be positive, but I have an idea that the driver was wearing a dark hood. So no, I couldn't tell what sex they were."

"Fair enough," said Tina. "So, then what happened?"

"I speeded up. I just wanted to get out of there as fast as I could. But the other car did the same and came at me again. I swerved to try to avoid it, but it hit me side-on again, only much harder this time. And I knew that whoever was behind the wheel of that car meant to harm me."

"That must have been very frightening," said JP.

"Frankly, I was terrified," said Anna. "And I know this probably sounds idiotic, but I just kept thinking about the sea and trying to remember what it was you're supposed to do and not do. You know, should you find yourself in a car submerged in water. But somehow, I couldn't actually remember a single thing."

"That doesn't sound in the slightest bit idiotic to me," said JP. Anna gave him an unexpectedly grateful smile. It was so very much the same smile as that of the girl in the silver framed photograph that Tina's eyes went automatically to the place on the dresser where it had been; the photograph wasn't there. She abandoned the minor mystery as Anna resumed her story.

"It came at me one more time," she said, her eyes full of the memory. "Even harder again this time, and I lost control of the car. It hit the rumble strip and went up onto the grass bank. I could feel it bouncing under me. I think I screamed. I was waiting for it to go over the edge. But instead, it came to a stop. I was so relieved. But I couldn't see anything, and I had no idea where I was. Then I got it into my head that my car might be balanced on the edge of the cliff. I was terrified to move. I just sat there trying to stay absolutely still, when this man suddenly appeared at my window and began yelling at me through the glass. He was telling me to open the door so he could help me. I thought he was the driver of the other car and I screamed at him to go away and leave me alone. And when he didn't, I leaned both hands on the horn and just kept them there. I feel bad about that now, the poor man was only trying to help me. A woman came then and spoke to me through the window, and I calmed down a bit, and opened the door. They were very kind to me, and I don't think I ever actually thanked them either."

"I'm sure they'll understand," said Tina. "So, have you any idea who the driver of the other was?"

"I have absolutely no idea," said Anna without hesitation.

"Can you think of anyone who might want to harm you?"

Anna considered for a moment, "No, I can't."

"You're quite certain about that?"

Anna's eyebrows rose. "Am I certain that I can't think of anyone who might want to run me off the road and into the sea? Yes, I'm quite certain. And I would like to say that there isn't anyone, that the whole idea is ridiculous. I would like to say that it must have been some lunatic who attacked me last night, simply because I happened to be in the wrong place at the wrong time."

"Are you telling us that you don't believe that?" asked Tina.

"Well, you two are here aren't you? Asking me to answer the same questions I already answered last night. So, I'm thinking that you don't believe it was some random lunatic either? You believe it has something to do with those photographs, don't you – the ones Rachel phoned you about."

Tina got to her feet and rolled up her copybook. "We're here because a serious offence was committed last night, and because it's our job to investigate that offence and find the person responsible. Can I ask, have you spoken to Rachel Quinn about what happened to you last night?"

"No, I haven't. I didn't want to upset her, frighten her. Are you saying I should talk to her, warn her?"

"Right now, if I were you, I'd get some rest," said Tina. "But if you do happen to remember anything further about last night, or if you have any concerns at all in fact, give us a call. Here's my mobile number, you'll get me anytime day or night. Please don't get up, we'll let ourselves out."

*

After she heard the sound of the outer door shutting, Anna pressed her back to the wall and closed her eyes. The interview with the two detectives had taken it out of her. She was surprised just how vividly simply talking about it, had brought back the events of the previous evening. So vividly that she had felt herself back there on that dark road, with the relentless rain thrumming the roof, windscreen wipers slapping, while the wind buffeted the car. She could see again the pinprick of lights in the rear-view mirror, the other car coming up behind, then alongside hers. Then the attacks, the strike of metal upon metal. The moment when her car went over the embankment and all she could think about was the cold sea crashing on the rocks below... Anna opened her eyes, the collar felt as if it were gripping her throat. She slipped her fingers between it and her neck in an attempt to loosen it and her skin felt warm and clammy to the touch. Her instinct was to claw the thing off and fling it to the floor, but instead she pushed herself away from the wall, picked up her phone and keyed in a number. Rachel should hear it from her first.

*

CHAPTER 20

Friday 6th March

"She's not quite as tough as she likes to let on," said JP.

Tina glanced across at him, his eyes were on the road ahead. "Are any of us?" she asked.

"I suppose not." For a while they were quiet, each thinking their own thoughts as the car sped along the coast road toward the scene of the attack on Anna's car. Tina broke the silence.

"The photograph wasn't there anymore," she said. "Remember the one I told you about? It was on the dresser that last time we were there, but it wasn't there just now."

JP threw her a quizzical glance, "So it fell, and the glass broke, or she fancied moving it to somewhere different. What's the big deal, Tina?"

Tina decided to let it rest and was silent as JP pulled into a layby close to the scene of the attack on Anna Fox. They got out and walked back along the winding pathway that skirted the coastline. The sunshine had held up and in spite of the stiff breeze blowing in off a choppy sea, it was a pleasant and bracing walk under blue skies. The spot itself was marked by fluttering blue and white tape. The area had already been sealed and swept, and a squad car boxed by traffic cones was still parked up close by. As they approached, the driver and passenger doors opened and the two officers who had responded to the incident the previous night, climbed out. Garda Kitty Malone and Garda Brendan Cleary; Tina knew them both. Cleary was wiping his mouth with the back of his hand and Tina was certain she smelled fried bacon.

"Cheers for hanging about," she thanked them, as all four made their way toward the taped-off area. "I know your shift ended some time ago. Is Anna Fox's car still in situ?"

"Yes, SOCO have already had a look and taken some shots." Kitty confirmed. "We're just waiting for you to see it for yourselves and then we'll have it taken away."

"Sound," Tina nodded. "Well let's do that and then you two can go too and get some kip."

"Sure, yeah thanks," Kitty led the way to the boundary of the taped-off area.

"You can see the skid marks running along here, where the car went off the road and up onto the embankment. If you follow me, I'll show you where it ended up."

Tina, JP and Cleary followed as she climbed the bank. It was wet and slippery, and mud squelched under their boots. On the far side, the bank sloped down to a stretch of grass which extended out to the edge of the cliff, beyond it was a sheer drop to the rocks and sea. They slip-slided carefully as they could down to the metallic silver Audi Q3.

"There's some damage to the rear," Kitty told them. "Consistent with it having been rammed. But most of the real damage is to the driver's side, as you can see."

"Shame, nice zippy little car," JP said appreciatively.

Tina turned to the two officers. "OK, thanks. Now you two can get off home, and cheers again for hanging about for us."

To JP she said, "Head back to the car, I'll catch you up, I'm just going to take a minute here and clear my head."

JP followed the two uniforms without comment, he was used to her ways by now. Tina turned back to the sea and gazed down at the waves crashing upon the rocks. She was reminded of the place where Nicole Brady had met her death. Was she, she asked herself on a completely wrong track here? But the sea gave her no answer.

*

JP was leaning against the bonnet of the car, face upturned to the sun. *Like a big beautiful, lithe, sun-worshipping ...*

"I hope you're not planning on getting into my car like that?" JP greeted her and she hurriedly turned her thoughts off.

"Like what?" Tina was mystified.

"You've got mud all over your boots."

Tina glanced down. "Crap! But you must have too." But a quick glance at JP's boots revealed no sign of his recent muddy climb.

"I cleaned them while I was waiting for you."

"What with?"

"A handkerchief."

"I haven't got a handkerchief."

"Here use this." JP held out a hanky.

"What, you carry two? Are you sure, it's very clean looking?" Tina stared doubtfully at the perfectly folded, spotless square of cotton. But she accepted the hanky and set about cleaning off the worst of the dirt from her boots.

"Thanks," she made to hand it back.

"Eh, you're grand," said JP. "Hang on to it, there's plenty more where that came from. My mother's given me six of them every Christmas since I was ten."

"I love your mother."

"You've never met her."

This was true, but JP mentioned her a lot and Tina had created a mental picture of a blonde woman in a floral dress, with a cinched in waist and wide skirt, floating about a garden with a basket on one arm, snipping at roses. Pure nonsense no doubt, in real life JP's mother was more likely a perfectly sensible woman who dressed in slacks and polo necked jumpers from M&S. And pearls, possibly pearls…

"Well, I like the sound of her then," she said, stuffing the filthy hanky in her jacket pocket.

"I'm pretty sure she'd like you."

"Yeah right," said Tina. But the idea pleased her.

"Do you believe in coincidence, JP?" she asked, when they were back in the car.

"Do I believe in it? I don't know, to be honest. The scientists say it's down to maths, don't they? That and the human need for order and patterns, and that any meaning we attribute to it is all in our heads."

"OK, don't blind me with science," Tina protested. "I'll put the question another way, would you say we have a pattern here?"

JP threw her a glance. "You mean this thing with these women, Nicole and Bethany and now, Anna Fox. Yes, I can see how you could argue there's a possible pattern here. But is that what is termed a coincidence or is it something else entirely. Are those three incidents connected and have they something to do with those photographs, that's what you're really asking me, isn't it? And the answer is, I don't know, Tina. But I do know that your gut is telling you there's a link. And that's good enough for me."

"It is?" Tina couldn't hide her surprise.

"Yes, and that's not to say that you're right. But it's clear you've had an instinct about this whole thing from the start, and well, after this thing with Anna Fox, I think you have to go with that instinct."

Tina was quiet for a moment. Then she said, “You know that means taking it to Colonel Mustard?”

“Yep,” said JP, his eyes on the road.

“Crap!” they said in unison.

*

CHAPTER 21

Monday 6th March

Tina wrinkled her nose. Coleman's office smelled as always, of aniseed. The DI was addicted to Fisherman's Friends. Coleman had granted them ten minutes of his time, making it clear that even this should be considered a major concession. But so far all they had done was wait while Coleman scratched away on some papers with his silver fountain pen. Tina had promised JP that she would try to keep her patience, not to mention her temper, in check, but already Coleman was pushing all her buttons. The truth was that everything about the DI grated on her nerves, even the way he looked. He had one of those pink, almost scalded looking complexions, thinning sandy coloured hair, barely-there blue eyes and thin bloodless lips. Unable to see a single reason why he could, Tina was nonetheless convinced that the man loved himself.

Why else would he tend that ridiculous moustache of his like a sickly plant? Why else keep a special tiny comb in his breast pocket and take it out regularly to groom the thing, when he thought no-one was looking. The moustache was tightly trimmed, and Tina could imagine Coleman standing before his bathroom mirror and measuring it to ensure it was strictly in keeping with the Garda code. The code which laid down that a moustache was permitted only on condition that no portion will extend below the corners of the mouth or fall below a line parallel with the lower lip. But appearance aside, the man, in Tina's opinion was a didactic little fusspot, and almost always the fusses he made were over things which she herself considered of secondary importance. Things like punctuality and blasted paperwork and standing on form, none of which were Tina's strong points, and all of which he used to try to squash her like a bug.

"Try taking it as a compliment," Joe Tynan, the Sergeant at Tina's first posting had advised her.

Tina had had massive respect for Joe and now retired, he and Tina kept in touch, meeting from time to time for a beer, or simply because she felt the need for an injection of sound sense coupled with compassion. Or to bemoan the fact that the DI seemed to have taken against her from the start. "Of course, he's going to pull you up on the small stuff," Joe had told her. "It's because that's all he can catch you on. Ever think maybe it's because he's afraid you're good? That you're better at the job than he is, and he knows you'll go places he never will? Coleman saw himself going right to the top and now he's hit a wall at DI. It galls him to see anyone with the potential to go further."

Tina had dismissed this with a self-deprecating laugh, but the truth was, Joe's opinion of her potential had given her an actual shiver of pleasure. She was ambitious, not for rank in and of itself, but to be the very best detective she could be. But Joe had brought her back to earth with his next remark. "Probably doesn't help that someone put it into his head that you're a 'gut cop'."

"Who told him that?" Tina demanded.

"Never mind who told him, they meant it as a positive, but men like Toby Coleman unfortunately equate intuition and instinct with imagination. Coleman is a dullard, and like all dullards, he has no imagination and is suspicious of anyone who does. But what do you care? Just do your job and let the results speak for themselves. And try not to antagonise him, if you can help it."

Thinking of all this now, Tina glared resentfully at the top of Coleman's head. He chose that moment to suddenly put down silver his fountainpen, looked up and caught her mid-scowl. "Now what's all this about?" he asked querulously.

For all the world, thought Tina, as though they were a pair of nuisance school kids wasting the busy headmaster's time with their nonsense. As though he hadn't been given her report already with all the facts laid out clearly. But she swallowed her resentment and made her case again, taking Coleman through the facts as she knew them, and on to the conclusion she had arrived at. The D.I. heard her out without interruption, his face devoid of expression.

"I see," he said, when she had finished. "And these photographs have been tested for prints, I assume?"

"Yes sir. But other than the people they were sent to, and the few family members the admitted showing the photo to, there's nothing."

"There's nothing," Coleman repeated, leaning his elbows on his desk and steepling his fingers. "I see." That was another one of his many habits which drove Tina almost insane, because he rarely did see.

"So, aside from these photographs, is there any hard evidence linking the deaths of these two women and the incident last night with this car being run off the road?"

"Hard evidence, no," Tina admitted. "But I don't believe we can afford to overlook the possibility that there is a connection, sir."

"You don't, don't you?" Coleman leaned back, causing his plush leather chair to expel a small whooshing sound. His shirt gaped slightly in front and Tina averted her eyes from the sight of his pink and hairless chest. "And these photographs, have you any real evidence to suggest they are linked to one or all of these incidents?"

"As yet we can't actually prove that there's a link, but I do think that in all probability..."

"Well then, there you have it, Detective Sergeant Bassett" Coleman sat forward again. "You just said it yourself. You are dealing in probabilities. And as you well know, I am interested only in certainties, in hard evidence. All this gut instinct is very well and good but it's no substitute for procedure and evidence.

"Yes sir, but…"

"And you Detective Garda O'Rourke?" Coleman cut Tina off. "Are you in agreement with DS Barrett's contention that we have a serial killer busy at work in North County Dublin?"

"Sir, I don't actually think…"

This time it was Tina who cut in. "Sir, I never said that" she protested. "All I'm saying is that we have six women who were sent a copy of that group photo, their own face scratched out, and now two of those women are dead, and one has narrowly escaped death. And one of those women came to us with her concerns about the photographs and…"

"And those concerns," Coleman interrupted once more, "have quite rightly been taken on board and looked into. And this other lassie, this Lisa…"

"Liz Warren, sir," Tina supplied.

"This Liz Warren who was suspected of sending these photographs has been interviewed, denies any involvement and was able and willing to account for her whereabouts on the dates in question. Remind me of the details would you please, Detective O'Rourke."

"Yes sir," JP pulled out his notebook and turned the pages. "So, at the time Nicole Brady is believed to have fallen to her death, Ms Warren says she was at home with her husband, that they didn't leave the house until three o'clock in the afternoon, at which time they went to a local pub for a carvery lunch, after which they stayed on to listen to a band that was playing that afternoon. Her husband corroborated that statement. On the night of the hit and run, in which Bethany Doyle died, Ms Warren, who is a nurse, was working a nightshift. This has been checked out and confirmed to be true".

"Excellent," said Coleman, once more the headmaster congratulating a favoured boy on his homework. A boy with a big-shot Daddy the headmaster didn't mind keeping on side. Which in fairness, Tina reminder herself was hardly JP's fault.

"But sir," she couldn't contain herself any longer. "All that proves is that Liz Warren wasn't responsible for the deaths of Nicole Brady or Bethany Doyle. There's no way of proving she didn't send the photographs, though actually I don't believe she did that either. But the point is, someone did. And once again, I feel I must remind you that of the six women who received them, two are now dead and the other…"

"And once again," Coleman's voice was tight with anger, "once again, I must ask whether your investigations into these three incidents have turned up any firm evidence to bolster your assertion that they are linked?
"The women are linked, as I told you sir. All three are past members of a teenage gang which…."

"Ah yes, this gang," Coleman leaned back in his chair again. "What was it they called themselves again - the A-Team? This link of yours, DS Bassett, comes down to a gang of teenage girls dating back twenty odd years. And the motive is a series of historic schoolyard pranks - ear piercing with stapler guns, girls going to school with no pants on. Yes, I've read your report and found it all vastly diverting indeed."

As Tina opened her mouth to speak, Coleman raised a warning hand and she shut it again. "And this A-Team business aside, just what other evidence do you have to support a link between these incidents?"

"But that's just it, sir, I believe that the A-Team is the link." Coleman smiled a humourless smile. "From which I take it that there is no further evidence. Which begs the question, isn't it just possible that you're barking up the wrong tree entirely here?"

"The wrong tree in what sense, sir?"

Coleman flashed a crabbed smile. "The wrong tree is the wrong tree in every sense, wouldn't you agree DS Bassett."

"Not if it isn't actually the wrong tree," Tina muttered. What the hell were they doing here wasting time talking about trees with this idiot?

Coleman eyed her with naked dislike. "Then you do believe that we have serial killer on our patch?"

"No sir, that's not what I'm saying. But I don't believe we can rule out a possible link between the deaths of Nicole Brady and Bethany Doyle and the attempt on the life of Anna Fox. And I'd like to continue to investigate that possibility. I may be wrong of course, but, if I'm right, then there are still four women out there whose lives could be in danger. And in the meantime, I think they should be made aware of that possible danger. Some of them already have the wind up, but I believe..."

"You believe they should have the wind put up them officially, is that it?"

"I believe it's our duty to warn them to at least be vigilant," said Tina stubbornly. "Because if anything were to happen to any more of these women and it comes out that we suspected there was a link, but that we did nothing about it..."

She let the sentence hang in the air and watched as the pink of Coleman's complexion shade to purple.

*

CHAPTER 22

Monday 6th March - Tuesday 7th March

"You do know you did yourself no favours in there, telling your DI his duty," said JP as they made their way back to the Detectives' Room.

"I don't care, he's nothing but a cretinous, moronic fucktard. Besides, I was reminding him what our duty is. That's not the same thing at all."

"Granted. But that's not how he'll see it. All you did was hand him another reason to wipe the floor with you."

"Like he needs a reason," Tina fumed. "It's alright for you, he's been brown-nosing you ever since you got here. Before you got here, actually. He gave you my fucking desk, for God's sake!"

"Are you seriously throwing my old man in my face?" JP rounded on her. "Take the stupid desk. How many times have I offered to swap?"

"I don't want the desk, it's not about the stupid desk. It's just that that bloody man never gives me a break, while you – well he's only ever short of patting you on the back and telling you what a good boy you are." The anger left her as quickly as it has arrived. "Shit, I'm sorry, JP. That was out of line."

She meant it. Not only was it not JP's fault that his Da was a former AG, but he had also never once played that card to get ahead in the force, and she knew he never would. The truth was she didn't deserve him as a partner. If she wasn't ticking him off, she was being a grumpy cow or pretending to be one in an attempt to cover up the way she really felt about him. Because God forbid, he ever realised how she lusted after him – no, face it, Tina, more than lusted after him - she liked him, really liked him. She pushed the thought aside, tried to concentrate on the advice JP was yet again giving her about how best to handle Coleman.

"Forget it," JP gave her a friendly punch on the arm. "But you have to stop letting him provoke you. Why bother when we both know that you're never actually going to let anything he says stop you doing exactly what you believe you should?"

"OK, but that's not the point. Just for once I'd like him to back me."

"He'll back you when he has no choice but to back you."

"Meaning what, when another one of those women turns up dead?"

"Well hopefully it won't take that," said JP. "But we do need to bring Mustard something concrete to back up your conviction of a link between what happened to Nicole, Bethany and Anna."

"Yeah, but what? You heard him, the photographs aren't enough, the A Team stuff isn't enough. We need something more. Because there has to be something, and whatever it is, we need to find it before somebody else gets hurt."

*

"It would help if we knew where to start," said JP. "Or even what we're looking for."

It was one o'clock in the morning and, thanks to a flu epidemic, they had the Detective's room to themselves for a while. It seemed as good a time as any to get to work on trawling the database as they had earlier decided to do.

"Well, we've agreed it's likely to be something historical," said Tina. "That's indicated by the old school photo. And we know the original was taken some time in 1995, so that's as good a starting point as any.

I mean the photo has to have some significance, otherwise why bother sending it?"

"Because all six women just happened to be in it?" JP suggested.

"True," Tina agreed. "This may have nothing at all to do with the photograph, and everything to do with the women themselves. Or at least with something they may have done or were involved in. Which is why we need to be looking for anything that could possibly tie in with all six A Team members."

"And I imagine it would have to be something fairly serious," said JP. "I mean it would be, to have suddenly triggered a killing spree. Which, let's face it, is what we're envisaging is happening here."

Tina sighed, "God, it all sounds so melodramatic when you say it like that. And its's the suddenly bit that makes the least sense. But let's leave that aside for the moment, and just focus on trying to find out what's at the root of this whole thing. So yes, I agree, we should be looking for something serious. Unexplained deaths, disappearances, that kind of thing. At least we know all six of them attended the same school and lived in the same geographical area, so that narrows it down a bit. And let's keep an open mind, so anything however tenuous, flag it. We can sort the wheat from the chaff later."

*

It was a disappointing hour and a half later, before Tina felt her pulse quicken as she read the report on the discovery of the body of sixteen-year-old Shauna Matthews in one of the stables of a riding-school near her home. Earlier in her teens, Shauna had had riding lessons there. But further reading showed that Shauna had taken an overdose, choosing to die in the one place, where, according to her devastated parents, she had been truly happy. They attributed their daughter's death to a systematic bullying campaign at her convent school. Unfortunately, for Tina's purposes, not the same school attended by the A Team girls.

"What do you think of this one?" asked JP, almost an hour later. "Rebecca Dunne, 17 years of age, went missing in Baldoyle, in

January 1995. She left her home to walk to the local shop and was never seen again."

He frowned at the screen, "Oh no, hang on! Turns out she was a heroin addict and there's reason to think she'd fallen foul of her dealers. And there's nothing linking her to our five, as far as I can tell. Still, I'll flag it just in case."

"Might as well," Tina agreed despondently. Her hopes were raised again in a report on a fifteen-year-old runway, Marie McDonagh. But Marie had turned up five weeks later, safe, sound, pregnant, and admitting to having run away for fear that "my mother will kill me".

Tina's frustrated sighs brought JP's head up. "No luck?"

"Nope. You?"

"Nada." JP got to his feet and reached for his jacket. "I think it's time for a break, I'm beginning to see double."

Tina perked up. "Good idea, go and get yourself some fresh air. And while you're getting it, grab me a spice bag from Charlie's Chips, would you? That's the thing about not going to bed, you want the meals you don't have while you're asleep."

"Killer shrew," said JP under his breath, as he made for the door.

"I heard that," Tina yelled after him.

*

It was over twenty minutes before JP returned, seventeen of which Tina had spent visualising the coming pleasure. Nowhere in Dublin did spice bags the way Charlie's did – the chips fluffy on the inside and crispy on the outside. The perfect ratio of teriyaki-marinated chicken to sweet and juicy veg and the spice beautifully and masterfully sprinkled over it all. But when JP came through the door, the unmistakable aromas preceding him, she did not even glance up from the screen. "Listen to this," she called to him.

"In the early hours of 10th November 1996, the body of a baby girl was found on the doorstep of a house owned by a Mrs. Rita Nolan, she was the local Parish Priest's housekeeper. The baby had been wrapped in a plain white towel, which had been placed inside a plastic Roches Stores bag. It was believed that the baby had been delivered alive, but had died some hours after birth, as a result of hypothermia."

"Jesus Christ, poor little mite." JP put the bag of goodies on his desk and came to stand behind Tina. "Did they find the mother?"

"No, they didn't. They did all the usual stuff, door-to-door enquiries, questionnaires, TV appeals for the mother or anyone with any information to come forward etc but no one did. What do you think? I mean, I know this happened in late '96 and the photograph was taken in '95. But we agreed the date the photograph was taken isn't necessarily significant in and of itself. It's the girls in the photograph that matter, right?"

"Right."

"And we wanted something reasonably serious, something involving teenage girls. And let's face it, an abandoned baby to my mind, means a desperate mother, which in nine cases out of ten involves a desperate young mother. I mean, we just might have something here, right?"

"Yeah, it's possible," JP agreed. "I mean I wouldn't be getting too excited just yet, but I don't think we can ignore this one."

Tina's eyes were shining. "Good, because I just stuck in a request to have the records pulled on this Roches Stores baby case. Now pass me that grub before it gets cold. If there's one thing, I can't stand it's a cold Spice Bag."

*

CHAPTER 23

Tuesday 7th March

This time it was Tina, woken by her phone, who broke the news to a sleep-sodden JP. Hardly surprising considering it had been four-thirty before they'd called it a night on their trawl of the database.

"Jennifer O'Keeffe's been found dead in her hot-tub."

That woke him up. "What the fuck! So, what is it, accident or…?"

"Don't know yet, SOCO are at the scene. Pick you up outside your place in fifteen" Tina rang off without waiting for a reply.

*

It was still dark when she pulled up outside JP's place, an imposing three storey detached affair, quite literally a stone's throne from the Clontarf waterfront. The first time she'd seen it she'd assumed he was a lodger there, particularly as he'd asked if she minded him stopping by to check Mrs C.

"Nice digs," she'd remarked. She wanted to stay in the car, but JP had insisted she come in with him. She'd assumed that Mrs C was his landlady, instead she turned out to be an enormous dusty grey cat, who eyed her disdainfully from an armchair which had been spread with a white fur rug for her comfort.

"That's Mrs C – my God, she's obese."

"She's not obese," JP looked and sounded as though she'd just insulted his child. "She's just a bit rotund, that's all."

"Rotund?" Tina laughed out loud. "I hate to break it to you, JP, but you're in denial. I mean look at her, she's like a basketball with ears and a tail."

"Don't listen to her, Mrs. C," JP crooned, and kneeling next to the chair he'd stroked the beast's ears. "And if she is a bit on the heavy side, it's my fault not hers. I probably overfeed her because I feel guilty about leaving her alone so much."

"Then why get a cat in the first place?"

"I didn't get her, she got me. She just turned up one day and then she kept on coming back."

"You fed her, didn't you, the first time she came around, you fed her?"

"Of course, I fed her. She looked hungry, so I gave her a saucer of milk and a tin of salmon I had in the cupboard."

"And you wonder that she came back?" Tina rolled her eyes. But as JP fluffed and crooned to Mrs C, she realised that JP really cared about his fat cat and laid off teasing him about her.

"How much does it cost to rent a room in this gaff?" she enquired. At which, JP admitted shamefacedly that it cost him nothing. The house was his, a gift to him when he'd started college from his mother who had inherited it from an uncle.

"Ya jammy fecker" said Tina, thinking a little enviously of her own one-bed apartment in Raheny. How nice it would be to live in a place like this, with it's lofty, elegant rooms and sea-views from the big windows. Still, she had the coast road not far away and St Anne's Park just down the road... Tina brought her mind back to the moment, as JP came hurrying down the steps, hood up, head down against the cold. As he climbed in next to her, she caught the scent of his aftershave and when he pulled back his hood, found herself gazing at his shower-damp hair. "Jesus, it's freez..." he began.

Tina stabbed the radio with her finger and drowned out his weather-moans with an ear-bursting blast of Ed Sheeran's *Perfect*.

*

A uniformed Garda stood on duty at the gates to Jennifer O'Keeffe's home and at the front door, open to the freezing morning air, another Garda handed Tina and JPa white paper suit, cap and blue plastic shoe covers. Having wrestled into these, they made their way inside the house. Tina glanced in passing into the living room, where so recently they had questioned Jennifer O'Keeffe and her friends. A blonde woman in a pale pink coat was standing by the window, her back to the room, one hand resting on the shoulder of the man sitting in the armchair next to her. The man's head was flung back against the chair's headrest, his eyes closed. Something in the tableau they formed, struck Tina as off. Possibly it was the set of the woman's shoulders, the suggestion of pent-up tension. Or the way her hand rested on the man's shoulder, which ought to have conveyed support, comfort even, but instead appeared somehow perfunctory. And the man himself – at the sight of him, Tina made an involuntary sound. The woman wheeled round, stared at Tina from pink-rimmed eyes. At the same moment, the man opened his eyes and looked directly into Tina's. Tina moved on quickly along the hallway and through the big gleaming white kitchen with its granite counters and high-end appliances flooded now with the icy morning air from beyond the open French windows. She was fleetingly aware, as she passed, of a white-face woman sitting at the table. And then she was outside on the wide flagged stone of the patio where she breathed in a breath of cleansing air.

"Are you OK, Tina?" JP, behind her, sounded concerned.

"I'm fine," Tina kept her eyes on the garden beyond, dotted now with figures in white paper suits. "It's just there are some people who, when you're near them, give you the urge to jump into the nearest body of water and scrub yourself clean. But come on, let's get on with this."

*

Jennifer O'Keeffe's body had already been lifted from the hot tub. To Tina she seemed oddly more attractive looking in death than she had been in life. Her eyes were closed but her face looked younger, softer. Something had gone from it - disdain, anger, pain - Tina wasn't sure, but whatever it was, the dead woman looked the better for its absence. And in the skimpy white bikini, black hair lying in wet and gleaming tendrils against the tanned and honed body, she might well have been a teenager.

"Tina," Tom Quigley, the local coroner nodded his recognition.

"How's it goin' Tom, so, what's the story?"

"Right now, the best I can give you is death by immersion and drowning."

"When did it happen?"

"Hard to say," Quigley gazed down at the dead woman. "The problem is the water in the tub. The temperature would have been set to the desired level and the mechanism would have tried to maintain that temperature. With someone actually in it, and the lid off, the water would have gradually cooled. But that's just it, it's gradual, even now the water isn't actually cold which means that the time of death can't be easily ascertained. Best I can do on a preliminary examination is a rough estimate – death is likely to have occurred sometime between 10.00pm and midnight last night."

"Is there anything to indicate why or how she drowned?" asked JP.

Quigley shrugged, "What can I say, hot tubs and alcohol just don't mix well. It's all been tagged and bagged now, but when I got here, there was a glass on the ledge of the tub and a couple of empty champagne bottles rolling about on the deck. Clearly the poor lady was having a little party for herself. But hot water lowers the blood pressure, alcohol relaxes the muscles as well as the brain and that combination can quite easily lead to someone passing out and slipping unconscious under the water."

"Are you saying that's what happened here? That she was drunk and simply passed out and slipped under the water. Isn't it possible it wasn't an accident?"

Quigley turned to Tina. "In answer to your first question, I can't say just exactly what happened here. I'll be calling in a pathologist. As for your second, there's nothing obvious to suggest it wasn't an accident, no sign of a struggle, no defence wounds or blunt force trauma or anything of that nature."

"It sounds like you're saying it was an accident?"

"It sounds like you almost hope it wasn't," Quigley sounded more intrigued than reproachful.

"What? God no. Look Tom, thanks a million, we'll get out of your way and go talk to the SOCO lads, see what they've got."

*

CHAPTER 24

Tuesday 7th March

The items bagged by the SOCO team included the glass mentioned by Quigley, a single crystal flute, along with the empty champagne bottles. The real thing, Tina noted – no Aldi's finest for Jennifer O'Keeffe. There was also a pair of matching towels, looking fluffily pristine and unused, as well as a pair of fit-flops covered in sequins and a mobile phone. "Drinking alone," said JP. "And drinking a lot."

"Who found her?" Tina asked Garda Breda Curran. They had worked together in the past and considered her sound. The other uniform, Garda Dara Tierney, whom she only knew by sight, replied, "The cleaner."

"Does the cleaner have a name?" Tina fixed him with a glacial stare.

"Irena Dudek," Curran supplied quickly. "She's been working for the dead woman for four years now."

That would be the white-faced woman in the kitchen, Tina decided. "So, what had Ms Dudek to tell us?"

"She came in at 7.30 this morning," said Curran, "her usual start time. She has a key to the house and the code for the alarm, but she says the alarm wasn't on this morning. Neither were the security lights, but apparently that's not unusual. Ms Dudek let herself in as normal but when she went through to the kitchen, she found the door to the back garden ajar. She took a look outside and saw Ms O'Keeffe's phone on the patio table, she recognised the diamante cover. She assumed

Ms O'Keeffe was still in bed and had left the phone outside all night. Apparently, when Ms O'Keeffe used the hot tub late at night, she sometimes left stuff outside, glasses, towels, that kind of thing. She sometimes left the door unlocked too. We've kept Ms Dudek here, and we've taken her statement and all her contact details. She's quite shook up."

"I imagine she is," said Tina. "Was it Ms Dudek who notified the dead woman's brother? I see he's here with his wife."

"Yes, she had his number for when Ms O'Keeffe is away, in case of emergencies or anything. She rang Mr O'Keeffe and he arrived along with his wife."

"So, who called it in, Irena or O'Keeffe?"

"Actually, it was Mr O'Keeffe's wife, Alison, who made the call," Curran explained. "It seems Mr O'Keeffe had tried to pull his sister out…"

"What, he touched her?" Tina asked sharply.

"Unfortunately, yes. But only, he says, to raise her head above the water. He says he couldn't just leave her lying there, so he held her up while his wife rang an ambulance and the police. He said he knew his sister was dead as soon as he saw her in the hot tub. His wife and Ms Dudek have already corroborated all of this."

"And we notified the techs of course," Tierney put in, "so his prints can be taken for elimination purposes. The tub's already been swabbed and printed."

"Right," said Tina. "Well, I think you can let Irena go now. Sounds to me like she's had enough to contend with for one morning."

As the two uniforms walked away, Tina crossed the deck and made her way down the few steps to the lawn, which stretched away to a boundary wall. The garden had clearly been professionally landscaped as well as professionally tended. The borders and flower beds showed signs of recent planting, and Tina refused to believe that Jennifer

O'Keeffe had done any gardening, not with those nails. Having walked as far the boundary wall, Tina eyed the wooden door set into it. There was no key in the mortis lock and bolts had been fitted at top and bottom.

"Is this locked?" she asked one of the SOCO crew who was working nearby.

The officer looked up and shook his head. "No, it was shut and unlocked when we got here."

"OK, thanks. "And what's behind it?"

"Some kind of laneway, I believe. We've someone out there taking a look."

"Great," Tina made her way back to the patio, where JP had been chatting to Breda Curran, who was gazing adoringly into his eyes.

"Come on," she told him, "Time for the fun bit, let's go talk to the family."

JP fell into step with her. "So, the brother, this Lorcan O'Keeffe, is this the same Lorcan O'Keeffe who…."

"Yep, one and the same," said Tina shortly.

CHAPTER 25

Tuesday 7th March

They were sitting side by side on the sofa where Jennifer O'Keeffe had been huddled, the last time Tina had seen her alive. Lorcan O'Keeffe was wearing a white shirt with a red tie, under a V-necked blue wool sweater that accentuated his paunch. His left breast strained against the Ralph Lauren logo. Tina reminded herself that on this occasion she was dealing with O'Keeffe not as a suspect but as a grieving brother. But as always, the sight of him impressed on her again just what a big guy he was and how very slight Orla was. And she was reminded too of Nicole Brady's parents sitting together in their grief on a sofa, except there was more space between these two and they weren't holding hands.

She knows, thought Tina. She knows that her husband is a lying, cheating sleazeball. She just can't bear for the world to know she knows it, poor cow. Hard to figure out whether she was more to be pitied than blamed. No, scratch that – what was there to pity? Paula O'Keeffe had been there in that courtroom throughout the trial. She'd heard Orla Reid's testimony. And if she suspected or if in her heart of hearts, she knew that her husband could be a rapist, and had still chosen to help him cover it up, then she deserved to be miserable. Tina waited while JP did the condolences bit and apologies at having to ask questions at such a time.

"Just doing your job, Detective," O'Keeffe got to his feet and flashed a perfunctory smile showing, in Tina's opinion, unfeasibly white teeth. She reminded herself again that the body in the garden was his only sister, his only sibling in fact. Reminded herself too that her aversion to O'Keeffe did not in all conscience stem purely from her conviction that Orla Reid had been telling the truth. She had, she recognised, an instinctive dislike for all that Lorcan O'Keeffe represented – privilege, connections, arrogant, smug entitlement.

"This is my wife, Paula," O'Keeffe was saying. "Anything she or I can do to help you find out what happened to my sister, you only have to ask."

Paula, who had removed her pink coat to reveal a little cream tweed jacket and matching skirt, favoured JP with a ghost of a smile, but blanked Tina. No surprises there, over the two weeks of the rape trial, Lorcan O'Keeffe's wife had made her feelings for the detective backing Orla Reid, very clear. As always, the lovely Paula's perfect turn out made her feel particularly unkempt. The blonde hair was perfectly groomed, there were pearl studs in her ears. It was all very Jackie O, thought Tina, the only thing missing was the pillbox hat. She glanced down at her own ill-fitting black work trouser suit, her easy-iron and slightly less than white shirt. How did women like Paula O'Keeffe do that - pull it all together and make it look so easy?

"We appreciate your cooperation, Mr O'Keeffe, Ms O'Keeffe," said Tina with steely politeness.

"Lorcan and Paula, please," O'Keeffe sat down next to his wife again.

"Great, well then perhaps you could start by telling me when you last saw your sister alive?"

"It was two days ago, but I spoke to her yesterday on the phone."

"And how would you say your sister seemed on that occasion?"

"She seemed fine."

"Not upset or worried, or anxious about anything?"

"No. And to save yourselves time, don't bother going down that road," O'Keeffe sounded suddenly belligerent. "Jen had had her problems,

I'm sure you'll find that out soon enough, if you haven't already. But she was doing better. She was looking forward to the kids coming home in a couple of days' time, for Christ sake!"

In the silence, Paula weighed in, by way of explanation. "Jennifer's kids are away on holiday with their father," she said. "Jason and Jennifer are divorced, and Jason married again. Lorcan had to call Jason earlier and let him know what's happened. Just how he's going to break the news to Stacey and Ryan, I don't know."

"How old are Stacy and Ryan?" asked Tina.

"Stacy is eighteen and Ryan is sixteen."

Tina was surprised, Jennifer had barely looked old enough to have children half that age. Her body looked more like that of a teenager than of a woman who had given birth not once but twice. "Did the children see a lot of their father," she asked. "I'm assuming that Jennifer had custody?"

Paula looked uncertainly at her husband "Jennifer had custody yes, but the children liked to spend time with their father…"

"Because the bastard turned them against their own mother," O'Keeffe growled.

So, Jennifer's kids had taken sides, thought Tina, and chosen their father over their boozy mother.

"I see. So, we know that Jennifer was found in the hot tub this morning. And while it's difficult to be completely accurate, it seems that the time of death was between 10pm and midnight. Was your sister in the habit of drinking while in the tub, late at night?"

O'Keeffe's phone rang just then. Glancing at the screen he frowned and stabbed at the keypad shutting of the ringing sound. "Sorry, this thing just keeps going off," he said. "You were asking if Jen often used the tub late at night? Well yes, she did. It was her newest toy and she said it helped her relax, and sleep afterwards. She's been having trouble sleeping for some time now."

"And would she often use it alone?"

"I guess so. Alone, with a gang of her gal pals – whatever. Like I say, it was her latest fad."

"And would you say that your sister was in the habit of drinking alcohol while using the hot tub alone and late at night?"

"Yes, I'd say she was in the habit of drinking alone in the hot tub," Lorcan gave a helpless shrug.

"Everybody tried to tell her it was a bad idea," Paula put in hastily. "Lorcan, Me, Nicole, Rachel, everyone, but…."

"What Paula is struggling to put into words," said O'Keeffe, "is that Jen didn't pay a blind bit of notice to what anyone said. She did things her way."

"OK. And your sister had security lights and an alarm system fitted to the house, I gather, but neither were on when her cleaner, Ms Dudek, arrived this morning. Was that unusual?"

Lorcan ran his hand over his head once more. "I'd like to say it was unusual, but I'd be lying. Jen's gotten more and more careless about stuff like that. Sometimes she remembered to turn the lights and alarm on, sometimes she didn't. It depended on how…it just depended."

"Right, and can I ask, the door, the one giving access to the rear garden?"

"Yeah, what about it?"

"It's been fitted with bolts and a padlock. Was your sister also in the habit of leaving that door unlocked?"

O'Keeffe shook his head. "Not as far as I knew. The key went missing years ago, but there's a bloody nuisance right-of-way behind the house, so it was kept bolted. Are you saying the door was left unbolted last night?"

"The SOCO team found it unlocked, yes," Tina admitted.

O'Keeffe frowned, was about to say something when his phone rang again. This time, with a glance at his screen, he got to his feet.

"Excuse me, I'm going to take this one." As he passed her on the way to door, Tina caught a whiff of his overly sweet aftershave. She caught too, the expression in his wife's eyes as they followed him from the room. Probably worried he's talking to one of his girlfriends, she decided. But as the door closed behind him, they could hear Lorcan's voice booming. "Rachel? Hi. No, no, it's fine honestly, I can talk."

Paula's face relaxed, "That will be our friend Rachel Quinn. Rachel is…I mean she was a very close friend of Jennifer's too. I thought she should know what's happened, so I texted her."

"And your husband and his sister, were they very close too, would you say?" asked Tina.

"Yes, they were very close. Lorcan's always been very protective of Jennifer and she of him."

Paula got up and walked across to the long window and stood with her back to Tina and JP. A moment later she wheeled round as Lorcan suddenly erupted into the room. "I've just spoken to Rachel Quinn," he boomed, voice tight with fury.

"Is it true what she told me, that she went to you with this story about scratched out faces in some photograph? Is it true that you've actually been investigating a connection between the deaths of Nicole Brady and Bethany Doyle?"

Tina and JP looked at one another. Awh shit, thought Tina.

"Lorcan, what are you talking about?" Paula O'Keeffe came toward him, but her husband pushed past her and glared down at the two detectives.

"Answer me, is this true" he demanded.

JP, his tone placatory said quietly, "It's true that Ms Quinn contacted us regarding some unease she'd been feeling as a result..."

"I don't fucking believe this," O'Keeffe exploded. "I do not fucking believe it! So, this is why you were asking me all that stuff about the garden door. You knew my sister's life might well be in danger, but did nothing about it?"

"Lorcan," Paula pleaded, "Would you please calm down!"

"Calm down," her husband roared. "Calm down? How the fuck am I supposed to calm down? My sister is dead, and now I hear that that might not be an accident. That some nutjob may have actually killed her, some nutjob the cops have known about, for how long now?"

"Your wife is right, Mr O'Keeffe," said Tina. "If you could try to calm down..."

O'Keeffe rounded on her, leaning in and looming over her as she purposely stayed in her seat. He was close enough that Tina could see how anger had set the bluish-purple vein in his forehead, pulsing. "Don't you dare tell me to calm down," he roared. "I'll calm down when I get some answers."

"And you'll get answers," said Tina evenly. "Just tell us what you'd like to know?"

"I want to know who sent those photographs? I want to know if there's a link between it and the deaths of my sister and her friends Nicole Brady and Bethany Doyle. And what's all this about Anna Fox's car almost being driven into the sea? What steps have you taken to protect my sister, did you even warn her that you believed her life was in danger?"

Tina, in an effort to diffuse his anger, kept her tone level. "OK," she said quietly. "To answer your first question, we don't know yet who sent the photos. As to any link between them and the deaths of your sister and her friends, we have no concrete evidence to support that theory. But yes, Jennifer was aware of our concerns, and at no point did she indicate that she shared those concerns. On the contrary in fact, Jennifer..."

"So now you're saying it's her fault?" O'Keeffe exploded again. "Jesus H Christ, this just keeps getting better. Actually, you know what, I'm not going to waste another minute of my time on the organ grinder's monkeys, but you better believe you haven't heard the end of this."

This time when he stormed out, the door crashed closed behind him. For a moment there was absolute silence in the room, then Paula fixed steely eyes on Tina.

"I think you should go," she said. It was clearly not a suggestion but an order. And without waiting for a reply, she marched from the room, high heels clacking on the wooden floor. With a glance at one another, Tina and JP got up and followed her along the hallway to the already open door, which, as soon as they stepped over the threshold, was slammed in their faces.

*

CHAPTER 26

Tuesday 7th March

"Well, that went well," said JP, as the car swept through the gateway. Then as Tina steered right instead of left toward the coast road, he threw her an enquiring glance.

"I want to take a look at this laneway behind the house," she said. "According to SOCO it's a right-of-way."

The laneway was too narrow to drive through, so Tina parked at the entrance, and they made their way on foot along the muddy, overgrown track, bordered on one side by the O'Keeffe's boundary wall and on the other by open fields. Nothing to stop anyone who didn't want to risk being seen approaching the house from the coast road, accessing this laneway via those fields, thought Tina. She glanced up at the wall which she figured was about twelve feet high.

JP, reading her mind said, "Anyone wanting to scale that wall would have had to come prepared."

"Unless it was someone who knew the gate was unlocked," said Tina. Her phone rang and she mouthed the word Coleman to JP. She spoke brightly into the phone.

"Yes sir? Well, yes sir, he did but we...yes sir. Yes sir, I understand sir, and we are actually on our way back right now and…sir? Are you there, sir?" Tina stared at the blank screen. "Bastard hung up on me."

"What's up with him?" asked JP.

"He wants us both in his office asap. Apparently, he's had the Super on, chewing his ear off. Looks like that little bastard O'Keeffe wasted no time getting onto the organ grinder."

*

On the way back to the station, JP said tentatively. "Look Tina, tell me to drop it if you want, but you never really told me what happened with O'Keeffe. I mean, I know about the trial and acquittal obviously. And I know you have no doubt he was guilty, and clearly it was all a big deal for you. But like I said, if you'd rather not talk about it..."

But to her surprise, Tina discovered that she did want to talk about it, needed to talk about it. Perhaps it was seeing O'Keeffe again for the first time since the trial. Whatever the reason, she found herself telling JP all about it. From her first interview with Orla, through how they had built their case. How they'd managed to trace the taxi driver who'd driven the pair to Orla's home that night, Jacko Dunne, a balding overweight Dub, well into his fifties. How Jacko, shown a photograph of Lorcan O'Keeffe, had wrinkled his nose as though he had suddenly detected a bad smell.

"I remember she was more than half his age," he'd said, "and yer man was all over her in the back of me cab." But also, how, later in court, pressed by Keith Brady, Jacko had admitted, albeit with obvious reluctance, that Orla, "didn't look like she minded too much."

How, when the cab pulled up, O'Keeffe had gotten out with the 'young one'.

"I heard her telling him he needn't bother, she'd to be up early in the morning for work," Jacko told the court. "But he got out with her, anyway, told me he'd see her to the door and be right back. I opened the window to keep an eye on him, you know, in case he was planning to do a runner without paying me. Then the next minute he was back on his own, shoving the money for the fare at me through the window. That was when I said to meself, this bloke isn't taking no for an answer, that's for sure."

She told him how her jubilation at Jacko's evidence had been short-lived, as an entirely different picture was painted of Orla Reid. A picture of a girl whose Instagram posts showed her posing repeatedly in skimpy clothes, with a drink in one hand and the hashtag #partyanimal. A girl who, by her own evidence, met Lorcan O'Keeffe in a bar while on a hen party night-out, prior to which she and her friends had been drinking for at least five hours. How Brady, with what seemed to Tina, salacious pleasure, had read aloud the website description of what Orla and the other hens had been wearing that night.

A short-skirted dress, a white-collar neckpiece and a wet look habit. Black fishnet tights, black stiletto heeled shoes, the outfit having been purchased from a website which advertised it, as 'a nasty habit costume for the naughtiest nuns!

And then there was the display put on by O'Keeffe himself, the repeated allusions to his wife and his regret at having betrayed and hurt her. The impression he managed to convey of shamefacedly, but manfully owning up having flirted with Orla, bought her drinks, and finally having left the nightclub with her. He even admitted to kissing her in the back of the taxi and insisting on walking her to her door, but with the sole intention of seeing her safely inside, he insisted. He had, he admitted, only changed his mind and let the taxi go without him, when Orla had repeatedly invited him in for some black coffee. This, he conceded, had been an enormous error of judgment on his part. He also conceded that he had had sex with Orla that night.

"It happened," he said. "I don't deny that. I have never denied that. It happened and I truly regret that it did. In particular, because of the hurt it has caused my wife and my family. But it was entirely consensual. I did not force her. I did not rape her."

"And they believed him," Tina finished. "They believed him, and he got off."

Into the silence that followed, JP spoke feelingly. "Christ, it's a sickener when they walk away, and you know they're guilty as fuck."

"It's not just that," said Tina. "It was my fault. Orla would never have gone through with the case if I hadn't pushed her. And two weeks ago, she tried to kill herself and I…"

JP said sharply. "Stop the car, will you, Tina?"

"What here? Why, what's up, have you forgotten that Coleman is waiting for us?"

"Forget Coleman," said JP. "Just pull over, please."

Frowning, Tina pulled into a lay-by and turned to face him. "What's going on, JP?"

*

CHAPTER 27

Tuesday 7th March

"What you said just now, it's absolute bollocks and you know it," said JP.

"Don't say bollocks," Tina smiled thinly.

"Why not, you say it all the time?"

"Yeah, well that's different, it doesn't sound right coming from a big girl's blouse like you."

"Don't try to change the subject," said JP.

"OK then, how is it bollocks," Tina demanded. "It was me who talked Orla out of doing what she wanted to do in the first place, which was to keep quiet and not take it any further."

"If that was the case, then why report it in the first place?"

"Come on, JP. We both know that not everyone who gives an initial statement alleging rape actually goes ahead with taking a case. Orla told us on the night she gave her statement that she knew she wouldn't be believed. If I hadn't convinced her she could win, she'd have let it lie."

"So, you're saying you forced her to go ahead with the case, actually forced her? Or let her believe it would be easy?"

"No, of course I didn't," Tina said impatiently. "The opposite in fact. It was explained to Orla that the prosecution process could be a long and drawn-out business, and that the legal system can be confusing and intimidating."

"But she still chose to go ahead, in spite of those warnings?"

"Yes, clearly she did," Tina agreed irritably, "But again, mostly because of me."

"Because you believed her," said JP. "You believed that O'Keeffe had raped her and that there was in fact a case to be made."

"A case to be made, yes. But there was practically no trace evidence and…"

"So what? You know as well as I do that trace evidence in a rape case doesn't need to be strong in order to get a conviction. So much of these things are down to the jury and how sympathetic they feel toward the alleged victim."

"Yeah, yeah, I know all of that. But I made her a promise that we'd get that bastard. I never should have done that."

"No, you shouldn't," said JP flatly. "You'll get no arguments from me on that point. But you won't make that mistake again, will you?"

"And what if I don't," said Tina, turning the key in the ignition. "A fat lot of use that will do Orla Reid. Now can we leave it please and let me get us back to the station before Coleman blows a gasket."

*

As Tina reached for the station door, it burst open and a man came barrelling out, almost ploughing into her. "Woah!" called Tina warningly.

The man gave her a filthy look. "Shower of bleedin' wankers!" he called over his shoulder as he hurried away.

JP stared after him. "I wonder what had him back again?"

"You know him?"

"Yeah, that's Anthony Fitzpatrick, the guy who witnessed the attack on Anna Fox's car? I wonder if he's remembered something more."

"That's Fitzpatrick?"

Tina was surprised. "He doesn't exactly strike me as the civic-minded sort."

"No, me neither," said JP. "Look go ahead, I'll catch you up, I'll just go check at the front desk."

"I'll come with you." But just then Tina's phone rang. Coleman. She held the phone a safe distance from her ear. "Sir? Yes sir. No sir, I mean yes sir, we did sir. We're just here sir. Yes sir. Right away sir."

"Coleman?" guessed JP, appearing at her side again.

"Yep, and like I told you, he's blowing a gasket. So has this Fitzpatrick guy remembered anything new?"

"No, he hadn't come in about that. He was done for driving his van without tax and insurance."

*

After a lecture on keeping him waiting, Coleman, who did not offer them a seat, demanded Tina bring him through what they knew so far about the death of Jennifer O'Keeffe.

"So, an unexpected death, but nothing as yet to suggest anything untoward."

"No sir, nothing definite," Tina conceded, "But Jennifer O'Keeffe was yet another member of the A-Team gang and I still think that it's not possible to be certain that there's no link …"

"Before you give us the benefit of your thoughts, DS Bassett," said Coleman nastily, "perhaps you could explain why I found myself earlier today in the position of having an official complaint relayed to me by my superior officer, on the subject of your attitude."

Tina blinked. "My attitude, sir? I'm not sure I follow."

"Then let me enlighten you. The complaint concerns the manner in which you dealt with the brother of this hot-tub lassie in Malahide, Lorcan O'Keeffe."

"Sir," said JP quickly. "Sir, I'd like to say that I saw nothing untoward in DS Bassett's demeanour toward Mr O'Keeffe, and I was there for the entire duration of the interview."

Coleman's eyes narrowed. "Be that as it may, Detective Garda O'Rourke, but Mr O'Keeffe's wife, who also was present for the duration of the interview, did in fact take exception to Detective Sergeant Basset's general attitude."

"So, it was Paula O'Keeffe who made the complaint," said Tina. "And what exactly was her problem with my attitude, sir?"

"That's just it," Coleman steepled his fingers. "Mrs O'Keeffe contends that it is you who has a problem with her husband. Let's face it, DS Bassett, we all know there's a history here. But I did not expect that you would need reminding of the fact that Lorcan O'Keeffe was found innocent by a jury of his peers, of all charges brought against him."

Next to her, JP shifted his weight and his arm brushed against Tina's. She thought she could almost feel him desperately willing her not to lose her cool. Summoning up a great fake smile, she said brightly, "Absolutely not sir. You need have no concerns on that score, sir."

She had her revenge in the non-plussed expression in Coleman's suspicious little eyes. He picked up his fountain pen and lowered his head. They were dismissed.

"Seriously, I'll end up doing time for that man," Tina fumed, as they walked away from Coleman's office. "And as for Paula O'Keeffe, her problem is that she knows that I know what a total piece of shite she's married to."

"Coleman has obviously had the ear chewed off him by the super," said JP. "And he's taking it out on you."

"Yeah, well that still doesn't…" She broke off at the sight of the archive box that was sitting on her desk.

"I hope that's what I think it is," she said and fell upon it.

*

CHAPTER 28

Tuesday 7th March

Lifting the lid, Tina's nose wrinkled involuntarily at the smell of dust, courtesy of the basement where the box had been stored for however many years since the case had last been re-examined.

"Yes! It's the Roches Stores baby files." She replaced the lid. "I'm going to take this somewhere quiet," she told JP, and carried the box along the corridor and into a vacant interview room.

It had seemed inappropriate somehow to examine the contents of the box amid the bustle and noise of the Detective's room. Because when all was said and done, it wasn't much to show for a human life – a single file, a couple of evidence bags. The first contained the white plastic carrier bag bearing the red Roches Stores logo: More Value More Choice More Service. The second held the towel the little girl had been wrapped in. It was plain white, well-worn and had a label attached bearing the Dunnes Stores St Bernard tag.

But could there really, Tina asked herself, be any link between the tragic death of this baby and what she had come to think of in her own mind as the Class of '98 case? In the hopes of answering that question, she sat down and read the file from beginning to end. It was just as the database records had already told them, the child had been born prematurely, but alive, and had died of hypothermia. House-to-house enquiries had been carried out, every possible lead followed up. Appeals had been made on national TV for the mother to come forward but to no avail; the mother had never been found. In the course of the investigation, forensic tests were done on the bag and the blanket, and a DNA sample was taken from the body of the child. Because the mother of the child had never been identified, those samples were still in existence on the Garda DNA database system.

But what use were they, thought Tina, with no-one to match them against? And the little girl – Tina read that the investigating Gardai had named her – Grace, had been laid to rest in one of the communal graves in the Angel's Plot in Glasnevin. But, thought Tina sadly, in truth there had been precious little grace for the little girl in this world at least.

She replaced the file and evidence bags back in the box and closed the lid. The whole thing had made her feel sad and depressed and angry too, angry at all the desperation and the pain that underlay the whole sad little affair. And to add to all of that, she felt herself no further along toward solving the current case. Back in the detective's room, JP, who had been swivelling in his chair, stopped as she came through the door, the box under her arm.

"Anything?"

"I don't know," said Tina, putting the box on the floor next to her desk, before slumping disconsolately into her chair.

"Tell you what," said JP. "You look like you could do with a coffee. I'll go out and get the good stuff, shall I?"

Tina shook her head, "No, I'm fine. I don't want coffee. Actually, I'm going to pop out, get some lunch, I'm starving."

"Want some company?" JP called after her. But Tina was already out of the room and heading for the door to the car park. It was true that she was hungry, and she stopped off at the nearest SPAR and picked up a tea and an all-day breakfast roll, which she ate in the car. Then she scrunched up the greasy wrapper, squashed it down into the empty cup which she flung onto the passenger seat. Then brushing off the crumbs, she belted up and started the engine.

*

It was peaceful in Glasnevin cemetery and though cold in the shade, there was actual heat in the March sunshine. The light picked out the green of the tall conifers, the glinting stone of the monuments. It didn't take Tina long to find the Angel's Plot, and from there, the final resting place of the little girl who had come to be known as the Roches Stores baby. She shared her grave with twenty-nine other babies, and although buried officially as 'unknown baby', the name bestowed on her by the investigating Gardai had subsequently been carved on the communal headstone - Grace. Above the list of names, four words had been carved. PRAY FOR OUR ANGELS.

Tina wondered how many, if any, had prayed for baby Grace by name. That said, the grave, unlike the others in the Angel's plot, all of which showed some small evidence of care – plaster angels, windchimes, ceramic birds and animals – had been planted, and recently by the look of the soil, with greats clumps of yellow tulips and daffodils. Rain and wind had taken its toll on the tulips, giving them a ragged, blowsy look, but nothing could diminish their vivid yellow beauty. Sighing a little at the sadness of it all, Tina turned away from the grave.

What had she hoped to gain in coming in here? The truth was that she didn't know the answer. She had acted on a whim, without really thinking it through and it had brought her no further along. Feeling tired and dispirited, she realised that she wasn't quite ready yet to return to the station. She looked about at the gravestones, the Celtic crosse. The sun was still shining, the birds were singing in the many trees. She made her way to a bench beneath a yew tree and sat down. Why was it, she wondered, that graveyards were always such peaceful places? And what was she doing here anyway? Had she really thought that the grave of a long dead baby would yield up any clues to who it's mother had been. And was she seriously considering that the mother may have been one of the six girls who had made up the A-Team?

Technically of course, it was possible. But even if that were the case, how would it tie in with the present series of deaths? Had someone found out who it was that had abandoned the little girl and had decided to punish them? But why now, after all this time? And what was she contemplating here anyway – that someone was exacting revenge for the life of the Roches Stores baby, by killing not alone the mother, but everyone connected with her? Because, if her theory was right, then to date, three women had now been murdered and another, Anna Fox, had almost lost her life. No, this Roches Stores baby was a red herring and she Tina, had gone haring off on the wrong scent. And yet, and yet…

And it came to her then, the reason this place, all such places, are so peaceful. It was because here the dead held sway. And the dead are not troubled by decisions or choices, whether good or bad, right or wrong. For them there are no more mysteries, no puzzles to be solved. And no more answers to be had because there are no more questions to be asked. For them, this was it. This was what it had all come down to and they really, actually did, rest here in peace. But, thought Tina, suddenly jumping to her feet, and shaking off the fanciful fugue which had somehow overtaken her, she was not dead. No, she was very much alive and inside her head there were mysteries and puzzles galore and questions that needed asking, and she strode across the sparkling sun warmed grass and left the dead to their rest.

*

CHAPTER 29

Tuesday 7th March

"I don't understand what's happening," Rachel told Tina miserably.

They were sitting together in the big messy living room. Rachel's mother having taken the children to another room to give them some quiet and privacy. "Is that why you're here? Have you come to tell me what's going on?"

"I'm sorry Rachel," said Tina. "For now, all we can tell you is that we are doing absolutely everything we can to make sense of it all."

"Lorcan doesn't think so," Rachel sounded reproachful. "Lorcan says that Jennifer would still be alive if the police had been doing their jobs properly. He doesn't believe that Jennifer died of natural causes. He thinks someone did that to her on purpose. Is that what you believe?"

"Rachel, I'm going to have to ask you to trust me," said Tina. "Can you do that?"

"I don't know," Rachel replied simply.

"Fair enough," said Tina. "I can understand why you might feel that way. But I'm going to ask you to trust me anyway. And part of that means answering some more questions we need to ask you. Even if the questions appear to have nothing at all to do with what's been happening. Do you think you could do that?"

"I think so. I want to help."

"Good. Then the first thing I need to ask is this. When I questioned you about Anna Fox's twin sister, Claire, you said Claire didn't finish school, even though she was just as bright as Anna. Instead, she went to London and took an office job. Why was that do you know?"

Rachel shook her head, "I don't really know. I don't think even Anna could make any sense of it at the time. I think Claire just sort of went a bit funny."

"In what way, funny?"

"Just funny. Weird, Anna called it. Like, Claire went and had all her hair cut off for starters, I mean short-short." Rachel gave what Tina thought was an unconscious toss of her lovely mass of curls. "And then she changed the way she dressed. Claire was always a real girly girl, that was one of the things we used to tease her about, but then she started wearing really shapeless gear, you know, really baggy. And she had a boyfriend, David. They were crazy about each other, but she just suddenly dumped him. Then again, their mother was really sick around that time, I mean she was actually dying. So that may have had something to do with it all."

"And can you remember roughly when all these changes in Claire began?"

"God, I don't know, it was all so long ago. Although…hang on, I do remember that it was around the time I had my appendix out, that Claire had her hair cut off. I remember that I met her on the very first day I was allowed out after the operation. I hardly recognised her to be honest."

"When did you have your appendix out," asked Tina.

"Exactly? Oh Lord, let me think. It would have been about a week before I was supposed to go to Wicklow for the transition year weekend field trip. I was absolutely gutted I had to miss it."

"And when did the field trip take place, what time of the year?"

"Just after the Easter holidays," said Rachel with certainty. "It was always held then. So yeah, it would have been just after Easter 1995."

Tina felt a small stirring of excitement. "Great, that's really helpful, Rachel. And this trip, to Wicklow, was it, do you think it's possible it was something that happened then, that triggered these changes you mentioned in Claire?"

Rachel frowned, "Something that happened on the trip to Wicklow, how could it be? Claire didn't go on the trip, it was only for transition students."

"Claire didn't go on the trip?" Tina echoed hollowly.

"No. Claire didn't do transition year, she went straight on into fifth year. Anna went, but not Claire."

"Not Claire," Tina repeated again stupidly.

The sudden deflation had left her flailing about in her mind for the other question she knew she had wanted to ask Rachel. With an effort she picked up the train of her thoughts, though she was no longer sure where she was going with all of this.

"Just one other thing, Rachel, I understand that Anna and Nicole had only reconnected quite recently?"

"That's right," Rachel nodded her agreement.

"And even that was only because Nicole happened to join the same yoga class as Anna, I believe. And I might have imagined it, but I thought I picked up on some tension between Anna and Jennifer when we interviewed you all together?"

"You didn't imagine it," said Rachel. "Anna and Jennifer never really got on. And then they had a big-time falling out over…well over boys. And the same with Anna and Nicole. But what you just said about Nicole turning up at Anna's yoga class, it was actually the other way around. Anna turned up at Nicole's yoga class."

"Right, but you think they'd put their falling out behind them?"

"I guess so," Rachel's eyes filled with tears, and she scrabbled in her sleeve for a tissue and dabbed her eyes. "I'm glad they did, because I always thought it was such a pity, them falling out over someone like Lorcan."

"Lorcan?" Tina pounced. "Is this Lorcan O'Keeffe you're talking about, Rachel? Are you saying Nicole and Anna fell out over Lorcan O'Keeffe?"

"Well yes, but this was when they were teenagers. Nicole really fancied Lorcan, but he never really took her seriously. And Lorcan liked Anna, but Anna had no time for him."

"And Claire? Was there ever anything between Lorcan and Claire?"

"Lorcan and Claire?" Rachel's tone was derisive. "God no! If you'd known Claire, you'd realise how funny that is. No, there was nothing like that. And to be honest, I don't know why you need to know all this, it was all just silly teenage stuff."

Tina said nothing. Silly teenage stuff, she thought, but unless she was very wrong, it was silly teenage stuff that was at the heart of this whole thing.

Back in the car, she made a call. "Joe? It's Tina. How's tricks? Good, that's good. Yeah, yeah, all good with me too. Listen, I'm actually calling because I'm hoping you might be able to do me a big favour?"

At the station, Tina was greeted by the news that Jennifer O'Keeffe's phone records had come through.

"Already? Someone's had a rocket put under them. Anything interesting?"

"Nothing that jumps out," said JP. "A lot of sarky texts to her ex-husband, mostly about the kids. Not a lot in the way of replies from him. A ton of calls and texts to the kids, calls and texts to and from Lorcan, same with Nicole Brady. Nothing of any real interest there though. A couple of texts to and from Rachel Quinn. A call from Anna Fox to Jennifer last week…"

"Just the one?"

"Yeah. Texts to and from Irena Dudek, just about the cleaning and that sort of thing. There's an incoming call to Jennifer on the morning of the day she died, just after eleven. That's been traced to an unregistered prepaid phone, lasted just over one minute. Jennifer's final call was to her daughter. She'd texted both her kids on the day of her death, to say she was looking forward to them coming home. Her son got back to her, her daughter didn't."

*

That evening, alone in her flat with a frozen pizza and a couple of beers, Tina found herself wondering what it must be like to have two parents fighting over you, fighting to keep you that is. Phyllis and Gerry had fought over her alright, but that had been a different thing entirely.

"We can't just send her back, Phil. For the love of God, she's a little child, not a coat that doesn't quite measure up. If she was our own, we couldn't just send her back, could we?"

She would never know how Phyllis might have replied because they had heard her just then. A creaking of the stair where she was standing listening perhaps. In any event Gerry had come hurrying up the stairs, scooped her up into his arms and carried her back to bed. Over his shoulder, Tina had seen Phyllis standing in the hall staring up at them. But after all, as she now knew, it happened; sometimes adoptions simply did not take. There was even a word for it – a disruption. And there were all sorts of reasons for it. Perhaps in her case, it had come down to the simple fact that Phyllis had believed she was getting a different kind of child, that Tina had simply not been the type of little girl Phyllis wanted, if indeed she had wanted one at all. Tina had concluded that Phyllis was not a particularly maternal sort of woman. Then again, if she had been a different type of little girl; more disarming, more loveable…

And after all, in the end, it had not been so bad, because they hadn't actually sent her back, like the badly fitting coat she was. And really, when she came to think about it, what had she to complain of? Phyllis and Gerry had raised her conscientiously. Instead, they had given her a home, fed her, clothed her, educated her. The trouble was nobody had ever told her in so many words that she was safe, that she was wanted and loved and would not be returned.

*

CHAPTER 30

Wed 8th March

Early the following morning, Tina and JP were summoned to Coleman's office.

"I thought you might be interested to know that we've received the preliminary autopsy results on Jennifer O'Keeffe," he told them, patting a buff-coloured file which lay on the desk before him. "Ms O'Keeffe's death will be ruled accidental."

"For Christ's sake!" Tina was too frustrated to hide it.

"I'm sorry the findings of the State Pathologist don't meet with your approval, DS Barrett," said Coleman dryly. "But the facts are that no drugs were found in the dead woman's system, other than a prescription anti-depressant, that and some traces of a low dose of some anxiety medication she'd also been prescribed."

"Yes sir, but..."

Coleman held up a warning hand and Tina fell silent.

"She had not suffered a stroke or heart attack, and there were no clear signs of any suspicious circumstances," Coleman continued. "Now, you may not agree, DS Bassett, but from the viewpoint of the dead woman's family, this is the best news possible in a situation where there can be no actual good news."

"And Lorcan O'Keeffe and his lawyers are satisfied with that, are they?" Tina asked incredulously.

Coleman eyed her coldly. "Not having spoken to Mr O'Keeffe or indeed, his lawyers, I am not in a position to answer that question. However, I imagine he will appreciate the fact that neither time nor expense has been spared in expediting these findings. Small comfort perhaps, but I hope going some way to allaying any suspicions which may have been aroused, in my opinion, unnecessarily aroused, concerning the circumstances in which his sister lost her life."

"But sir, you said yourself only yesterday that you were prepared to consider the possibility that…"

"Enough!" Coleman snapped. He picked up the buff file and shoved it at Tina.

"Take it," he said. "Take it and read it for yourself. Acquaint yourself with the facts and after you've done that, I don't expect to hear another word about your fantastic theories and spurious connections. You have other cases on your desk to be getting on with, so I suggest you do just that."

"But sir…."

"I said enough!" Coleman barked. "Take this and get out!"

Tina got out.

*

"So, it's right back to me barking up the wrong tree, then," said Tina.

They were in the car park behind the station, to which JP had practically manhandled her so she could let off steam without anyone to hear her do it. Once there, he said nothing while she paced and ranted until the worst heat of her anger had begun to cool.

"What's in it anyway," JP indicated the file she was still clutching in a clenched fist.

By way of answer, Tina shoved the file into his hands. JP opened it, ran an eye over the report. "Nothing here we didn't already find out at the scene, unless you count a lot of additional facts about the effects of heat on blood vessels and how, combined with alcohol that can lead to a drop in blood pressure. Apparently, it's pretty much equivalent to fainting. And if you faint in a hot tub, well…. "

"Yeah, yeah, spare me," said Tina.

"But no sign of her having overdosed," JP continued. "If it had been suicide, and she'd chosen the hot tub as the way to go, you'd expect that she'd have overdosed, wouldn't you say? Wash the pills down with champagne?"

Tina slid to her hunkers, let her head rest against the station wall and closed her eyes. "So, we're left to believe she drank too much, passed out and slipped under the water?"

"At the risk of pissing you off even further," said JP, "it's possible that's exactly what did happen. Death by hot tub is actually a lot more common than you might think. I googled it. Apparently, an average of 335 Americans drowns each year in a hot tub. And half of those are able-bodied aged between five and sixty-four. Then again, I suppose there are a lot more people with hot tubs in American than there are here. But here's the interesting bit…"

"You mean there actually is an interesting bit?" Tina raised her head wearily.

"…there's some serious speculation that about 20% of those deaths are homicides that go undetected. Or so says Google."

"Yeah, and if you can find that out, then so could anyone else."

"Meaning you don't buy it that Jennifer O'Keeffe died as the result of an accident?"

"To be honest I'm not sure I know what I believe," said Tina. She got to her feet again. "Look, you go back in, I just need a minute or two on my own."

"You sure you're ok?"

"I'm sure I'm OK." When he had gone, Tina walked to her car, unlocked it and slipped into the driver's seat. From under the passenger seat, she pulled out the plastic bag she thought of as her 'emergency supply' and dug out a Snickers bar. Tearing open the wrapper with her teeth, she bit off almost half and began to chew. JP was right, she seriously needed to cool off and calm the fuck down. She also needed to recapture some of that sense of purpose she had felt while sitting under the tree in Glasnevin Cemetery. That determination to follow this trail, and regardless of Coleman, follow her nose wherever it might lead her. Questions, she reminded herself, there were still questions unanswered, and shoving the remainder of the chocolate bar into her mouth, she shoved the wrapper into the plastic bag, threw it back under the seat, licked the chocolate off her fingers and climbed out of the car. And the first question was one for JP. She fired it at him as he came through the door, two coffees in his hands.

"You know this Anthony Fitzpatrick, the guy who witnessed the attack on Anna Fox's car?"

"Sure, what about him?" JP handed Tina her coffee.

"I ran him through the system. Did you know he has a history of petty theft and a suspended sentence for an attempted breaking and entering? Hasn't done any time yet but…"

JP shook his head, "I didn't, actually." Then, catching the look in Tina's eyes, "Eh, where exactly are you going with this?"

"I'm not sure yet, to be honest," Tina admitted. "But you know, I think it might be interesting to have a little talk with Mr Fitzpatrick all the same."

JP raised his eyebrows, "What, you mean bring him in?"

Tina grinned, "Why not, as long as we ask him nicely."

*

CHAPTER 31

Wed 8th March

The interview room was a study in grey. Grey floor, grey walls, greying ceiling. Even the table, fixed to the floor was a dark shade of grey. And it was cold, Tina could tell that JP was feeling it, even if the bull-necked man sitting opposite them was immune. Fitzpatrick had taken off his leather jacket and hung it carefully across the back of the chair and was sitting there in a short sleeved black tee-shirt and black jeans.

"Detective DS Bassett and Detective JP O'Rourke interviewing Mr Anthony Fitzpatrick," said JP, for the benefit of the video cameras. "You are not obliged to say anything unless you wish to do so, but anything you do say will be taken down and may be used in evidence. Do you understand?"

"Thought you said I wasn't under arrest," Fitzpatrick scowled under the glare of the strip lights

Tina looked him over, the shaven head and thick tattooed neck, the small suspicious eyes. You're not under arrest, Mr Fitzpatrick, but we are obliged by law to warn you. But then you know that as well as I do, so let's not pretend this is your first time, OK?"

"I'm sayin' nuttin' coz I did nuttin'", Fitzpatrick muttered.

"You were driving without insurance, Mr Fitzpatrick," JP reminded him.

"You brought me in for that?" Fitzpatrick turned an incredulous look on JP. "Yiz must have fuck all else to do, that's all I can say."

But Tina thought she detected a slight loosening of the muscles in his thick tattooed neck; could that be relief, she wondered. "What other reason would we have for bringing you in, Mr Fitzpatrick?" she asked pleasantly.

"Fuck would I know?" Fitzpatrick ran a stubby finger round the metal rim of the table.

"It is a serious offence, Mr Fitzpatrick," said Tina mildly, "driving without insurance."

"Yeah, well I thought the job had it covered, didn't I?"

"The job? You drive a van for Dino's, delivering pizzas, is that correct?"

"Yeah, that's bleedin' correct. And the job's insurance covers me. So, like I said, I thought I was OK. A misunderstandin' is all, could happen to anyone."

"But the driving without insurance charge doesn't relate to a van owned by Dino's, does it, Mr Fitzpatrick?" said Tina. "The charge relates to a van registered in your own personal name. Is your employer in the habit of insuring your personal property, Mr Fitzpatrick?"

Fitzpatrick transferred his gaze to the wall between the detectives' heads. "Like I said, it was a misunderstandin'. I got me wires crossed, but I'm sorting it now."

"The misunderstanding being," said JP, "that you mistakenly believed that your employer's insurance policy covered your new van, is that it?"

Fitzpatrick nodded his agreement and JP raised an eyebrow at Tina, as though asking a question of her.

Tina pretended to think about it for a moment. "Fair enough," she said, closing the file which lay on the table before her. "Let's park this there, for the moment then."

As JP made a show of getting to his feet, Tina saw the naked relief on Fitzpatrick's face, as he too got to his feet.

"Just one other thing, Mr Fitzpatrick," she said. "If you wouldn't mind sitting down again?"

Fitzpatrick's face fell. "Fuck sake, what other bleedin' thing?"

"You were recently a witness to an incident involving a car being run off the road, is that correct?"

"What about it?" Fitzpatrick's tone was surly as he sank back down in the chair, but Tina noted how the beady little eyes flitted from one detective to another.

"In your statement," said Tina, "you say you actually saw the car being driven by a Ms Anna Fox being deliberately run off the road by a second vehicle. Is that correct?"

"If it says so in me statement then yeah, it's correct. Look what's goin' on here? Why are you asking me about this again? Is this the bleedin' thanks I get for trying to do the right thing?"

"Not at all, Mr Fitzpatrick," said Tina sweetly. "We do greatly appreciate your civic-mindedness in coming forward as a witness to this..."

"Yeah right," Fitzpatrick scoffed.

"...to this incident, please believe me, we do. But can I just clarify, on the night in question you were driving a van, the property of your employer, Dino's Pizza's, am I right?"

"Yeah, so what? I was on me way home from work, wasn't I?"

"So, I gathered from your statement. And would you be in the habit of driving your employer's van outside of your working hours, then?"

Fitzpatrick looked momentarily puzzled. "Yeah, I get the use of it sometimes. Look, what are you getting at?"

"Just that it must be handy. Having the use of a van, especially when you don't have any wheels of your own"

"I've got me own wheels," Fitzpatrick shot back.

"Yes, you're a man with a van now, aren't you Anthony, a brand-new Ford transit, is it? That must have cost you a bit. Pizza delivery must be paying very well these days?"

"The name's Ant," Fitzpatrick growled. "Only me bleedin' Ma calls me Anthony. And what if I have got a new van, last time I checked there was no bleedin' law against it."

"That sort of depends on where and how you go it," said Tina. "On finance, was it? Got the agreement handy, have you, if anyone wanted a look at it?"

"Never said I got it on finance, did I?" Fitzpatrick muttered.

"You're saying you bought it outright?" Tina's eyebrows climbed her forehead. "Nice. Had a bit of a windfall, did you? Enough of a windfall that you could buy yourself a brand new, top of the range Ford transit van?"

"Might have," Fitzpatrick crossed his arms and stared at the wall once more.

"Prove it, can you?"

"I don't need to prove it. Bloke owed me some money, didn't he? And I got a good deal because I paid cash."

"A minute ago, it was a windfall," Tina reminded him. "Now it's a bloke paying back a loan. Which is it Ant?"

"You were the one that said windfall," said Fitzpatrick. "I'm saying a bloke that owed me had a bit of luck and paid me back."

"A bloke that owed you the price of a new van. Bullshit. Come on Ant, pull the other one."

"I've got contacts in the trade, what can I tell you?"

"And I suppose you have the receipt to prove it?"

"Yeah, I have got the bleedin' receipt," Fitzpatrick looked so pleased with himself, Tina guessed this at least was the truth.

“Glad to hear it,” she said. “I’d hold onto that because we might need to take a look at it. But in the meantime, why not take me through the events of the night you so kindly came to the assistance of Anna Fox?”

“Fuck sake! What do you want me to do that for, it’s all in me bleedin’ statement isn’t it?”

Tina leaned across the table, smiled brightly into the furious face just inches from her own. “Humour me, Anthony,” she said. “Tell me again.”

*

After Fitzpatrick had gone, leaving a trail of obscenities behind him, JP turned to Tina.

“OK, so I know that none of that had anything to do with him driving without insurance. But I’m damned if I know what you’re driving at, Tina? You can’t seriously think Fitzpatrick had anything to do with what happened to Anna Fox? How could he have, we picked him up in that pizza delivery van at least three times on CCTV that night, driving toward Anna, not behind her. And what was all that about this new van of his, and why…”

“I don’t know,” Tina cut across him. “I don’t know what it was. And I know you’re right, and I’m probably a million miles off. But there’s something, JP, I just can’t help feeling that there’s something.”

*

CHAPTER 32

Thursday 9th March

Tina's shift began at three the following afternoon. Before she had stepped over the threshold to the office, JP was on his feet. "There you are, Coleman is waiting for us."

"Ah for… can I at least get a cup of tea first?"

"Did I mention that he wants us yesterday?"
Coleman greeted them without preamble. "Paula O'Keeffe has just reported her husband missing."
"Actually missing, sir, or just didn't come home last night?"

Coleman fixed Tina with a warning glare, "He didn't come home last night, and he's not been answering his phone. So, I want you two over there, quick smart. And mind, DS Bassett, I don't want any more complaints about your attitude. I expect Mrs O'Keeffe to be treated with respect and sensitivity; is that understood?"

Then why send me, Tina fumed inwardly. Why not find someone else to brown-nose Paula O'Keeffe and hold her hand because her rat of a husband stayed out all night ratting? But she forced herself to swallow her disgust and smiled brightly at Coleman.

"Absolutely sir. Respectful sensitivity it is, or should that be sensitive respect? Either way, Mrs O'Keeffe shall have it from me."

"And up yours, sir!" she said as JP pulled the door behind them.

"You're getting better at this," JP grinned appreciatively.

*

"Oh, it's you again!" Paula O'Keeffe greeted the two detectives, though clearly the remark was intended for Tina.

Coleman's warning ringing in her ears, Tina responded with an insincere smile. "I'm only sorry it's under these troubling circumstances."

Paula turned on her heel and Tina and JP were left to follow her through to a spacious living room. Paula threw herself into a green leather armchair, crossed her arms and legs and said nothing. With no invitation to sit forthcoming, Tina took the initiative and settled herself on the matching sofa, where JP, obviously dithering in an agony of etiquette, eventually joined her.

Paula who had been eyeing Tina resentfully, said suddenly, "You know I recognised you at Jennifer's house? You're that cop who was in the courtroom every day, cheering on that lying little slut who tried to destroy mine and my husband's life."

Tina again managed to stop herself saying what she really wanted to. "But right now, Mrs O'Keeffe," she said instead, "our concern is actually for your husband."

Paula sniffed and tossed her head. She was wearing pink again – a jumper that looked so touchably soft it had to be cashmere teamed with tight jeans and caramel coloured Ugg boots.

JP, whom Tina had decided should try his charm on the woman, began the interview in his gentle way. "I understand that this must be very worrying for you, Mrs O'Keeffe. But it would really help if we could ask you some questions concerning your husband?"

"Paula," said Paula, less than graciously.

"Paula, thank you," JP managed to make it seem as though she had bestowed an enormous favour on him. "So, Paula, perhaps I could begin by asking when you last spoke to your husband, to Lorcan?"

Paula uncrossed her arms and began to fiddle with her hair. "He texted me at 6.33 yesterday evening. I've checked the time on my phone.

He'd gone out without saying where he was going, and I was a bit worried. Lorcan's been very upset about Jennifer. He texted back to say he was just about to go to the gym. That was the last time I heard from him. I rang him around 8.30 but it went to voicemail, and it's been doing that ever since. And no one has seen or heard from him since then either. None of his friends, I mean. I rang everyone I could think of."

"Which gym does he use, as a matter of interest?"

"It's called XRcize. It's the handiest one for his office. I think I have a card for it somewhere with the address on it, I'll get it for you, before you go, if you like."

"That would be very helpful, thank you Paula. So, I assume Lorcan would have used the gym car park?"

"Actually, the gym doesn't have a car park, but there's one close by that gym members have the use of."

"I understand. So, Paula, we're going to need a description of Lorcan's car, make and model and registration number, if you happen to have those details handy at all?"

"It's a brand-new BMW 3 Series in platinum silver." Paula rattled off the registration number.

JP noted down the details. "And tell me, was Lorcan in the habit of attending the gym regularly then?"

"He used to go regularly, but…" Paula fired an accusatory look in Tina's direction. "Well anyway, with things getting back to normal again, he's started going again. He usually goes after work, though obviously with what's happened he wasn't working yesterday. But I suppose he thought a work-out might help take his mind off things."

Back to normal, thought Tina indignantly, nothing was back to normal for Orla Reid, nor ever likely to be.

"And how long would he usually spend at the gym?" JP continued.

"Well, it depended really, anything from half an hour to two hours, if he used the pool and the sauna, and he mostly did that".

"Good, and you said you've been in touch with Lorcan's friends?"

"Nobody's heard from him. And this morning, I rang the office and spoke to Julie, Lorcan's secretary. He's taken bereavement leave, but I just thought I'd check. But Julie hasn't seen him since the day before Jennifer died."

"OK. And you say Lorcan's been quite upset about his sister's death. Were they very close?"

"Very," said Paula. "They always have been. Both their parents are dead, so there's just the two of them left of the family. Lorcan's taken it badly. It was a terrible shock to him, to me too."

"Of course," said JP, "it would be." "And Paula, do you think it's at all possible that Lorcan may have felt the need to have some time to himself? People do sometimes behave a bit strangely when they're grieving."

Paula shook her head, "No, that's just not Lorcan," she said resolutely. "I know some people might react that way, but Lorcan likes to be around people when he's feeling down. And he doesn't stay out all night without letting me know in advance."

Which was not to say, thought Tina, that he never stayed out all night, just that this time he hadn't told her he was planning on doing it. "Did he take any belongings when he left the house yesterday?" she asked abruptly. "Extra clothes, his passport, anything that might suggest he was intending on going somewhere?"

Paula's eyes sparked anger. "Are you asking if I think my husband was planning on leaving me?"

"I'm sure that DS Bassett didn't intend…"

Paula cut JP short. "My husband's passport is where it always is, and as far as I can tell, nothing else is missing either."

Then she did check, thought Tina. "Would you object to us taking a look, all the same, Mrs O'Keeffe?" she asked.

"I just told you there's nothing missing."

"And you're probably right," Tina kept her tone even. "But there's always the possibility we might notice something you've overlooked, that might help us in our efforts to find your husband."

"Fine. Look, then," said Paula curtly.

*

The bedroom, monopolised by a big dark wood sleigh bed, smelled of Paula's perfume. She opened the double doors to a spacious walk-in wardrobe and walked to a section of drawers. "Here's Lorcan's passport, if you don't believe me," she said.

"There's no question of us not believing you, Mrs O'Keeffe," said Tina. "No question at all. Believe me, we're just doing our job."

Paula's phone rang and she quickly stepped back into the bedroom to answer it. Tina gazed about her in awe. One entire wall of the wardrobe had been given over to what was obviously Paula's enormous collection of clothes. The other held a long row of designer suits; too many surely for the needs of one man, most of them flashy, with a rail of equally flashy shirts. Clearly O'Keeffe had invested in a couple of sober dark outfits especially for his court appearances. Shelves held stack after stack of polo shirts and perfectly folded cashmere jumpers. "How can she possibly be sure that nothing's missing out of this lot?" Tina mused.

JP shrugged his shoulders, "Damned if I know. Passport's here anyway."

Paula returned and shook her head in response to the mute enquiry from both detectives. "It was just my mother wanting to know if there's any news."

Back in the bedroom, Tina asked if she could use the bathroom. Looking like she wanted to refuse, Paula said tightly, "To the right and straight ahead."

Tina thanked her and made her way along the corridor, glancing back to be sure that Paula wasn't watching her, but she and JP were heading back downstairs. The first door she tried, revealed what was probably a guest room, spick and span but unoccupied. This was followed by a walk-in airing cupboard, but she struck gold on the third attempt. The bedroom looked like it was definitely in use. A pair of grey pyjamas were neatly folded at the foot of the bed, a bedside table held a reading lamp and a copy of *The Crucifix Killer*; somehow Tina doubted it would be the bedtime reading of choice of pretty-in-pink Paula O'Keeffe. Still, you never could tell. But that scent - Tina sniffed the air - she was certain she knew where she had smelled it before. To be sure, she darted toward the open doorway of the en-suite bathroom. A glass shelf above the wash-hand basin held a black leather washbag, an electric razor next to it. Back in the bedroom, Tina opened the door of the wardrobe – four or five shirts and a couple of suits, all shrieking Lorcan O'Keeffe. Shutting the wardrobe, she sprinted along the landing and down the stairs where JP and Paula were standing waiting, Paula eyeing Tina suspiciously.

*

"What the hell took you so long?" asked JP as soon as they were outside. "She was just about to go looking for you."

"They're sleeping in separate rooms," Tina told him.

"So what?" JP shrugged. "Hardly surprising really is it, when you consider that he recently stood up in front of a courtroom full of people and admitted to having sex with another woman. It doesn't prove that he's run off and left her if that's what you're thinking. And sleeping apart or not, she seems genuinely worried to me."

"She's worried alright," said Tina, "maybe because she knows exactly what she's married to. But come on, let's get out of here, and go see what we can find out at this gym O'Keeffe is supposed to have been so fond of. Probably only used it for the sauna and to perve on hot, lycra-clad women."

*

CHAPTER 33

Thursday 9th March 2017

It was a miserable day, rain like a grey veil draped the city as they drove through the late afternoon traffic. At XRcize they were greeted in reception by the manager, whose name was Chad. He was clad in black lycra shorts which to Tina looked to be in danger of bursting their seams at any moment. A blazing white vest showed off an impossibly muscular physique and an implausibly mahogany tan. He ushered them to his office along a corridor that reeked of that odour Tina always associated with gyms; sweat, testosterone and way too much effort. She had joined a gym on at least five separate occasions in her life but in spite of her best intentions had never managed to last more a couple of weeks at any of them.

Installed in Chad's office and pressed to a bottle of mineral water each, Tina kicked off the questions. Chad confirmed knowing Lorcan O'Keeffe by sight and having himself been on duty the evening in question. He remembered having spotted O'Keeffe about the place and further enquiries from another staff member Chad summoned to his office, evinced the information that O'Keeffe had done a circuit of the weights room then spent the rest of the time in the pool and the wet room. "Any idea when he left?" asked Tina.

"We can find that out easily enough," said Chad, and was as good as his word. A quick phone call confirmed that Lorcan O'Keeffe had signed out at 9.15."

"That's very helpful," Tina told Chad.

"No problem, do you mind me asking, has something happened to Mr O'Keeffe?"

"At this stage we're not in a position to say," said Tina. "But we appreciate all the assistance you've given us, Chad. Now any chance you could make my day and tell me that the CCTV on your parking area is similarly state-of-the-art."

"'Fraid I can't help you there. Actually, we don't strictly speaking have a car park, but we have an arrangement with the operators of one just three minutes away. It allows our members two hours free parking. They take a ticket at the car park, and have it validated here before they leave the gym."

Chad gave them directions to the car park and thanking him, they took their leave.

"Where to now," asked JP.

"Let's go see if there's anything worth finding out at this carpark," said Tina.

*

What there was, was Lorcan O'Keeffe's snazzy BMW in the place where presumably he'd left it on the first floor of the underground car park. While JP rang it in, Tina snapped on gloves and tried the driver's door. It was locked and she had to be satisfied with circling it and peering inside. While they waited for forensics to arrive, Tina tracked down the security guard, a dour looking man somewhere in his sixties, who reluctantly admitted to being called Dan. He appeared to take umbrage at the request to view the CCTV footage and reluctantly agreed to call 'the boss' for authority to do so.

There was a further delay when, having been given the go ahead, Dan grudgingly admitted that 'this technology stuff' wasn't his thing. Someone called Wayne, who's thing it apparently was, had to be sent for. Meanwhile the forensics team arrived, and Tina and JP watched on as they checked the boot and then set about examining the rest of

O'Keeffe's car and the surrounding area. Wayne finally showed up, a hulking young giant with ginger curls and full matching beard. All four of them sardined into the tiny security hut.

Dan reluctantly vacated the single chair so that Wayne could sit down to do his thing. "I'm off for me tea break," he announced and left, muttering under his breath.

"Cheerful chappie!" said JP

"Gas man altogether, when he gets a few scoops into him," Wayne assured them.

Within minutes he had pulled up reasonably decent footage of the silver BMW pulling into the space on the first floor underground. All three of them watched as O'Keeffe climbed out, leather hold-all in hand. He crossed the carpark, was momentarily lost to sight before reappearing on the stairwell where he made his way up to ground floor level before disappearing again. Wayne fast-forwarded to 9.15pm and picked up O'Keeffe on the stairwell again as he returned to his car. He was still carrying the bag and his hair was slicked back now, presumably damp from the shower. Then nothing.

"Where did he go?" Tina asked, after Wayne had let the tape run on for a while, then at her request, rewound and replayed the footage. "I mean we know he didn't go back to his car."

"I'm guessing there's a blind spot," said JP. "Am I right Wayne? I noticed we lost him for a second or two on his way out too."

Wayne nodded, "Yeah, there's a couple of blind spots on every level. With this particular system you get between ninety-five to ninety-seven percent coverage at most."

He began waffling about density of cameras and wide dynamic range and the plans of the management company to upgrade the system. "Not much use to you though," he added ruefully.

"Not much," Tina agreed. "But that's not your fault, Wayne, but do you think you could show us exactly where this particular blind spot is?"

"Sure thing." Wayne lumbered to his feet and the two detectives followed him at his own leisurely pace, across the carpark where a sign on the wall showed a red arrow which pointed to the left. Beneath it were the words TO STAIRS. Wayne led them around the corner to where a door with a square inset of reinforced glass showed a flight of stairs.

"So, what – this whole area is a blind spot?" asked Tina.

"From here to just beyond that silver Volvo," Wayne confirmed.

"Then anyone coming out from the stairwell and getting into a car parked just here, wouldn't get picked up by the cameras. Except of course he had his own car," said JP.

"That doesn't mean he left in it," said Tina. She turned to Wayne. "Is it possible he carried on down the stairs to a lower level?"

"We can take a look," Wayne offered. Tina nodded agreement and Wayne started back at an amble to the hut where he ran the footage of the stairwells on all three levels, but there was no sign of Lorcan O'Keeffe.

"So now we know he didn't carry on downstairs," said Tina. "And we know that he didn't leave the carpark in his own car. Wayne, could you run the footage of the car park exit, say from about 9.15 onwards for that night?"

Wayne obliged and JP and Tina leaned in, and eyes glued to the screen, scrutinised each vehicle as it emerged. The tape had been running for just over ten minutes when Tina raised her hand.

"Stop it there, please Wayne!" She jabbed at the still image with her index finger. "There, JP! See that? Is that or is that not a suspiciously new-looking white Ford transit van?"

"Ring any bells?"

"Fitzpatrick!" said JP. "Our charming and civic minded witness!"

"The very one," said Tina. "JP, get onto the station and check the reg of Fitzpatrick's van. They'll have it on the report into that tax and insurance evasion charge."

"Already on it," said JP, phone to his ear.

"Cheers." Tina turned to Wayne. "Is it possible to zoom in on the reg?"

"I can do better than that. This system may not have 100% camera coverage, but it has got automatic number plate recognition. Give me a second and I can give you what you need."

"Got it," said JP, phone between ear and shoulder as he scribbled on the back of his hand.

"Here you go," said Wayne.

"Can you call out the reg, please JP," Tina leaned in close to the screen, as JP obliged.

"Bingo!" Tina punched the air. "That's definitely Fitzpatrick's van. Wayne, has anyone ever told you you're a diamond?"

Wayne's big, good-natured face flushed redder than his beard.

*

But Anthony John Fitzpatrick was not to be found, neither at the house where he rented a room from a mate, nor at his former place of work, for as his one-time boss informed them, Fitzpatrick had packed in the job just under a week ago.

"So, he packs in his job," said Tina, "and he's been driving around in a new van. He was there on the spot when Anna Fox's car was driven off the road and his van was there on the night Lorcan O'Keeffe disappeared. What the hell does it all mean?"

*

CHAPTER 34

Thursday 9th March

They were on their way back to the station where Coleman, apprised of developments had hurriedly called a team meeting.

"Let's drop in on Anna Fox at her practice," said Tina. "I'd like to talk to her again about what happened that night."

But Anna's dental nurse informed them that Anna had not turned in for work that morning, in spite of having six patients scheduled for treatment before lunchtime and a further four in the afternoon. "She's not answering her phone either," Niamh O'Brien told them, worriedly.

"Has anything like this ever happened before?" asked JP. "That Anna wouldn't turn up without an explanation."

"Never," said Niamh. "She took a bit of time off when her father died last year, but she'd organised a locum in to cover her appointments. The same when she had flu after Christmas. And she was involved in a car accident very recently and had to cancel two day's appointments."

"Well, no doubt there's a simple explanation," JP reassured her.

But as soon as they were outside again, he said, "I don't like the look of this."

"Me neither," said Tina.

She tried Anna's phone, but the call went to voicemail. She left a message for Anna to call her urgently. Almost as soon as she hung up, her phone rang, but it was just Coleman enquiring icily whether she and her partner intended to honour the rest of the team with their presence.

"On our way, sir," said Tina. "And you should know there's been another development." She filled him in on the seeming disappearance of Anna Fox.

"All the more reason to get here asap," Coleman snapped, and hung up.

*

An incident room had been set up and the entire team stood about waiting for Coleman to begin. "As you will all know by now," he told them, when the required level of hush had been achieved, "Lorcan O'Keeffe has been reported missing."

"Now, we know that he visited his city centre gym on the evening he disappeared. From there he returned to the city-centre car park where he had left his car. We have CCTV footage of him there, where he was last seen in the stairwell. He did not however make it back to his car which was found where Mr O'Keeffe had left it. Nor, we know, did he leave the car park on foot. Unfortunately, the CCTV system does not provide 100% coverage, which means we are unable to say what happened to Mr O'Keeffe. Did he leave the car park in another vehicle, perhaps – whether willingly or under coercion? What we do know however, is that a vehicle belonging to one Anthony Fitzpatrick, was seen leaving the car park on the night in question and in the relevant time frame. Fitzpatrick, as some of you will be aware, is a petty criminal and no stranger to the Gardai. Efforts to bring Mr Fitzpatrick in for questioning have so far failed. Mr Fitzpatrick is not at his home and has, it transpires, recently resigned from his job, delivering pizzas."

"Now you may wonder," Coleman continued, "what connects Fitzpatrick to the disappearance of Mr O'Keeffe. You may also wonder why we are taking this level of interest in Mr O'Keeffe who has been missing now for a relatively short time. To answer these questions, I will hand over to DI Bassett. DI Bassett if you will?"

"Thank you, sir."

Tina raised the hand that held the school group photo. "This is a photo taken some time in 1995," she told the room. She went on to explain how the photo had been posted on Facebook by Liz Warren and how defaced copies of it had been sent to the six women, all once members of the teenage gang known as the A Team.

"Those six women," she continued, "are Nicole Brady, now deceased, Bethany Doyle, now deceased, Jennifer O'Keeffe, who incidentally was the sister of Lorcan O'Keeffe, now deceased, along with Anna Fox, Rachel Doyle and Megan McGrath."

She then outlined the circumstances in which the three women had died, as well as the attack on Anna Fox, who it now appeared, had gone missing.

"The attack on Anna Fox," she explained, "was allegedly witnessed by Anthony Fitzpatrick, who in an uncharacteristic attack of civic mindedness, not only reported the incident, but remained on the scene and subsequently provided a full witness statement to Gardai. Mr Fitzpatrick was subsequently pulled over for driving without tax or insurance. The van he was driving, a spanking new Ford transit van, is the same van seen leaving the car park on the night Mr O'Keeffe disappeared." Tina paused for a moment, before finishing, "I'll let you draw your own conclusions."

First to react was Patterson. "The implication is that Fitzpatrick is in some way involved," he said, "not just in the disappearance of Lorcan O'Keeffe, but possibly in the attack on Anna Fox?"

"That does seem indicated," Coleman agreed.

"Whoever it was, had obviously done their homework on the blind spots in the carpark CCTV coverage," said Con Kearney.

"So, if Fitzpatrick is implicated in the attack on Anna Fox," said Patterson, "are we saying he's also involved in the deaths of these other women?"

Before Tina had a chance to reply, Coleman jumped in swiftly. "Let's keep in mind," he said smoothly, "the fact that the deaths of Nicole Brady, Bethany Doyle and Jennifer O'Keeffe were all fully investigated. All three were, based on the evidence then available, put down, and quite correctly in my opinion, to accident or misadventure. As indeed they may yet prove to be."

Here, Coleman shot a glance at Tina. "However, in light of subsequent events, and with the caveat that as yet no motive has been shown to exist, we cannot now ignore the possibility of a link between the deaths of these three women as well as a possible link to the disappearance of Lorcan O'Keeffe."

Hallelujah thought Tina. At last!

"Sir?" It was Chilli again. "Isn't it the case that Lorcan O'Keeffe was recently acquitted on a charge of rape? Is there any reason to believe there might be some connection between that fact and his disappearance?"

Seeing Coleman about to speak, Tina got in first. "Personally, I believe that possibility cannot be ruled out."

"DS Bassett!" Coleman's eyes shot poisonous arrows in Tina's direction. "I would remind you that while it is true that Mr O'Keeffe recently stood trial on a rape charge, it is equally true that he was acquitted of all charges brought against him."

Just then, Tina's phone vibrated in her pocket. Seeing the name on the screen, she turned her back on Coleman, and making for the door, calling over her shoulder. "Sorry sir, urgent call. Related to the case. Have to take it!"

Out in the corridor, she said, "Jim, any joy? No shit! Jim, you're an absolute treasure, and I owe you a serious load of pints."

*

CHAPTER 35

Thursday 9th March

"JP?"

"Tina? Where the hell have you been. Coleman's been trying to get hold of you for hours now."

Tina rolled her eyes at the phone in her hand. "Why do you think I've been keeping out of his way? But never mind that now and listen. I've got hold of something, JP. It turns out Anna's twin sister, Claire, didn't die of natural causes after all. She died of strangulation. Or to be more specific, suspension by a ligature, she hanged herself."

"Ah Christ! Poor kid."

"Yeah, I know. But listen, there's more. The PM showed that she'd definitely given birth at some stage."

JP whistled down the phone. "Where did all of this come from?"

"I called in a favour, or rather my old Sarge did. I knew Claire died in London, but her death was never registered in Ireland. I got a copy of her death certificate from the English authorities, but I needed to get my hands on the PM report asap. Jim has contacts in the Met and was able to speed things up for me. But you see how this changes things, right?"

"Yeah, I guess it does," said JP slowly. "We're right back to the Roches Stores baby, aren't we?"

"I think so. Look, can we chew this over properly, face-to-face?"

"Sure, why don't you come round to my place?"

Tina hesitated, "You sure? I don't want to be interrupting anything?"

"You won't be interrupting anything."

Tina smiled broadly but kept her tone casual. "OK. When?"

"Now is good. Have you eaten?"

"Nope. And I'm so hungry I could swallow a buttered hedgehog whole."

"Would you settle for my famed spag bol. Oh, and get a cab, I think we both need a few drinks right now."

*

Twenty minutes later Tina was knocking at JP's door.

"Wow. You dressed up!"

Tina glanced down at the green dress, the new and so far, ladderless, Primark black opaque tights, her best knee-high boots. "Nah, I just threw these on."

She nervously licked her lip, they tasted of strawberry lip gloss, gave her freshly washed hair a shake, and sniffing the air, hastily changed the subject. "God, that smells good."

"So, do you," said JP. "New perfume?"

"No, just my new deodorant," Tina lied.

"Well, dinner is almost ready," JP stood aside and ushered her along the hallway which was redolent of basil and garlic. "I lit a fire in the living room, thought we could make ourselves comfortable while we eat. I'll just go grab an extra glass."

Left alone, Tina flopped down into the depths of the plush grey leather sofa, let her bag drop down next to her and feasted her eyes on the rarity that was a real fire. Then she let her eyes close and listened to the gentle hiss and spit of the sappy logs. She opened them again as

JP returned with the glasses and sat down next to her, watched as he filled first hers then his own.

“Cheers! So, Claire Fox, fill me in.”

“Cheers! Well, it’s like I told you, Claire didn’t die in a road accident. She hanged herself. And like most people who attempt suicide by hanging, she ended up dying of strangulation, which as you well know is altogether a very unpleasant death.”

“Poor little soul,” said JP quietly.

“Yeah, really nasty. She did it in the wardrobe of her bedsit in London. Her body wasn’t discovered for almost a week. Seems she had precious few friends looking in on her.”

“Ah Christ!” JP took a slug from his glass, then went back for more and drained it dry. He reached for the bottle and Tina knocked back what was in her own glass, held it out for a refill.

“And like I told you, she’d definitely given birth at some point in her life.”

“But no sign of a child.”

“No sign of a child. And wasn’t that what we were looking for, with this Roches Stores baby angle? A young girl who had lived in the area, who had given birth but had no baby to show for it.”

“Agreed, but…”

“So, what I want to know is what happened to Claire Fox’s baby? Was it stillborn, did it survive? Was it given up for adoption?”

“Anna must know.”

“Anna does know, I’m certain of it. But Anna told us that Claire died in an accident.”

“Yeah, well, people do that sometimes, don’t they? People who have lost a loved one to suicide.”

“No, there’s more to it, I’m telling you. That photograph of Claire she had on her dresser, the one I told you about. Why remove it like that?”

"Jeez Tina, there's any number of reasons why, maybe it fell, and the glass got smashed and she hasn't had a chance to replace it yet. Maybe…"

"Yeah, yeah, yeah, you don't have to list all the possible scenarios." Tina frowned into her glass, it was empty again, but she couldn't remember having finished the wine.

JP saw her staring at her empty glass and got to his feet. "I'll go get us another bottle."

While he was gone, Tina pulled out the report Joe had had faxed through to her on Claire Fox's PM and re-read it. As JP came through the door, she picked up where they had left off.

"I just know in my gut that Anna was uncomfortable when she saw me looking at the photograph," she told him. "Just like I know in my gut that there's some connection between Claire Fox and the Roches Stores baby case."

"And like I told you before, I respect your gut," said JP. "It's what led you to checking out Claire's death in the first place."

"Yes, it is," Tina agreed, "and look where that's led. We know now that Anna Fox's twin sister, who was widely believed to have died in an accident, whom Anna herself told us died in an accident, actually took her own life. And now we know that Claire had given birth."

"All of that is absolutely true," JP agreed. "But we still have no way of knowing that Claire was the mother of the Roches Stores baby, which I know is what you believe. The only person likely to know the truth and be able to tell us it, is Anna. But Anna seems to have disappeared. So right now, all of this, fascinating as it is, is surmise."

"It wouldn't be surmise if we could prove it," said Tina obstinately.

"And how do we do that?"

"There are DNA tests that can be done to test familial relationships."

JP stared at her in undisguised disbelief. "Tests on whom exactly? Anna? And on what grounds? Look Tina, I hate to remind you, but the Roches Stores baby case is not the case we are supposed to working on. What we're concerned with is supposed to be the possible link between the deaths of these women; that and the disappearance of Lorcan O'Keeffe."

"And I happen to think it's all connected in some way," said Tina obstinately again.

"And maybe you're right. But right now, I need to go boil some pasta, so let's just give this a rest. We can come back to it later."

*

CHAPTER 36

Tuesday 7th March

But somehow, they didn't come back to it later. They ate - the famous spag bol was only mediocre, in Tina's opinion, the garlic bread the kind that comes frozen in a packet from Tesco; Tina knew because she'd spotted the wrapper on the draining board when she carried the plates to the kitchen. Dessert was an enormous wodge of vanilla ice-cream served with a bottle of M&S Raspberry Sauce.

But for all its lack of sophistication, Tina enjoyed everything immensely. Besides, it was nice to discover that JP was not actually brilliant at every single thing. After the meal, he opened a third bottle of wine and dropping down next to her on the sofa, pointed a remote control at the sound system and the room filled with the sound of Rory Gallagher.

"Lord, I'm shattered," he said. "Sometimes I think it must be nice to have a job that you can leave behind you at 5.30 and not think about it again until 9.00 the next morning."

"You'd hate it, and you know you would," said Tina.

"True. And so would you," JP agreed. "Did you always know you wanted to join the force?"

"Oh absolutely," said Tina. "As a little girl I dreamed of standing for hours in the rain and the cold doing checks, or of seeing dead bodies."

JP grinned. "OK, so what made you decide this was for you, then?"

"Would you believe me if I told you, it was on account of a postman with a glass eye?" said Tina. "No, don't laugh, I'm actually serious. His name was Jack Weston, and he'd been the town's postman forever. He'd only just retired, about two weeks earlier or something like that, and was cycling home from the pub one night, when he was struck by a car. He was thrown from his bike and left to die on the side of the road like he was a dog."

"The car didn't stop?"

"The car didn't stop," Tina nodded. "I overheard Phyllis telling…I mean I overheard my parents talking about it, and how Jack had lost his glass eye in the accident. They thought it must have rolled away down the hill somewhere. As soon as I heard that, I wanted to go and look for it. But my parents said no, that the place where Jack died was far too dangerous, there was no footpath along that stretch of road. I got really upset at the thought of Jack being buried with a hole in his head where his glass eye should have been. But what upset me even more, was that the person or people who knocked him down and left him to die were still out there. And I just knew that if I'd been old enough, I'd not only have found Jack's eye so he could be buried with it, but I'd have caught whoever had killed him too."

JP shook his head, "You know something, I just know you'd have done both. I only wish I'd known you as a little girl. We could have gone and found poor old Jack's eye together."

Tina laughed. "No, but all joking aside," said JP, "you're amazing, Tina Bassett. So, how did your parents take it when you told them what you wanted to do?"

"Well, there was only Phyllis, my mother by then. She wasn't impressed."

Which, thought Tina, was only the understatement of the year. She could still clearly recall the taut silence punctured by a prolonged stirring of her tea, always a sign of discontent in Phyllis.

"I take it you don't approve then," Tina had said.

"As if it makes a blind bit of difference whether I approve or not," Phyllis had informed her cup.

"I just thought you had more of a head on your shoulders. Why would any girl with a chance to go to university and be a teacher or a nurse or something nice, want to go in for a job where she'd be dealing with criminals and God only knows what else every day of the week? One thing's for sure though, it's not something Gerry would have been happy to see you doing."

Tina was almost certain that Gerry would have wanted her to do what made Phyllis happy, or at the very least to try. And it was for that reason she decided to postpone her application. Instead, she had gone travelling for a year which had run into two years. On her return home, she'd begun a degree in sociology in UCD, choosing the course because she'd read that it was one looked on favourably by the force. She had even managed to stick it out for a year and a half before packing it in, before applying for and being accepted as a trainee Garda. She had left Templemore Training College with her uniform, her badge, and her radio and a hunger to get on with the job she had always known she was made to do.

And, as it turned out, Phyllis had not been entirely wrong – her work had brought her up against aggression, violence, death and people at their worst, or their lowest and most desperate. But working for communities, helping people who were victims of all the unpleasantness, that was why she had wanted to do the job in the first place, and she had never regretted her choice.

*

"I bet you're sorry you asked now, aren't you?" Tina said ruefully, with a glance at JP.

"Not at all," JP shook his head. "It's nice hearing you talk about yourself. You so rarely do."

"Nothing much to talk about," said Tina. She was feeling curiously awkward and all sorts of other things too. She made to drink from her glass but found it empty.

"Hang on, there's a drop left in this," JP reached for the bottle, then leaned in to pour. But somehow, Tina moved her glass just a moment too soon. A little of the wine spilled and they both spoke at the same time.

"Shit, sorry," said Tina.

"Sorry, that was my fault?" said JP.

They turned to one another and laughed. JP's face was inches from Tina's own. Afterward she tortured herself replaying the moment, trying to capture exactly the moment when their eyes had met. Trying to figure out how she had misread the signals so very badly; had there even been any signals? Trying to visualise the expression on his face when she had said, "You know that I really like you, JP?"

And he had replied, without hesitation, "And I like you too, Tina."

Trying to forget the spring of happiness deep inside her as, like a fool, she had gone on,

"No, I mean, I really like you, JP."

Trying to convince herself that it was he who had moved toward her, not the other way about. Trying to edit out that moment when their lips had touched, which just for a moment had been as perfect as she had always imagined it would be. Until he drew back from her, and she opened her eyes and saw the expression in his, unadulterated dismay. Which was when she had leaped to her feet, toppling her glass; red wine staining the beautiful hardwood floor. But there was no edit button on life, all there was, was the feeling of blood thumping painfully to her head as she scrabbled to gather up the email print-offs and shove them into her bag, before haring for the door, racing down the stairs, fumbling for the doorlatch.

And all the time there was JP trying to reason with her, placating, pleading, and finally calling after her into the cold dark night, "Tina, don't go Tina. Please let me explain… Tina…."

*

CHAPTER 37

Friday 10th March

Tina woke to the feeling that while she slept, someone had superglued her tongue to the top of her mouth. Then she remembered what she had said and done, and how that had played out. At which point, the pain in her head gave way to a sick heaviness in her stomach, much as though she had swallowed a turnip whole. The only comfort to be found was that she needed to be in court that morning, giving her a legitimate reason to steer clear of the station for a few hours. The case dragged on into the afternoon and rough as she felt, she was grateful for that, giving her as it did, an excuse to avoid JP.

By the time she eventually got there it was gone two-thirty and there was no sign of him. As she hung up her coat, she noticed that his jacket wasn't on the back of his chair. Relieved, she slid into her own chair, turned on her PC and tried to concentrate. It was almost an hour-and-a-half later before he made an appearance. Tina didn't hear him come in, just looked up and found him standing there. She thought she hid her surprise well, staring at him blankly and treating him to her best double eyebrow-raise, which she hoped translated as - Something I can do for you?

"Look Tina, can we talk?" he said, glancing over his shoulder.

They were alone in the office aside from the Gannett, who was on the phone at his desk in the far corner, and he was talking so loudly there was little chance he'd hear anything that was going on around him.

"Nothing to talk about!"

"Come on, Tina, of course there is."

"OK, then let me put it another way, there's nothing I want to talk to you about. Is that better? Now, if you don't mind, can we get on with the job in hand please?"

At that moment, the Gannett got to his feet. He came toward them, slipped in behind Tina's desk to grab his jacket from the coat rack, grinning at JP as he passed, "How's it hanging?"

JP returned the grin but said nothing until the door closed behind the other man, when he turned to Tina again.

"Tina, at least let me explain. It's not what you think at all. It's complicated."

"Actually, it's not complicated," said Tina. "It's really very simple. You don't fancy me, that's all. And let's face it, why would you? I get it, of course I do. But please, please, JP, do not insult me by trying to make it into something it isn't."

She got to her feet, grabbed her own jacket and without knowing where she was going, made for the door. Wrenching it open, she came face-to-face with the Gannett on his way back in again. He was grinning all over his stupid face. Please don't let him have heard, please don't let him....

"Sorry," his grin widened. "Forgot my phone. Didn't mean to intrude on anything private, guys."

"Oh, shut up Alan!" Tina snapped and pushed past him.

He yelled after her, "Been punching above your weight, have you, Bassett? Seriously, would you ever wise up?"

Tina kept going. *Fuck. Fuck, Fuck. Fuck. Fuck.*

*

She was racing across the car park, eyes blurring, battling tears, battling fury and humiliation when she heard him calling after her.

“Tina! Tina, wait! Tina, we need to talk about this! Tina!” He caught her up, put his hand on her arm. “Tina, will you listen to me, for God’s sake. It’s not what you think. I’m not into women, OK. I’m not into women full stop, because I’m gay. OK? I’m gay.”

Tina wheeled round and faced him. “Oh no,” she said, “Please, please no. Tell me you’re not going to try pulling that one on me. At least show me some fucking respect, JP.”

“I’m not trying to pull anything on you Tina. I’m telling you the truth, OK! I’m telling you the honest to…”

But Tina was not listening to him, was already in her car and slamming the door behind her. He was battering on the driver’s window as she was shoving the key into the ignition. And as she was driving away with a screech of tyres, she could see him in the rear-view mirror, standing there staring after her, arms hanging by his sides.

*

For a while she just drove. Then she parked and sat for a while by the side of a quiet road and let herself feel what she was feeling. Anger, disappointment, hurt, she was feeling all of them. But there was outrage too, outrage that he could have so little respect for her as to make up a yarn like that. If he’d had any regard at all for her, he wouldn’t have insulted her intelligence in that way. Gay? JP O’Rourke whom everyone knew had women falling all over him. And anyway, what the hell had she been thinking. As if! As bloody if JP O’Rourke would look twice at her in that way. He was outrageously gorgeous for God’s sake, and he was funny and kind and charming and she… well she was Tina Basset. Of course, he didn’t want her. And in her misery and self-disgust she comforted herself with just one thought – at least now she wouldn’t be spending every last minute, moping over him. At least now she’d be able to keep her mind on her work.

It was after seven when she got home. She ordered a pizza, ate it, had a bath and got into her leopard print onesie, then lay on the sofa watching Netflix and willing herself not to start drinking again. Looking at Netflix, not watching, because it was impossible to concentrate on anything when her head just kept replaying the real-life drama of last night and its cringeworthy sequel in the station that afternoon. More than anything, she wanted to call Carol and tell her everything – the dinner, the wine, that stupid kiss, the mortifying knock-back. But much as she longed to wallow in the sympathy, the indignation on her behalf, which she was certain would be forthcoming from her best friend, she couldn't quite bring herself to pick up the phone. Something held her back. She was just about to go to bed when the intercom buzzed sharply. Before she had gotten to her feet, it sounded again, just as loudly and then repeatedly as thought someone was leaning their weight against it.

"Who the hell is that?" she yelled into the phone, unable to see anything but a black blur on the video screen.

"Teenaah! Teenaah, lemmein!"

"Piss off JP!" she said into the phone.

"Teenaah, please! Isme, JP! Lemmein!"

"I know who it is. Go away, JP, you're drunk and it's late and I don't want to talk to you. Go home and go to bed."

"Teenaah! Open the door! Open the door and lemme in!"

*

In the end she gave in, because of the racket he was making, and because he quite simply would not go away. But in spite of having buzzed him in and waited at her open door for him to appear, the corridor remained empty. In the end she had to go grab her keys, pull the door behind her, and go look for him. She found him in the foyer standing and swaying as he stared at the lift door.

"For God's sake, you big feckin eejit! It's out of order, can you not read?" Her voice was harsh, but JP turned to her with a great drunken smile on his face.

"Teenaah!" he lurched toward her and almost fell, but she caught him just in time.

"Christ, you're maggoty!" she said, hooking her arm under his shoulder. JP flopped to one side, leaning his weight on her so that she staggered a little.

"Work with me will you, for God's sake," she hissed at him. "Come on now, one foot in front of the other, you know how it's done."

Somehow, she managed to get him up the stairs and inside her apartment without injury to either one of them. Then she guided him toward her sofa, where he flopped down heavily. "Stay there," she ordered. "I'm going to make you some coffee and you're going to drink it."

But when she came back with the coffee, he was already asleep, head hanging over the back of her sofa, mouth open, snoring loudly.

"Damn you, JP," he told him. She thought about trying to wake him, but he was clearly comatose, so she went to the airing cupboard and grabbed the duvet she kept for the blow-up bed she used when anyone stayed over. She flung it over the sleeping man unceremoniously, he stirred and made what sounded like a moan and then he began to snore.

"Pig!" said Tina, aloud. "Asshole!" "What did I ever see in you?"

But she knew she was talking out of her backside; even drunk, even comatose and snoring, he was beautiful, and she turned her back on him, switched off the light, shut the door and went to her bed alone.

*

CHAPTER 38

Saturday 11th March

Tina woke to the sound of the shower running and remembered her uninvited guest. She groaned out loud and made the decision to stay in bed in the hope that he would get dressed and go. She heard him on the stairs, then moving about downstairs, then silence. No sound of a door closing, but he'd likely gone out quietly so as not to wake her. She hoped he was sick with embarrassment. She stayed in bed a little longer to be on the safe side, then got up, pulled on a dressing gown, and went downstairs to the kitchen. JP was there, drinking coffee at her table, hair still damp from her shower.

"Morning," he said. His tone was light but his eyes betrayed discomfit. "I hope you don't mind, I had a shower."

"You certainly needed one," said Tina, tersely.

"Yeah, sorry," JP put the mug down and ruffled his damp hair, a sheepish look on his face. "I don't seem to remember much about how I got here last night, but I imagine I was in a bit of a state."

"You were maggoty, is what you were."

"Jeez, I'm sorry, Tina."

"Yeah, everybody is sorry," Tina walked to the fridge and took out a carton of milk.

There was silence as she made her coffee, a silence so thick you could almost touch it. She had her back to him, stirring sugar into her coffee, when JP spoke again.

“I wasn’t lying Tina,” he said quietly. “What I told you in the car park yesterday, that wasn’t some stupid story I made up. It’s the truth, plain and simple. I’m gay, Tina, I’m gay. At least tell me you don’t think I’m lying about that.”

Tina carried her mug to the table, sat down as far from him as possible and gazed silently into her coffee.

“Come on Tina, I know you're mad at me, but at least tell me you believe I’m not lying to you about that.”

“OK, OK!” Tina met his gaze. “I don’t think you’re lying. But come on JP, can you blame me? I mean I’ve seen the way you are with women, the way they are with you. I’ve seen how you look at them. I mean, Anna Fox for instance, you were practically drooling over her.”

“So what,” JP shook his head. “Are you saying that a gay man can’t appreciate beauty in a woman? And as for Anna Fox, sure she's very good looking, but any drooling you think you saw me doing, was in your imagination.”

“But what about all the women you pull, the girlfriend you had in Cork?”

JP ran a hand over his head, “I don't pull women and there was no girlfriend in Cork, or anywhere else for that matter.”

“But I’ve seen you when we’re all out drinking, women giving you their numbers. You attract them like a giant bloody magnet.”

“Yes, women give me their numbers, that doesn’t mean I ring them.”

“Then that whole babe magnet thing is just a cover, is that it?” Tina demanded. “It’s just a great big lie?”

JP grimaced, “I suppose if you put it that way, then yes, it is a lie. But I don't string women along and I don't deliberately try to deceive people. It's just that if the lads think I have a string of women, then that makes it easier to keep below the radar. It's the only way I know to protect myself and my career.”

“But why?” said Tina. “Why do you feel the need to live a lie to protect your career? Aren't we all about diversity now? Diversity, inclusiveness, all that good stuff. They’ve even done reports on it for Christ sake.”

JP laughed out loud. “Yes, they’ve done reports on it,” he said. “But homophobia doesn’t magically go away because it says so in some report, certainly not institutionalised homophobia. I've seen it myself, the mistake some detective makes being put to down to the fact that they happen to be gay. As though their sexual orientation somehow makes them less competent to do the job. And I’ve seen people passed over for promotions they'd worked hard for and deserved, purely because they’d come out.”

“But there are laws about this sort of stuff, complaints processes…”

“Oh, wise up Tina, you know as well as I do that anyone who speaks up or makes an official complaint is marked down as a troublemaker and you know the repercussions of that too.”

Tina knew she couldn’t really argue with that. She had known officers who had gone the route of formal complaints and had their lives made a misery as a result. And not only because they were gay.

“But that wouldn’t happen to you, JP,” she argued. “You’re popular, you’re really popular, all the lads like you.”

JP smiled wryly, “Yeah, I’m one of the lads now, but how long would that last if they knew? And sure, there are some great guys in there, some great women too. But Coleman is as homophobic as he’s misogynistic. And you've heard the Gannet talking, Tina, you’ve heard the language he uses. And he’s not the only one either.”

It was true, Tina had heard it, she'd experienced it too. Not homophobia in her case, but she’d been on the receiving end of sexist comments more often she cared to remember.

JP got up and walked to the window. “I told my parents, you know," he said, his back to Tina.

“And?” My mother said she wasn’t surprised. Want to know what my father said?"

“What?”

“He said – I imagine you know best who and what you are. But you do know, don't you son, that you can't be gay and be a Guard too?”

“But that's just nonsense,” said Tina. “I mean, maybe it was true once, but things have moved on since your Da’s day. And they’ll keep on getting better if gay members of the force talk openly and honestly about their lives. Surely you see that, JP?”

JP said dully, “Maybe you're right, maybe they have. But I’m just not prepared to take that chance. As far as I'm concerned, my private life is my business and I’ll do what I have to, to keep it that way. And yeah, that means there are people I can never get truly close to.”

He turned and faced her. “But you’re not one of those people, Tina. And before you say it, yes, I know I didn’t confide in you. But I would have, eventually. I know I wanted to, I even came close to telling you once or twice. At least believe that, will you?”

“I believe it,” said Tina. “But God Almighty, JP, the energy it must take every day!”

“You're not wrong there,” JP's smile was rueful. He came back to the table and sat down again.

“Look Tina, I'm under no illusions. If I stay with the force my whole life, I know I'll never be the copper you are. You’re a natural Tina. You have a nose for the job, and that’s something you’re born with. No, don’t pull a face, you know it's true, so take the compliment. But I also know that I do a good job. And I know that I wouldn’t want to do anything else. And if I might never get to the top, I intend to get as far as I can. So, for now anyway, this is just how it’s got to be. Do you understand that, Tina?”

“Yes, I understand. It’s your decision, I get that. But just for the record, I happen to think you’re a very fine cop. I just....I just wish you could have felt more able to honest with me. Not wait until I tried to stick my tongue down your throat and made a complete and utter arse of myself."

"I'm the arse," said JP. "And if you only knew how sorry I am for that. The very last thing I ever wanted to do was to hurt you in any way, Tina."

"Listen, don't flatter yourself," Tina forced a laugh. "Truth is, that was down to the wine, nothing more."

She got to her feet, "I'm going to go have my shower."

As she made for the door, JP stopped her. "OK, just one last thing. What you said about how someone like me could never fancy someone like you - that was pure rubbish, you know that, right?"

"Was it though?"

"Come on, Tina, you know it was."

"If you say so. Though actually no, I don't think it was nonsense. People like you just don't end up with people like me, that's just the way the world works."

"People like me?" JP raised an eyebrow.

"Yes, Marbles, people like you. Posh boys who went to private schools, whose Da's are somebody. That sort of boy doesn't end up with someone like me, who doesn't have an actual clue who her Da was. Now if you don't mind, I'm going for that shower, and you better not have used all the hot water."

"Well, if I'm a nob," JP's reply followed here into the hall, "then you're a bloody snob, Tina Bassett."

CHAPTER 39

Saturday 11th March

There was a text from JP on Tina's phone when she got out of the shower. He'd gone home to change and would see her at the station. She had just put the phone down when it rang again, Con Kearney.

"Ant Fitzpatrick was picked up," he told her. "He was trying to board a ferry at Rosslare. They're on the way back to Dublin with him now."

"Excellent, thanks for letting me know, Con." Tina hung up and texted JP the news.

It was, she told herself, a good start to a day she had already decided would be a fresh start. Because as Gerry had been fond of saying, there's nothing like knowing where you stand, and now she knew for sure where she stood with JP.

Driving to work she attempted to examine her feelings honestly. She would, she knew, get over having made a fool of herself. And a lot of what she was feeling was the hurt of knowing he had not known her well enough to be truthful with her. She had thought she knew pretty much all there was to know about him. Because in fairness, working ten-hour surveillance shifts together, as they so often had, was surely one way of getting to know someone. Drinking coffee from the same thermos, seeing one another in all sorts of moods, whether that be psyched up at the possibility of seeing something significant, something that might break a case, or exhausted and bored to the point of stupor on those soul-destroying nights when nothing at all happened.

But, thought Tina wryly, nobody ever really fully knew another person, and let that be a reminder to her. Besides, she reminded herself, having JP for a partner as well as a friend was not such a bad deal really.

*

Fitzpatrick met them with protests as soon as Tina and JP set foot inside the interview room.

“This is bleedin’ harassment,” he moaned. “I know my rights, and this is bleedin’ harassment.”

“Nobody is being harassed Mr Fitzpatrick. We simply need to ask you some further questions.” JP’s tone lacked its customary mildness. He’s feeling rough after that skin-full he had last night, Tina decided. Serves him right.

“I already answered all your bleedin’ questions, and I’m not answering no more,” Fitzpatrick folded his thick arms, stuck his chin in the air and gazed at the ceiling. “Anything I had to say, I said in me statement.”

“Would that be the statement you made regarding an alleged attack on Anna Fox on the night of 6th March,” asked Tina. “What makes you assume that’s what we want to ask you about?”

“What the hell else would it be?” demanded Fitzpatrick.

“Well for starters, you could tell us about your whereabouts on the evening of 8th March.” Tina watched as Fitzpatrick’s chin came down again and he stared at her, small eyes bulging.

“What are you on about?” he blustered. “Me whereabouts?"

“Fair enough,” said Tina genially. “Let's say we’re talking about a spot of abduction and false imprisonment. How’s that for starters?” She saw with satisfaction how just for a moment, all signs of bluster disappeared, before Fitzpatrick rallied once more.

“Now hang on a bleedin’ minute here, I know nuttin’ about no abduction or false imprisonment. But I know me rights, and I’m not saying’ nuttin’ else until I get a bleedin’ solicitor.”

*

“Looks like he’s sticking to his bleedin’ story,” said JP. Fitzpatrick had been led way and he and Tina were alone in the interview room.

“Give me strength,” Tina implored. “Does he seriously expect us to believe that he doesn’t know who was paying him to claim he saw Anna Fox’s car being run off the road? And that he didn't know what he was transporting from that car park?”

“You heard the man,” said JP. “Same as he expects us to believe he waited at some roadside, though where exactly he can’t quite recall, while someone he doesn’t know and didn’t see, unloaded the 'package'. You thought there was something fishy about that statement he gave on the attack on Anna Fox, didn’t you? That’s why you ran the check on Fitzpatrick.”

“It wasn’t anything in the statement,” Tina admitted. “I just couldn’t square the Ant Fitzpatrick we saw coming out of the station that day, effing and blinding at us, with the type of person who goes to the trouble of giving a witness statement to the cops. And when I heard he was driving around in a new van, well, I couldn’t help thinking – what if? What if Fitzpatrick is lying?”

Her phone rang and she got to her feet, “Hi Rachel, what’s up?”

On the other end, Rachel sounded breathless. “Something’s happened,” she said.

“OK, just try to stay calm and tell me exactly what’s happened. Are you in any immediate danger?” Tina motioned to JP to follow as she made for the door.

“No, it’s not me, I’m OK,” said Rachel. “It’s Megan, Anna’s just been over there and scared her half to death.”

“OK. Is Anna still there with Megan? Are you?”

"No, Anna's gone, but Megan is frightened that she'll come back. She was acting really crazy, Megan said. And I'm in the car outside my house, I thought I should call you before I went over to Megan's."

"You did right. But I want you to stay where you are. We're on our way, and we'll pick you up and go to Megan's together. Give her a call and stay on the phone with her. Tell her not to open the door to anyone until we get there."

Tina hung up and turned to JP. "Did you get any of that?"

"Think so," JP's eyes were on the road. "Megan's had a visit from Anna Fox, right?"

"Yeah, scared the living daylights out of her apparently."

"What the hell is going on?" said JP.

*

"Any idea what exactly it was that Anna did to frighten Megan so badly, Rachel?" Tina asked the question over her shoulder to Rachel, who was now sitting in the back seat of the car, tense and silent.

"Just crazy stuff that Megan says made no sense."

"What kind of crazy stuff?"

"Stuff about Nicole and Bethany and Jennifer. Megan said it almost sounded as if Anna had something to do with what happened to them. But that just can't be true, can it?" Rachel sounded bewildered.

Tina ignored the question. "What else did Anna say?"

"She wanted Megan to tell her everything she knew about what happened on the school trip to Wicklow."

"Do you know what happened on that trip, Rachel?" Tina glanced back and met Rachel's worried frown.

"How could I?" Rachel sounded weary. "I've already told you, I didn't go on the trip, I was in hospital having my appendix out."

Tina had another question on the tip of her tongue, but JP was slowing the car to pull into a leafy cul-de-sac. They had arrived at Megan's home.

*

CHAPTER 40

Saturday 11th March

Megan had coffee ready and waiting. It was clear from the blotches of mascara beneath her eyes that she had been crying. "I needed it, my nerves were in shreds," she informed them woefully. "Help yourselves, my hands are honestly still shaking."

"Yes, sounds like you had a bit of a fright," Tina conceded, as she poured herself a coffee. As everyone settled themselves around the big oak table, Tina glanced about her. An old-fashioned kitchen in an old-fashioned house she thought. Megan, as she knew from Rachel, still lived in her parents' home with her widowed mother.

"Would you mind telling us exactly what happened when Anna came to see you?" Tina asked Megan.

Megan wrapped both hands around her mug. "OK, well the doorbell rang and kept on ringing," she said.

"I opened the door and Anna just shoved in past me, no hello or anything like that, she just marched through into the lounge. I followed her, asked her what she wanted. She said she needed answers and I had better tell the truth if I knew what was good for me. I said I didn't know what she was talking about, and she told me to shut up. I told her not to speak to me like that, and that was when she came across and shoved me."

Megan's big blue eyes widened at the memory. "She shoved me really hard and I fell backwards into one of the armchairs. I couldn't get up, because Anna just stood there, looming over me. You should have seen the way she was looking at me. I was actually frightened."

"I can imagine," Tina tried to hide her impatience. "So, what were these questions Anna wanted answers to, Megan?"

"It was crazy stuff," Megan circled the mug in her cupped hands. "Stuff about a trip we all went on years and years ago. Back when we were at school, I mean."

"What about the trip, Megan?"

"She said I was to tell her exactly what happened, and that I was to be very careful how I answered, because... because my life might depend on it."

"That must have been really frightening," said JP.

Megan looked at him gratefully. "It was. She didn't even look like Anna; it was almost like she was a completely different person. I was afraid of her, I really was."

Rachel laid a sympathetic hand on Megan's arm. Megan flashed her a smile before continuing with her story.

"I tried telling her I didn't know what she was talking about. But she said that that was the wrong answer, and I should try again. She said it was really important that I understand she was trying to judge whether or not I was culpable."

"Culpable?" Tina repeated the word. "Did Anna explain what she meant by that?"

Megan shook her head, took a mouthful of coffee. "No. And I hadn't got a clue what she was talking about. But she said a heap of things that didn't make any sense. I think she's lost her mind or something."

"What other things did she say?" asked JP.

"Well, stuff about Nicole and Bethany and Jennifer. She used that word again – culpable, she said they were culpable, and that they deserved to die. And then she started talking about the way they died. It was so weird and creepy, almost as though she was there when it happened."

Megan looked from JP to Tina, eyes wide and puzzled. "But that can't be true, can it?"

It was almost exactly the question Rachel had posed a short time earlier and once again Tina side-stepped.

"Can you tell us exactly what Anna said about the way Nicole and Bethany and Jennifer died?"

Megan frowned, "I don't remember exactly, but it was something about watching Nicole falling. And then she said something about how Bethany died like a dog in the road."

A little cry of distress from Rachel made Megan pause for a moment, but at Tina's request, she went on.

"She said something about Jennifer too, about how she didn't even struggle. Like I said, it was creepy, and it gave me the shivers. It was almost as though she'd actually seen them, seen them die, I mean. But that's not possible is it, I mean you don't actually think that Anna…"

"Let's not get ahead of ourselves just yet," said Tina quickly. "I'd like to hear about this school trip to Wicklow, Megan. The one Anna asked you about."

Megan put her mug down. "What do you want to know?"

"You went with Jennifer and Anna and Nicole and Bethany, is that right?"

"Yes, all of us, except Rachel, she was in hospital. But there were lots of other girls there too. And teachers. They took us hiking and canoeing and we did survival skills, that sort of thing."

"And you stayed overnight?"

"We stayed for two nights actually."

"So, what was it, camping or…?"

“No, we stayed in a hostel.”

“What, just your school group, or were there other schools staying that weekend too?”

Megan threw a swift glance at Rachel, before replying. “No, it was just us at the hostel.”

“So, all girls then,” Tina probed, “no boys around?”

Again, the quick glance at Rachel before Megan replied, “No, it was only girls at the hostel.”

“You keep looking at Rachel, Megan, why is that?” asked Tina. “But Rachel can’t help you can she, considering she wasn’t on the trip? That right isn’t it, Rachel?”

Rachel nodded, “That’s right, I couldn’t go because of having my appendix out.”

“All the same,” said Tina. “I think you do know something about what happened on that trip, Rachel. You were uncomfortable last time we spoke about it and you’re clearly uncomfortable again now. What is it you’re holding back?”

Rachel shook her head, “I don’t know what you’re talking about. I’m not holding anything back. I’ve never known what happened on that trip, how could…”

“But you know that something did,” Tina pounced. “Was it something to do with Anna, Rachel?”

“I told you I don’t know,” Rachel looked distressed now.

“Why don’t you leave her alone,” said Megan hotly. “You just said yourself that she wasn’t even there, so why keep asking her about her about it?”

Tina, her eyes still on Rachel, ignored the interruption. “It was, wasn’t it? It was something to do with Anna. Did something happen to her on that trip, Rachel? Did something happen to Anna?”

"No. I mean..." Rachel paused, shook her head as though confused. "Maybe...I can't be sure..."

"Rachel," Megan's voice sounded a warning.

"You can't be sure, Rachel, that's OK," said Tina. "Just tell us what you think might have happened to Anna."

Rachel glanced at Megan, looked away again quickly. "It's only because of some things I heard, and something Jennifer said."

"What did Jennifer say, Rachel?"

"She said... she said that if I ever heard Anna saying things about Lorcan, I was to shut her up. And I was to come to her straight away and tell her, tell Jennifer, I mean."

Tina, aware of a quiver of excitement at the nape of her neck, exchanged a look with JP. "Is this Jennifer's brother, Lorcan O'Keefe, we're talking about, Rachel?"

Rachel nodded wordlessly.

"OK. And what has Lorcan O'Keeffe to do with the trip to Wicklow?" Tina turned to Megan. "Didn't you say that there weren't any boys there, Megan?"

Megan said sulkily, "I said there weren't any boys staying at the hostel. And it's true, the boys didn't stay at the hostel, they stayed at some sort of retreat centre, about a mile away from where we were."

"The boys?"

"The sixth year St Malachy boys," Rachel took over, as Megan remained silent. "They were staying not far from the hostel in Wicklow. They were there on a retreat before the Leaving Cert exams, their school did it every year."

"Then Lorcan O'Keeffe was there that same weekend," said Tina, "staying in the same area as you girls." The quiver in her neck had turned to a positive tingle of excitement. "OK, so let's go back to

Jennifer, Rachel. From what you say, it's clear she was anxious to stop Anna badmouthing her brother. Any idea what sort of stuff Jennifer worried Anna might say about Lorcan?"

"No, Jennifer didn't say, and Anna never mentioned anything at all to me about that trip."

"But even so," Tina persisted, "you must have some idea what Jennifer had in mind when she warned you like that? Come on Rachel, help me out here."

"I don't, really I don't," Rachel shook her head, spread her hand in a show of helplessness. "I mean, I suppose I thought that Lorcan might have…well, that he might have tried it on with Anna, something like that?"

"And did he," Tina's eyes moved to Megan. "Did Lorcan try it on with Anna, Megan?"

"No, of course he didn't!" Megan said contemptuously.

"And yet, Jennifer thought that Anna might say he had. Why do you think that was, Megan?"

"I don't know. Maybe because Anna made up stuff like. If you must know, she'd done it before, told a pack of lies about Lorcan in fact."

"What sort of lies exactly?"

Megan eyed Tina stonily. Tina turned to Rachel. "What lies did Anna tell about Lorcan, Rachel?"

Rachel bit her lip, said slowly, "I think Megan is talking about Ross's party."

"Ross?"

"Yes, Bethany's brother. He was eighteen and there was a party at their house. We were all there, Anna too. And afterwards, Anna said… Anna said that Lorcan tried to… that Lorcan attacked her."

"Lies," said Megan, with a dismissive toss of her head. "No one believed her."

"I believed her," said Rachel, quietly, but firmly.

"Yeah, well you would," Megan fired, "Jennifer was right, you always were under Anna Fox's spell."

Ignoring her, Tina said, "You believed Anna when she said Lorcan attacked her at this party, Rachel? But you say she never mentioned anything of that sort having happened on the trip to Wicklow?"

"Never," Rachel confirmed with obvious conviction.

Tina brought her attention back to Megan. "But something did happen on that trip, didn't it, Megan? So why not tell us about it?"

"She's right, Megan," Rachel turned to her friend, "You need to tell them. Something did happen, I know it did."

"You know nothing, Rachel," Megan snapped. "So why don't you just stay out of this."

"I can't stay out of it," said Rachel. She turned to Tina. "I don't know anything much really, but there is something that I should have mentioned before. It was something Bethany said one night when she was drunk, about the trip to Wicklow."

Tina nodded encouragement, "OK. What did Bethany say?"

"Well, she was going on about how something being a mess. How we had only meant to teach Anna a lesson. She said *we* – like she'd forgotten I wasn't on the trip. I asked her what she was talking about, and she must have remembered then, because she told me to forget it, that it was nothing. It was almost like she was annoyed with me. She muttered something, I can't remember what exactly, but it was something like – I'm surprised big mouth Megan didn't tell you all about it." Rachel threw an apologetic glance at Megan. "Sorry, Megan."

She turned back to Tina, "Anyway, I asked Megan about it, but she said she had no idea what Bethany was going on about. But I knew by the look on her face that that wasn't true. It wasn't true, was it,

Megan? Something did happen that weekend, and whatever it is, you need to tell the detectives."

"Rachel is right, Megan," said JP. "If there's something you know, now is the time to tell us, before someone else gets hurt."

"Did you hear that, Megan?" Rachel said urgently. "Someone else could get hurt. You need to tell them what you know. It's something to do with Lorcan and Anna, isn't it? Did he hurt her, did Lorcan hurt Anna? Megan, for God's sake, will you please just..."

"Stop it!" Megan jumped up so violently the chair rocked behind her. "Just stop it, all of you. You don't understand. None of you understand. It wasn't Anna, Anna wasn't even there that weekend. It was Claire, OK? It was Claire!"

*

***

So, have I always been a bitch?

Because I always thought that bitches are born, not made. And yet one of my earliest memories is of Claire and me praying, side-by-side at the bed we shared, reciting the words we'd been taught by our maternal grandmother and said every night before we went to sleep.

There are four corners on my bed.
There are four angels round me spread.
Saint Matthew, Saint Mark, Saint Luke, and Saint John.
God bless the bed that I lay on.
If I should die before I wake,
I ask you God, my soul to take.

Then again, I have another memory of Claire and me praying. This time we are kneeling back-to-back, each facing our separate beds. We had been sick, some illness from which I had recovered first, as I invariably did. Mum said it was probably because I had been born three minutes before Claire. I liked that - being the oldest, being the strongest, being the first. In any event, Claire had somehow gotten it into her head that she might never get better this time. As we climbed into bed, she piped up, "If I die, will you die too, Anna?"

"No, I won't!" I said without a moment's hesitation, outraged at the idea I should be expected to die just to keep my sister company.

"You can die on your own. Just because we're twins doesn't mean we have to do everything together."

I think the incident sums up quite neatly our respective attitudes to being a twin. Claire loved it and I, quite frankly, resented it. Though in fairness to my mother, there was never any nonsense about dressing us in matching dresses, or that kind of thing. But she did expect us to do things together, and from the age of four to fourteen I went along with that for the most part. Besides, I have to admit there were aspects of being identical twins that had its compensations. Well, almost identical – in our stocking feet, I was just a little over an inch taller than Claire, but otherwise, we were so alike that only our parents could positively tell us apart. We both had the same waterfall-straight shiny brown hair, our mother's caramel-coloured eyes and dark lashes and our father's sallow colouring.

"Aren't they a picture?" people said. "Aren't they a perfect pair?"

But the trouble was, I didn't want to be one of a pair. I wanted to be different. And in many ways, we were different. Claire was quiet, gentle, reflective, her head always stuck in some book, or she was writing little stories or poems. And she noticed things, things in nature especially, flowers and animals. And she was thoughtful and kind too. I suppose what I am trying to say really, is that Claire was a better person than me. No saint, but as a general rule if she did get into mischief, it was usually me who had led her there. But for all my resentment, it was not until we became teenagers that my feelings about not being uniquely me, really began to fester. My chance to actively rebel came when I was fourteen and my father set up his own dental practice. This meant we moved not just house, but to a different town, which for Claire and me, also meant a change of school. Up to now, Claire and I had been placed in the same class, sitting side by side, Mum had insisted on it and I had gone along with it without protest.

But now there was a new principal to contend with. Sister Margaret-Joseph was a formidable woman with strong feelings on the subject of individuality, among other things. She took one look at our grades from our previous school, and informed Mum that it would be better for both Claire and me if we went into different streams for second year. The problem was maths; unlike me, Claire struggled badly with figures of any kind - English and history were Claire's strengths. Of course, my mother resisted the plan to separate us, but Sister Margaret-Joseph triumphed in the end, finally convincing Mum that Claire would really struggle with maths in 2A. I think Mum honestly expected us both to be devastated when she broke the news. Instead,

I could not hide my jubilation at the idea of us being separated. And I said as much. There was a row, Mum lectured me on selfishness and thoughtfulness and a lot of other stuff I don't recall. What I do remember is that Claire said nothing until Mum threatened to ring the school to inform Sister Margaret Joseph that she'd changed her mind and wanted us both in the same class after all.

"I'd rather go into 2B," she said suddenly. "I don't want to be behind everyone else in maths."

And that was that. Nothing Mum said could change her mind. That was the thing about Claire, she could appear as mild as milk for the most part, but when it came to the things she felt really strongly about, she could be the most obstinate person in the world. When she chose a path, she stuck to it to the bitter end. Of course, I knew perfectly well that I had hurt her. I knew it even before overhearing Mum later that evening, making excuses to Claire for my behaviour.

"You have to understand that Anna is just growing up a little bit faster than you, Claire," Mum told her. "She feels the need to do some things by herself, but this has nothing to do with you." To all of which, Claire simply insisted over and over that she didn't mind, really, she didn't. Mum of course was dead right about one thing at least - it had nothing to do with Claire. It was all about me; it was always all about me.

It was all about me that first day at school too, when on the way home on the school bus, I sat next to Rachel Quinn, leaving Claire to sit wherever she could find a seat. I had been happy enough to sit next to my sister on the way to school that morning, but then I had known no one, and the world had felt strange and a little bit frightening. Even my body had felt different under the long woollen skirt and the starchy newness of my school blouse. But all that had changed by the time we caught the bus home. I have often wondered since whether, if things had happened otherwise than they did that day, everything might have turned out very differently. Perhaps if my period had not come when it did, announcing itself with that little dragging pain in the small of my back, as I walked with Claire toward the main hall for morning assembly. Because of that, I had turned back, telling Claire to go on ahead. Legging it to the toilets, I sat in a cubicle cursing the cramps that had gripped me by now, and grateful for the box of tampons that my mother had thought to put in the pocket of my school backpack.

Afterwards, while I was drying my hands, I heard a creaking sound behind me. Glancing round, I saw the door to the last cubicle open slowly and a dark curly head emerge. The girl saw me and pulled her neck back like a startled tortoise. I realised she had thought I'd gone, and she was alone in the toilets. But a moment later, her head reappeared, followed this time by the rest of her. She saw me and smiled, in relief I suspect, that I wasn't one of the nuns. Some friendships are born on a smile; ours was, mine and Rachel Quinn's. And, the smile widening to a beam, she came toward me, a little lopsided under the weight of the school bag hanging off one of her slight shoulders. She was much shorter than me, small and petite in every way, with perfect features, a skin so creamy it looked almost waxen beneath her dark springing curls; I thought she looked like a pretty little doll. As I straightened up, I caught the smell of smoke on her breath, then she dropped her bag with a dull thud on the tiled floor and, as though she had read my mind, said, "You haven't any gum, have you?"

I shook my head, "No, sorry."

"Crap, I forgot mine and Maggie Joe will smell us a mile off."

It took me a moment to realise that Maggie Joe was a reference to Sr Margaret Joseph. I also realised with a small thrill that she had assumed that I too had been smoking in the cubicles. I opened my mouth to tell her otherwise but shut it again, because I had made another realisation in that moment – which was, that more than anything, I wanted this girl to go on lumping us together in that way. I liked it, I liked her, and so I kept my mouth shut. I bent down to pick up my own school bag and was about to make for the door when the girl said urgently,

"Where are you going? Assembly's not over yet, the bell didn't ring. Oh, hang on, you're new, aren't you? What's your name?"

"Anna, Anna Fox. Today's my first day."

"Figures. I'm Rachel, Rachel Quinn. What class are you in?"

"2A."

"No way, me too! But we can't go out yet, we need to hang on here until the bell rings. Then when they all come out, we do too. That way no one will notice us. Look, just follow me and when I say it's good to go, you go. OK?"

"OK."

"OK. Oh, and by the way we've Maggie-Joe for Irish, first period. She has a nose like a shark, but don't worry, Jennifer always has gum, so I'll get us some."

*

And that was it, we were us. I remember feeling a warmth spreading through me at the thought. It made me forget about being new and feeling nervous. It even helped me forget the niggling pain in my back. Instead, I waited excitedly until the bell finally sounded, then a little longer again until Rachel said it was safe to go. Then, side-by-side we slipped quickly out into the corridor resounding now to the roar and chatter of pupils and teachers and blended with the crowd. Rachel led the way to the open door of a classroom at the end of the corridor. Inside, a crowd of girls were talking and laughing and, once again, I remembered that I knew nobody. Nobody apart from Rachel who had left me standing in the doorway while she made her way to the back row of desks.

I watched as she bent down and said something in the ear of a girl who suddenly turned her head and stared at me, then looked me up and down. I thought she was very pretty, in a quite different way to Rachel. She was much taller and had long straight black hair and high cheekbones and long narrow eyes, green eyes as I later discovered. And those eyes were fixed on me, unblinking it seemed, and their expression was so cool that I fought my instinct to smile at her. But I held her stare with my own, as though I already knew that this was the opening gambit in some sort of contest. And in the end, it was Jennifer who looked away first. She turned to Rachel, who took something from her and came toward me, a big smile on her face.

"Here, chew on that," she said. "I knew Jennifer would have some." She handed me two pieces and crammed another two into her own mouth and began frantically chewing. I did the same, in spite of knowing I had nothing to fear from Sr Margaret Joseph's olfactory powers.

A voice boomed behind me. "That will do now, girls. Term starts here!"

I turned and saw a tiny nun standing in the doorway. Rachel grabbed my arm, pulled me after her, hissing in my ear as we went. "I wasn't joking, nose like a shark! Don't get anywhere near her. Just follow me, Nicole kept me a place and you can sit next to me."

And there I was - sitting next to Rachel Quinn who sat next to Nicole Brady who sat next to Jennifer O'Keeffe. And separated by a short gap, sat Bethany Doyle and Megan McGrath.

Did I even like them? Rachel, yes, without a doubt. Bethany, with her wavy auburn hair and striking hazel eyes, a smatter of detested freckles across her nose and cheeks – I can't say I disliked her. She was opinionated and bracing to be around. As for Nicole - blonde, blue-eyed, beautiful Nicole – I thought her vain and none too bright and I despised the way she followed Jennifer's lead unquestioningly. Then there was Megan, who got all the boy's attention with her enormous boobs and waist length white-blonde hair which I envied quite a lot. She also had a curiously flat looking face – a pancake face, I used to think of it as – which I envied not at all. She had lovely big eyes, though, even if their somewhat vapid quality made her appear a bit stupid, which I thought she was, a little.

In any event, it didn't matter a great deal whether I liked them or not, the important thing was to be accepted by them. And Rachel saw to it that I was. She presented me to them that first day, like a prize she had cleverly picked up – the cool new girl she'd found skipping assembly to smoke in the loo. Which I told myself was only half an untruth – after all, I was the new girl, and I would make myself cool if it killed me. And so, I became one of them. I sat with them in the back row of the class and whispered and sniggered and pulled faces and acted the fool just as they did. I smoked in the loo at breaktime for real, came to school wearing pierced ears and my newly and hastily acquired, as well as forbidden Dr Martens. I even skipped classes from time to time. It was fun and exciting and best of all, it was yet another way to set myself apart from Claire, but it really bothered Mum to see us moving in different circles, not that Claire ever had a circle. Claire wasn't unpopular, people were drawn to her kindness and gentle patience, but for a long time there was no special friend to replace the long-time companion she had suddenly lost – that is to say – me. Mum nagged me from time to time. Friends come and go, she told me, but a sister, especially a twin sister was someone I could depend on forever. What she didn't tell me, was that she had been diagnosed with breast cancer; that she kept to herself. But, in any case, what did I care about forever – I was fourteen and I was part of the A Team! I can't even remember when or why we began calling ourselves that. But somehow identifying ourselves in words in that way, as a discrete group within a group (by then we had all followed Bethany's lead and were identifying as Grungers) set me even further apart, at least in my mind, from my sister.

But, while I had my doubts about Jennifer O'Keeffe right from the start, I took an instant dislike to her brother, Lorcan. He was a year and a half older than us, an up-and-coming rugby star, if you were to believe all you heard, with women falling at his feet; I could never really understand why. Nicole was mad about him, she never admitted it, but it was obvious from the way she behaved when he was around.

He knew it too, and he teased her and called her Blondie, which she pretended to hate, but clearly loved. As for Jennifer, she thought the sun shone out of her brother's backside, while she, in my opinion was the only person in the world he really cared much about. There were just the two of them in the family and from what I could gather, their parents were pretty crap. Their father at least was an actual shit, rumour had it he hit his wife. He was also obnoxious in other ways, with his loud grating voice and orange sunbed tan, shirts worn with the collars up and brightly coloured argyle socks. He had a habit of sitting with his legs spread wide, right ankle on left knee; Lorcan sat exactly the same way. He was always 'away with work' which was something to do with property development, which I imagine was a blessing for all concerned. Jennifer's mother 'drank a bit'. Actually, she was an out and out alcoholic, everyone knew it, not that anyone would dream of saying so or even hinting at it, not in front of Jennifer at any rate. All of which was probably why Jennifer rarely brought us home - in all the years we hung about together, I think I saw the inside of the O'Keeffe house maybe three times. It was on the first of these occasions that Lorcan first tried it on with me. It was a Saturday afternoon in summer, Jennifer's mother had gone to some spa hotel, or that was what she told us. Rachel told me 'in confidence' that she'd actually gone somewhere to dry out. They had a tennis court and we planned to play a few games, but when we arrived, Lorcan was already having a game with Bethany's brother, Ross. Jennifer had a go at Lorcan, complaining that she'd 'bagsied' the court first, but although Lorcan refused to give way for us, he said he and Ross would play a doubles match with two of us.

"Me and Foxy against Doyler and whoever. Take your pick mate," he called to Ross. Ross said nothing, just grinned like an idiot at Megan's tits.

"The Fair Megan it is then," Lorcan grinned, and Megan, tossed her hair happily and joined Ross on the court.

But I had seen the look on Nicole's face when Lorcan had chosen me, added to which I hated being called Foxy and had taken umbrage at that 'take your pick mate' comment. I told him, truthfully as it happens, that I wasn't much good at tennis, and that Lorcan should play with Nicole, Nicole played much better than I did.

Lorcan said, "Suit yourself. Come on then Blondie."

Nicole perked up immediately and trotted toward him happily, but I could tell that Lorcan was peeved at my refusal. I sat on the grass with Rachel and watched them play. Jennifer disappeared into the house with Bethany and came back carrying between them, a full bottle of gin and two bottles of red wine.

"Dad locked the drinks cabinet," Jennifer informed us with obvious disgust. "But I found this in Mu... I found this."

We all knew she had discovered her mother's stash, and although I doubt any of us liked the taste of neat gin, we passed it around among the four of us. When the match ended, the others joined us and there was no more tennis as we finished the gin and started on the wine. Rachel was the first to feel sick and she ran for the house. A couple of minutes later, Nicole puked her guts up on the lawn and she too staggered inside. I was feeling queasy myself and followed them into the house, but Rachel was still hogging the downstairs toilet, so I ran upstairs to use one of the other bathrooms. When I came out onto the landing again, Lorcan was standing a short distance away, leaning against the wall with his arms folded and a grin on his face.

"Feeling rough, Foxy?"

I didn't answer, and as I tried to pass him, he stepped in front of me. "What's your hurry?"

"My name is Anna," I told him curtly and again tried to get past him. He lunged at me and tried to kiss me. I was pushing him away when I heard a sound from behind. I turned and saw Nicole standing a little further along the landing, having just come out of one of the rooms. Lorcan laughed and let go of me and disappeared into the bathroom I had just vacated. Nicole and I were left standing and staring at one another; I remember thinking that if looks could kill, I'd have died on the spot.

*

We didn't know it, but that was Mum's last Christmas. It was also the year that Claire got a guitar. In January she began taking lessons and that was how she met David Power. She brought him home with her one evening for dinner. "This is David," she announced. "He doesn't eat meat."

Mum made him some sort of risotto with rice and mushrooms and afterward he and Claire disappeared upstairs to her bedroom. To watch videos, she said. Nobody raised an eyebrow. My father wouldn't have anyway, he was a mild and placid man who enjoyed reading and doing crossword puzzles. His dental patients came back to him, not just on account of his skill but because of his gentleness. He loved Claire and me and indulged us, but he left the real business of child-rearing to my mother. It was she who made the rules and imposed discipline. And I knew for certain that she would never have allowed me to bring a boy up to my room. But then again, it never occurred to me either that there might be anything to object to in David Power being alone with Claire. Because, just like my parents, I never for so much as a nano-second, viewed him as anything but Claire's geeky friend. He was lanky and skinny, with long greasy hair. He wore oval metal framed glasses that magnified his eyes; I thought he looked like an owl on stilts. Anyone less suited to pretty, girly, Claire, it was hard to imagine. But Claire liked him - really liked him. I walked into her bedroom one day looking for something, and they were there, lying on the big yellow bean bag on Claire's bedroom floor. Claire's head was on David's chest, and his arm was around her. Their eyes were closed. It gave me a sort of shock and I turned on my heel and left them there together. I watched them after that, noticing the way Claire looked at him, and I knew for sure that she cared for him, really, really cared for him. And illogical as it may seem, considering the way I had behaved toward her, I resented him for that, because it seemed to me that stupid, geeky, lanky David Power had usurped my place in my sister's heart.

*

Claire did better in the Junior Cert exams than I did, to my disgust but not surprise. I had been messing about all year to the detriment of my grades. As a result, nobody was too surprised when I decided to take the option of doing transition year, instead of moving on to fifth year. The real reason of course was that Jennifer had decided she wanted a doss year, which was what everyone knew transition year was really. Of course, the rest of the gang followed suit. In truth, I'd have preferred to go on to fifth year, but I was worried Jennifer would use that as an excuse to get me out of the A Team. If my mother had not been too ill at the time to be bothered by such matters, I would never have been allowed to do transition year. But she was visibly fading by then, had lost her lovely hair and as a result of cycle after cycle of chemotherapy, was almost unrecognisable from the big, handsome woman she had been. My father had become fiercely protective of her and did all in his power to keep anything of a troubling nature from her. As a result, when he saw that I had made up my mind, he gave in.

Only Claire challenged me about it. "Why would you," she asked me wonderingly. "Everyone knows it's just a doss year."

"That's exactly the point. God, are you absolutely sure we're twins?" It was in these and a myriad of other petty ways that I hurt my sister. And doss we did. We were continually in trouble of one sort or another. Sr Maggie Joe called my father in to talk about my deteriorating schoolwork, as well as my behaviour. He put it down to my mother's illness, while Maggie Joe implied it might have something to do with the company I was keeping, by which she of course meant A Team. Maggie Joe was right. We were out of control by then, Jennifer it seemed to me, was on a mission to make as many people's lives as miserable as she possibly could. Teachers as well as the other girls' lives – girls like Liz Wade, whom Jennifer seemed to delight in humiliating. But she had other targets too, like my sister Claire. Jennifer had had it in for Claire from the start really, making fun of her hair, her clothes, her taste in music. Claire wore her hair in plaits, hated smoking, loved Boyzone and wasn't even ashamed to admit it. Jennifer, I was pretty certain, had a go at Claire mostly to get at me. She made snide comments about her, even when Claire was not around to hear them, in the hope, I knew, that I would snap. The truth was Jennifer didn't like me; she resented my friendship with

Rachel and would have liked an excuse to cut me off from the group. But that year, she really upped the ante, not just teasing, but mocking my sister and poking fun at her at every opportunity. There were times I did come close to turning on Jennifer, but that would have been to let her win. So, the fact is that I never once actually called her out on Claire's behalf.

*

Something else happened that year. Bethany's older brother, Ross, turned seventeen and threw a party at their house to which we were all invited by Bethany. I decided to go, but only because I thought Michael Casey would be there, he and Ross played rugby together. I knew that Jennifer liked him too, but I'd recently got the feeling it was me, Michael was interested in. But on the night, there was no sign of him, though it felt as if just about everyone else had come. Ross and Bethany's Dad were away that night; their mother, I knew from Rachel, had left a long time ago, when they were still just kids. According to Rachel, she had gone to live with 'some hippy artist' in San Francisco but was killed shortly afterwards in a motorbike accident. As a result, their father pretty much let Ross and Bethany do whatever they pleased. There was a lot of booze that night and everyone was drinking their heads off. Things got messy and I would have left early but I kept hoping Michael would turn up. I had actually just made up my mind to go when I was grabbed from behind. It was Lorcan O'Keeffe.

"Hey Foxy!" he yelled over the sound of the music, "Looking hot tonight."

I tried to break free, but he held me hard against him and tried to stick his tongue in my mouth. I managed to push him off and yelled at him to get his greasy paws off me and made my way to the conservatory, where the coats had all been thrown in a heap on the wicker sofa. I was still trying to extricate my own jacket from the pile when Ross came up behind me. He yelled something about hoping I wasn't leaving already. I said I was, and that was when he told me that Lorcan wanted a word with me.

"He wants to apologise. Apparently, he was a bit of an asshole to you just now."

"When is he anything else," I retorted, and Ross laughed and said it was hard to disagree with that.

"But seriously, Anna, he knows he was way out of line tonight. He told me so, and said he wants to tell you that himself. He really likes you, you know that, right?"

"Well, I don't like him," I said firmly. "If you must know, I'd rather date outside my species."

Ross laughed again, then turned all serious again. "OK, fair enough, but all messing aside, Anna, you'd actually be doing me a huge favour. Lorco is refusing to come out until he sees you and apologises, and well the thing is...I kind of need to use my bedroom, if you get my drift?" Ross inclined his head toward the kitchen where the party was still in full swing and I suddenly remembered seeing him there earlier, snogging the face off Samantha D'Arcy.

I gave in "OK. OK, I'll go up, but I'm not going into your room. If Lorcan wants to apologise he can come out to me and do it."

So, I followed Ross upstairs and stood outside his bedroom door while Ross knocked and called to Lorcan over the boom of the music from downstairs.

"Lorco? Lorco, mate? I've got Anna here. I told her you want to say sorry for being such a dickhead." Ross grinned at me, but the door remained shut.

"Right, I'm going," I said.

"No don't go," Ross put a hand on my arm. "He probably thinks I'm winding him up, so he'll open the door and then I'll turf him out. Tell you what, just let him hear your voice, then he'll know you're really here and come out."

Ross stood back then, and like a little fool, I moved closer to the door and yelled at Lorcan that if he'd something to say to me, he'd better say it, or I was going home. I remember being aware of Ross suddenly standing too close to me, so close his body held me pressed against the door. Next thing I knew, the door opened inwards, and I almost fell into the room. I managed to stop myself from actually falling and swung round just as I heard the sound of the key turning in the lock. I fell on it, hammering and shouting to Ross to let me out. I did that over and over again, but Ross didn't answer. And eventually, not wanting to, I turned around. The room was dimly lit by a bedside lamp, but I could see Lorcan O'Keeffe clearly enough. He was sprawled on his back on the bed, head resting on his arms against a bank of pillow. His legs were crossed at the ankles and his eyes were fixed on me. And he was smiling. No way was I going to let him know I was nervous, though I was.

"I suppose this was your idea?" I said with disgust. "Well, you've had your fun now, so tell Ross to open the door."

But Lorcan just stayed on the bed smiling at me with that awful smile. I began hammering on the door and yelling to be let out. And then he was on me, arms around my waist. He spun me round and then his mouth was on mine. I raised my arms to fend him off, but he pinned them to my sides as effortlessly as though I were a butterfly. So, I bit down on the soft flesh of his lip and he yelped and let go of me, just long enough for me to get to the door and beginning hammering on it again and screaming for help. Then he was on me again, his arm around my neck this time, forcing my head upward so that my scream became a gurgle in my throat. He dragged me backwards, and then I felt a thump in the small of my back, which had the effect of sending me falling forward onto the bed. My face and nose were pressed into the duvet, I was conscious of the smell of stale sweat. Then he was on top of me, pushing the breath out of my body. I felt his mouth on the skin of my neck, his breath on my earlobe and I heard his voice, a vicious hiss. "Shut up like a good little bitch, Foxy, and just enjoy it, why don't you?"

And for a moment I did lie quite still because there was nothing else for me to do. I was a punctured thing, flattened beneath the great weight of him. And then blessed relief when the weight lessened as he dropped back onto his knees, hands still pressing down on either side of my hips. Perhaps he thought I would play along. I don't know, I only know that it gave me the chance to raise my face from the suffocating, nauseating duvet and twist my head a little so that I could see again. Just the bedside locker at first, then the lamp, the alarm clock with its bright green digital numerals, then the item just next to it...

"That's better, Foxy" he said. "Now let me see you better why don't..."

His hold on my hips loosened, his hands, moved around and under me. He was pulling at my jeans when I took him by surprise, scooting my body forward toward the head of the bed. He lunged after me. My right arm shot out and my hand closed around the base of the wine bottle. I twisted my body with all my strength and brought the bottle down on his head.

I thought it was blood at first, the wetness that spattered my arm and face, I just wasn't sure whose. It hardly seemed to matter, I wasn't thinking, I was just processing – thoughts and feelings would come later. All I knew was that he had let go his hold on me. I was off the bed and at the window, one knee up on the sill, the other leg still dangling, while my hands pulled and pulled at the latch which would not give, would not open. Open! Open! Please, please open!

I don't know if I was actually shouting the words or just silently begging. But I became aware of him moving behind me again. Then suddenly the window was open. It was only afterward that I stopped to think and knew that had the garage roof not been there a safe drop below, I would have jumped anyway.

*

I woke the following morning feeling as though every bone in my body had been crushed. The rush of adrenalin that had got me safely from that room had given way to flu-like symptoms and I stayed in my room until the evening, feeling shivery and sweaty in turn. I didn't want to talk to anyone, and it seemed that no one wanted to talk to me either. It was almost night before I heard from Rachel, which was unusual, especially after a party. I knew immediately I heard the breathy tone of her voice on the phone asking if I'd had a good night, that she'd heard something. When I told her I hadn't, there was an uncomfortable pause.

She said weakly, "Oh, how come?" She tried to convince me she'd only called to find out why I'd gone home without telling her I was leaving. But Rachel never had been a convincing or comfortable liar and I put her out of her misery.

"Look I know you've heard something Rachel, so why not just come out and tell me?"

"Well, only that you'd got off with Lorcan," she said, then added with a hint of reproach, "Nicole isn't too happy about that, Anna."

"Nicole isn't happy!" I almost laughed. Then I told her what had really happened, from Ross shoving me into the bedroom with Lorcan, to my jump from the first-floor window. I could tell she was genuinely shocked.

"Oh God, Anna, I'm so sorry," she told me. "I had no idea. Did you hurt yourself?"

I wanted to shout at her that no, I hadn't hurt myself; Lorcan O'Keeffe had hurt me. Instead, I told her I was OK. Rachel said she was glad about that but added, "Listen Anna, I think you should know that's not what people have been saying."

I demanded to know just which people she had in mind, and exactly what they had been saying.

"Well, Ross and..." Rachel began.

"What's Ross been saying?"

"Only that he was on his way upstairs and you asked him where Lorcan was. And then when he told you Lorcan had gone up to use

the en-suite loo in Ross's room, you followed him up. And Ross said he saw you going into his room and shutting the door."

"Then Ross is a filthy liar!" I felt sick to my stomach.

"I'm sorry, Anna," Rachel sounded miserable. "I'm just telling you what Ross told Bethany."

"And who did Bethany tell?"

"Jennifer, she told Jennifer, and Jennifer told me and Nicole and Megan. But Anna, Lorcan is saying it too, that you came onto him and..."

Again, I cut across her, "And who do you believe, Rachel, Lorcan or Me?"

And Rachel said quietly but unhesitatingly, "I believe you, Anna."

*

Perhaps Rachel did believe me. Actually, I think she did. But it didn't matter in the end. Because the first rule of the A Team was that Jennifer made the rules, called the shots and decided what everybody did or did not believe, or at least what they were prepared to admit before witnesses, that they believed. And Lorcan was Jennifer's brother and could do no wrong in her eyes. Which meant that I was the liar and Lorcan had done nothing more than kiss me, but only after I'd come onto him. As for Bethany, well, Ross was her brother and why would he lie? Besides, as she said, when I challenged her - I had been seen by loads of people going upstairs with Ross, who had come down a few minutes later on his own. And Nicole, I imagine Nicole needed, even if she didn't want to, believe Lorcan's version of events. While Megan, finding me alone in the school toilets one day, warned me "for your own good" not to be saying things about Lorcan having tried it on with me.

"He didn't try it on with me Megan," I told her. "He tried to rape me."

She must have reported back to Jennifer, who confronted me after school that day and threatened me that if I knew what was good for me, I'd stop telling lies about her brother. And so, I was frozen out of the A-Team, and to be honest it bothered me very little. Certainly not as much as the injustice of being labelled a liar, while Lorcan O'Keeffe and Ross Doyle got off scot free. The truth was I had already begun to outgrow the appeal the group had held for me. I was tired of getting into trouble at school. I was already on a last warning and had only avoided being suspended after being caught skipping off school, on account of my mother's illness. I was also growing increasingly uncomfortable with the things the A Team did and said. It was all beginning to seem either childish or just downright nasty. That initiation nonsense we had subjected Liz Wade to, had left a bad taste in my mouth. But most of all, I was growing increasingly ashamed of having failed to stand up to Jennifer's targeting of Claire. So that, all in all, it came as a relief almost to have a reason for distancing myself from the members of the A Team, just as they, with the exception of Rachel, were distancing themselves from me.

Besides, something happened to take the sting out of being blanked by Jennifer and Co. Michael Casey asked me to his band's first live gig. I was practically beside myself with happiness until I realised the gig clashed with the school's transition year weekend trip to Wicklow. The trip wasn't even optional, it was part of the transition year programme. The only obvious way out of it was to fake being ill, but if I did that, I could hardly suddenly recover in time for Michael's gig. Even my father wouldn't swallow that one. Regardless, it never once occurred to me to ring Michael and tell him I couldn't go after all.

There was, I decided, a solution; there just had to be.

*

CHAPTER 41

Saturday11th March

"You're not making any sense, Megan," Rachel sounded bewildered. "What do you mean, it wasn't Anna?"

"I mean what I said," Megan was impatient now. "Anna and Claire swapped places. Claire came on the trip to Wicklow that weekend, pretending to be Anna."

Tina looked at JP as Rachel repeated stupidly, "Anna and Claire switched places? But why would they? I don't understand."

"How the hell would I know," Megan snapped. "If you want to know, you'll have to ask Anna. All I know is that's what happened. Anna stayed home and Claire came on the trip pretending to be her. Nobody knew. Claire fooled us, she fooled all of us. Lorcan as well. He thought it was Anna at the lake that night. So, Claire had no one to blame if… it was her own fault is all I'm saying."

"What was Claire's own fault, Megan?" said Tina. "Did something happen to her at the lake that night? What did Lorcan do?"

In the ensuing silence, Rachel said wonderingly, "Megan?"

"What?" Megan turned on her, eyes blazing. "Why are you asking me? Why is everyone looking at me as though it were my fault? I had nothing to do with it. I wasn't even at the lake that night. I didn't go with them. I wasn't feeling very well so I stayed in bed. And none of it was my idea anyway. It was all Jennifer and Nicole, they cooked the whole thing up."

"Cooked what up?"

"The…the plan. The plan to trick Anna. Jennifer was mad jealous because of Michael Casey."

"Who the hell is Michael Casey" Tina was trying to keep a lid on her patience, as well as her excitement.

"Anna's boyfriend. Except Jennifer was mad after him. Plus, she was mad at Anna for the things she'd said about Lorcan trying to attack her at Ross Doyle's party. Nicole was pissed off too, because Lorcan fancied Anna. And Bethany had it in for Anna for accusing Ross of locking her into his room with Lorcan at his party."

Tina shook her head in an attempt to clear her mind. "OK, what's this party you keep talking about?" The question was addressed to Megan, but it was Rachel who answered.

"Bethany's brother Ross had a party and Anna said that Ross tricked her into going upstairs with him to his room. She said Ross told her that Lorcan was up there and that he wanted to apologise to Anna. He'd made a grab at her or something and tried to kiss her. Only, Anna said that when she got upstairs, Ross pushed her into his room and locked her in with Lorcan. She said Lorcan tried to attack her, and that she only got away from him, by jumping out of the window."

"Nobody believed her," said Megan mutinously.

"I believed her," said Rachel.

*

***

There was a solution of course, but it raised a whole new problem – how to get Claire on board. I couldn't do it without her, but when I told her what I needed her to do she laughed in my face.

"Are you crazy? They'd know straight away I'm not you."

"How would they?"

"Because I'm not you, Anna! That's how."

"But that's the whole point," I argued. "Don't you see? For those two days and nights, you will be me and I'll be you. Remember how you always used to say that we never did any of the things twins do in books and films? Trade places; pretend to be one another – well here's your chance. Come on Claire, it'll be fun!"

"It wouldn't be fun for me," said Claire. "I'd be worried sick the whole time, that we'd be found out."

"But we wouldn't be found out. We can pull it off, I just know we can."

"Maybe you can, but I couldn't."

"But you can, Claire, of course you can. Look, come here for a second."

I grabbed her arm and led her to the full-length mirror on the door of her wardrobe. Then I reached up and pulled the bands from the end of each of her plaits. Ignoring her protests, I moved my fingers through the rippling stands of her hair and let it fall loose about her shoulders. Then I stood next to her. "Look at us," I commanded, "just look at us."

I was remembering what Nicole had once said to me. "If it wasn't for those stupid plaits your sister wears, and the way you dress so differently, I'd never be able to tell you and her apart."

And she was right; aside from the minor difference in height and the ripples the plaits had left in Claire's hair, the only difference between the two girls staring back at us from the mirror was the clothes we were wearing.

"All you need to do to pass as me, is to wear your hair loose and dress the way I would," I told her. But Claire shook her head.

"It's not that simple, Anna. It's not just about the way we look. Your friends will be there, those girls... I can't fool them. They know you, and they'll know I'm not you."

"No, no they won't." I pulled her down onto the bed, sat next to her, my arm about her shoulder.

"You see, that's the beauty of it, Claire. Rachel won't even be there, she's in hospital having her appendix out. And the others, the thing is, we're not friends any longer. I'm sick of them, they're nothing but a pack of bitches."

Claire looked at me "You're only finding that out now?"

I grimaced but pursued my purpose. "So, you see, they'll give you a wide berth, which means there's nothing for you to worry about. All you have to do is keep a low profile and... I don't know... be a bit more me! You can do it Claire; I know you can. So please, please, please, will you? For me, Claire, will you do it for me, and I swear I'll never ask you for a favour again as long as we live?"

But she wasn't convinced and so, to my everlasting shame, I used my mother's illness to persuade her.

"You know if I get into any more trouble in school, they'll exclude me," I wheedled. "And then what do you think that will do to Mum? And Dad for that matter, do you not think he has enough to worry about right now?"

"Then don't go to the gig, go on the trip," Claire argued with infuriating reasonableness.

I got angry with her then. I told her I wasn't going on the trip, no matter what. I said that if the tables were turned, I'd do it for her. I said that all her talk about loving being my twin was just that – talk. I said a great many things, I wore her down in fact and in the end, more out of weariness than anything else, I suspect, she gave in.

*

We met in the school toilets after final morning period on the morning of the trip. Locked into the end cubicle, we took off our uniforms, then for authenticity as hers was neater than mine, I put on Claire's. Meanwhile, Claire dressed in the clothes I had chosen and packed for her in my haversack. Every item in it screamed me! Jumpers and shirts, tee-shirts, and jeans that I had worn again and again. I insisted Claire let me lash on a few coats of mascara for her and had also packed my make-up bag for her and warned her to stick on some lipstick at every opportunity. There were no nuns going on the trip, and Mr O'Dea and the three female teachers who were accompanying us, always relaxed the make-up rule when we were off the school premises. We had solved the problem of the rippling hair by Claire having worn pigtails instead of plaits for a couple of days prior to the trip. And now, her hair hanging lose about her shoulders, I stood impatiently while Claire plaited mine. The result was, that emerging from the cubicle and seeing our reflections in the long mirror over the handbasins, even I could hardly believe that I wasn't Claire, and she wasn't me. In fact, the transformation was so complete, in spite of her nerves, Claire joined me in a fit of the giggles. I was nervous too, but it was an excited nervousness, and if I am honest, as soon as the coach taking them to Wicklow had pulled out of the car park, I pretty much forgot about my sister. All my attention now was focused on the part I had to play. It was Friday afternoon, the concert wasn't until tomorrow night, which meant I had to get through an evening at home without Dad suspecting I wasn't Claire. I never doubted I could do it, after all my father expected to see Claire, so he would see Claire, it was that simple. All that was needed was for me to mouse about the house Claire-like, while keeping well out of Dad's way as much as possible. I skipped dinner and kept to my room with the excuse that I had cramps; my father shied like a nervous colt at the whisper of 'women's problems'. When he looked in on me, before he went to bed that night, I just needed to smile a little shyly, the way Claire would.

If I had to speak, I simply needed to keep my voice low and gentle. I had one bad moment only – when I looked in to say goodnight to Mum. Sometimes, she could suddenly emerge from her drug induced fugue and just for a moment, appear her old lucid self. If that were to happen, just as I was leaning over to kiss her, as I knew Claire did every night, I wasn't at all sure that she wouldn't immediately know I was Anna. But when I slipped into her room, Mum was asleep and lightly snoring and I said good night silently before escaping to my room.

*

On Saturday, I got up late, the palliative care nurse was with Mum, while Dad went out for a round of golf, so I was free to spend the afternoon supposedly preparing for the party to which David was supposed to be taking me. David - he had always been the potential fly in the ointment. It wouldn't have done for him to turn up at our door looking for me and have Dad ask him in and find me dressed as my sister; whatever about Mum, I was almost certain that however good an actress I fancied myself, David would be able to tell the difference.

"You'll have to tell him your class is going on the trip to Wicklow too," I had urged Claire. "He won't know any different."

Claire had frowned unhappily. "But I'd be lying, and I never lie to David."

"But you are going on the trip, remember? How is that lying?" I argued.

"I don't know, but it still feels like lying," Claire had insisted.

And so, I found myself having to coax her all over again. But at least now there was no David to worry about, just Dad who expected him to call for me to take me to the supposed party. I got around that by flying down the stairs while yelling at him that we were running late, and David was picking me up at the end of the road. I didn't give him a chance to argue, being out the door and haring down the path before he had a chance to get out of his armchair. Besides, why would he doubt me, I was Claire after all, and Claire didn't tell lies.

*

I feel I should say at this point, that I honestly had no idea Lorcan O'Keeffe was going to Wicklow that weekend. It wasn't part of the same trip - St Malachy's, the school to which he and Ross Doyle went, took them there on a sixth year pre-Leaving Certificate retreat. The venue just happened to be half a mile or so from the hostel at which we were to stay. Of course, had I been in the loop with Jennifer and the others, I would have known that. Would it have made any difference if I had known? Probably not, if I am completely honest, though I might have warned Claire to give Lorcan a wide berth if she happened to come into contact with him. But in fairness there was no reason to imagine their paths would cross.

***

CHAPTER 42

Saturday 11th March

Tina turned to Megan. "OK, but can we get back to the night at the lake in Wicklow now? What happened to Claire?"

"I just told you I wasn't there," Megan flared. "Is anyone listening to me? I wasn't there."

"I heard you," Tina kept her tone calm and even. "You weren't there, but you've just pretty much admitted that you knew there was a plan, Jennifer's idea you say. So, what was this plan?"

"I didn't know," said Megan. "I mean, I knew that we were all to pretend to Anna that the St. Malachy boys were planning a midnight barbecue at the lake. We told her we had all been invited. Jennifer said we all had to be really nice to Anna, so she'd agree to come with us to the lake - we hadn't really been talking to her since Ross's party. Once we got her to the lake, we were all to get in for a swim and when she wasn't looking, we were to get out, steal Anna's clothes and run off and leave her there."

"Leaving her there, alone?" Tina clarified.

"Well, alone with Lorcan. I mean that was the whole point."

"But that doesn't make any sense," said Rachel. "Why would Nicole go along with a plan like that? She knew he fancied Anna something rotten?"

"She didn't like it," Megan admitted. "But Jennifer told her that Lorcan hated Anna's guts on account of the lies she'd told about what happened at Ross's party. She convinced Nicole that Lorcan just wanted to have it out with Anna and teach her a lesson."

"Just exactly what sort of lesson was Lorcan planning to teach Anna, Megan?" asked JP.

"Don't ask me," said Megan defensively. "I don't know. None of it was my idea."

"But you knew that Anna was to be tricked into being alone in the middle of the night with a boy she'd already accused of having attacked her," said Tina. "So, just what did you think was going to happen to her that night, Megan?"

"I didn't think," said Megan. "I didn't think, and I didn't know. I still don't know. Claire said something happened, but Jennifer said not to believe a word that came out of her mouth. She said Claire was a liar just like Anna."

"So, what did Claire say had happened," asked Tina.

Megan lowered her gaze. "She said that Lorcan raped her."

Rachel made an inarticulate sound. Megan turned to her quickly. "That's what Claire said, Rachel. But I swear, Jennifer was right, you couldn't believe a word out of her mouth. I mean she told us she was pregnant too, but then she changed her mind."

"Claire was pregnant?" Rachel looked as stunned as if she'd just been slapped across the face.

"No. I said she told us she was pregnant. Not me, she didn't tell me, but she told the others, the others who were there that night at the lake." Megan looked flushed and flustered now.

"When was this?" Tina demanded.

"I don't know, a few months after we got back from Wicklow, I think. Claire came looking for help, at least that's what she said. But the next day she changed her story. Suddenly she wasn't pregnant after all. I only found out about it afterwards."

"You found out, how was that?"

"I overhead Bethany telling Jennifer and Nicole that she'd seen Claire in the loo at school," said Megan. "Bethany said Claire had told her that she'd made a mistake and there wasn't any baby after all. I asked Bethany about it later, and she told me everything, but she made me swear not to tell anyone else."

Megan glanced at Rachel. "Jennifer didn't tell you because she thought you'd make a fuss, I think," she said apologetically.

"I don't understand any of this," said Rachel plaintively. "Was Claire pregnant or not?"

"Of course, she wasn't," said Megan. "She was lying, just like Anna lied about what happened at Ross's party, Jennifer was right, it was all a pack of lies."

Rachel shook her head. "I don't believe that", she said. "Claire wouldn't lie about something like that, she just wouldn't. If she said she was pregnant, then she must have believed she was. But if she believed she could be pregnant, then that means...that must mean something did happen at the lake that night." Tina watched Rachel's eyes widen as realisation hit home.

"She was telling the truth," said Rachel, slowly. "Claire *was* pregnant. She was telling the truth. It all makes sense now, the way she changed. The baggy shapeless clothes, what she did to her hair - her beautiful hair. It was because of what he did to her, what Lorcan did to her. He raped her. He raped her and she was pregnant. She was telling the truth, but no one believed her. He did that to her, to Claire. Beautiful, gentle, little Claire. Oh God, I think I'm going to be sick."

Rachel buried her face in her hands, and with Megan showing signs of bursting into tears too, Tina spoke quietly to JP, "Get onto the station, would you? Get them to send an unmarked car."

As JP made for the door, Rachel looked up suddenly, her face streaked with tears. “The baby, Megan,” she said. “What happened to Claire's baby?”

Megan shook her head. “I don’t know, I swear I don’t,” she said, almost sobbing now.

“Anna kept asking me that too. What did I know about Claire’s baby? I told her I knew nothing. That I never even believed there was a baby. None of us did. Maybe Bethany, I don't know, but only at first. But come on, Rachel, did Claire ever look pregnant to you? Don’t you remember how we actually thought she was anorexic or bulimic or something - she got so skin and bone.”

Rachel didn’t answer and as both women dissolved further into tears, Tina chose that moment to interrupt. “Look, we need to move this to the station now,” she said briskly. “We’ll want statements from both of you. There’s a car on its way, Megan, you might want to grab a coat or something?”

Megan got up without a word of protest. “I’ll get my jacket,” she said.

Rachel immediately turned wet and pleading eyes on Tina.

“You know, don’t you? You know about Claire's baby. Please tell me. There was one, wasn’t there. What happened - did she have it? Please tell me, please.”

Tina said quietly. “I believe she did.”

“But what… where…?”

“That’s as much as I can say right now, I’m sorry Rachel.”

Before Rachel had the chance to argue, Megan came back with her jacket on. She had stopped crying and appeared composed enough to Tina.

“I don’t suppose Anna gave any indication of where she might be going, when she left you earlier?” Tina asked her.

"No. All she said was that she'd decided to give me the benefit of the doubt, though she was almost certain I didn't deserve it. Then she just went. She didn't even bother to shut the front door behind her. "I'd count myself lucky you got off that easily, if I were you," said Tina grimly.

*

***

The evening of Michael's gig went perfectly. To be honest I enjoyed myself so much I doubt if Claire crossed my mind more than once. And when it was over, and Claire had returned from the trip, my only concern was to know that she had managed to pull it off alright. Which apparently, she had. She was unforthcoming with details and seemed if anything, even quieter than normal. I put that down to her having sprained her wrist in a fall while hiking. She'd managed to scratch her face into the bargain as well as hurting her hand. I caught her wincing once or twice, but when I asked about it, she said it was nothing. She got snappy with me too, when I had a go at her for having managed to lose not only one of my jumpers, but also a pair of my favourite jeans. In fact, she got so snappy, it occurred to me that maybe she'd enjoyed being me so much she was feeling resentful it had come to an end.

*

And Claire wasn't the only one acting oddly around that time. Back at school, Jennifer, Nicole and Bethany seemed to be behaving differently around me. I'd have put it down to sour grapes on Jennifer's part, assuming she'd heard bynow that I was seeing Michael Casey, except that this time around it wasn't the usual dagger's looks and snide comments. It was more a sense I had that all three of them were watching me, almost as though they were waiting for me to say or do something. I asked Claire if anything had gone on with them while they were away, but she just shook her head. When I pressed her, she flew off the handle and yelled at me that she'd done what I'd asked her to, and now would I please just leave her alone. So, I dropped it, and after a while the funny looks from Jennifer & Co stopped.

In any case I had decided to put as much distance as I could between me and them, even changing desks at school. As a direct result, my schoolwork improved, and I felt good about that; I was too bright to have ever really enjoyed playing the fool. So, between that and Michael I felt pretty satisfied with life. The only place where things were not good, was home. We knew for certain now, that for Mum, time was running out and sadness lay siege to the house like a creeping fog. Because of that, I see now, it was understandable for both Dad and I to have overlooked the real causes of the changes in Claire. She was growing increasingly withdrawn, isolating herself from everyone, even a devastated David, whom she suddenly and unceremoniously dumped. But Claire changed in other ways too. The pretty girly, dresses were replaced with loose trousers and maxi skirts, baggy sweatshirts, and jumpers. She even had her hair cut into a boyish and frankly unflattering crop. I was so shocked when I first saw it, I asked her if she'd gone mad, cutting off her beautiful hair in that way.

"What do you care," she snapped. "You've always wanted us to look different, well now we do."

Mum died in October of that year, too deadened by drugs thankfully, to suffer any real pain. The fog of grief finally engulfed our home. Dad was laid low by it - no surprise – I had always known he worshipped my mother. What hit me like a kick in the face was my own grief. I think it was because Mum had been slipping away from me, from all of us for so long, that I had come to believe I was in some way prepared for the final loss. I wasn't. It may sound strange to say that it surprised me; the depth and force of it. And yet, as bad as it was, I remember thinking that whatever I was feeling, Claire was feeling it even more. It was just after the funeral, we were standing about the graveside when I looked up and saw my sister's face. I mean really saw it for the first time in a long time; the hollow cheeks, the huge suffering eyes, but most of all, how lost she appeared to me.

*

And it didn't get any better, not for Claire. Dad and I, over time, picked up the pieces of our lives as best we could; Dad engrossing himself in his work, me by keeping busy at school and spending time with Michael. But Claire just withdrew further and further into herself. She rarely spoke unless spoken to, spent more and more time alone in her room. Her schoolwork began to suffer, which worried my father, because Claire was in fifth year now and supposed to be working hard for her Leaving Certificate exams. I was also convinced that she had developed bulimia, I'd heard her throwing up more than once. Once, I heard her crying in the bathroom and called to her through the door, telling her Mum wouldn't want her to make herself sick with sadness. But all I got in response was silence and when I asked if I should go and get Dad, she said no, she was just having a bad period. After Christmas, Claire announced she was leaving school and nothing I, Dad or Sister Maggie Joe said could dissuade her. She signed up for some office skills course and got a job working in the office of a veterinary practices. Meanwhile I went on to fifth, then sixth year and did a really good Leaving Cert. I also decided about my own future – I would follow Dad and study to become a dental surgeon.

Then, at just gone nineteen, Claire, with little or no warning, announced she was going to London. There was no arguing with her and within days of telling us, she had gone. I missed her more than I could ever have imagined. Even depressed, and withdrawn, she had been my sister and my twin for all of my life and now I realised for the first time, just how much I had depended on her always being there. The feeling it appeared, was not mutual. For every four letters I wrote, I was lucky to receive one, and that often nothing more than a brief note telling me little of her day-to-day, and nothing at all of her inner life.

*

And then, in June 2002, came the news, broken to me by our devastated father, that Claire had died in a car accident. He tried to comfort me, insisted she'd have suffered no pain, her death had been instantaneous. I grieved for her more than I had imagined possible. But as it turned out, I had yet to discover what is possible when it comes to grief. Dad travelled to England alone, to formally identify my sister's remains; he point-blank refused to even hear of me accompanying him. My going with him now, with a post-mortem having to be done, on account of Claire having died in an RTA, would, he argued, only cause me, and therefore him, further unnecessary pain and stress. I gave in and he went alone and brought her home to be buried alongside her mother. He brought home some of her belongings too, books, a few framed photographs. One of them was a shot of the two of us standing side-by-side, I remember being happy that she had had it in her flat, the flat I had never even seen. There were some bits of jewellery, a couple of handbags, as well as a journal. It had birds of paradise on the cover, and inside, a lot of doodles in red and black, dark, intense drawings very unlike anything I had ever seen my sister do in all the years I had known her. In the past her drawings had been of trees, close studies of plants and flowers, animals, sunny landscapes, or birds in flight. Aside from the doodles, there were snatches of poetry that Claire had copied out in her still somewhat childish handwriting. Most of these I did not recognise, Claire had been the English literature buff not me. But they all reflected the mood of the drawings, maudlin reflections on grief and death. I found no comfort in it. So, I tried to bury my sense of loss and grief in the work I took so little real pleasure in, as well as a series of relationships with men I really only valued for the physical comfort I could derive from their temporary presence. Dad's early onset dementia began with little things - mislaying items, forgetting words, or getting lost in the middle of sentences. The disease then progressed through various stages until his personality – all that made him uniquely himself, had deserted him. Aggression set in, he struck me several times, once over the head with a tray so that I needed several stitches. And when it was no longer feasible for him to remain at home, I found a decent nursing home where he could be as comfortable as possible and well cared for by others. Even so, I often found myself thinking that Claire would have cared for him herself, right to the end. A great deal of my life since my sister's death had been punctuated by similar thoughts - what Claire would or would not have done in any given situation. By the time he died, a beautiful May morning in 2016, I felt I had already done a great deal of my grieving for him while he was still alive – at least for the person he had been before the disease robbed him of that. Or perhaps I was just all grieved out.

*

I found the envelope while I was going through his things one day. It was at the bottom of an old suitcase, one he used for his record collection. It was wrapped in a pink and navy paisley scarf I had not known he possessed. It wasn't at all his style and more like something a woman would wear. I unwrapped the scarf and there was the envelope, a brown, perfectly ordinary A4 envelope, seal intact, my name in capitals on the front. There was nothing to warn me it contained the power to alter my life irrevocably. At first, I thought it was something Dad had intended giving me, but in a confused moment, had put inside the suitcase and forgotten about. He had once posted a packet of fishfingers instead of the dental mould he had intended wrapping. As a result, I was half afraid to open the envelope, but when I did, I discovered it contained just two more envelopes. The smaller of the two had words written across it, again in block capitals – ***TO BE READ FIRST****.*

Intrigued, I tore it open, pulled out the single sheet of unlined writing paper and read the closely written letter. Turns out nothing can prepare you for your sister's suicide note. Even now it is impossible to put into words what I was feeling after I had read what Claire had written to me. I suspect I was almost numb when I finally picked up the second, bigger envelope. This contained some typed sheets of paper which had been stapled together at one corner. I began to read.

***

My name is Claire Sarah Fox. I was raped by Lorcan O'Keeffe. It happened beside the lake near Roundwood, County Wicklow on the night of Saturday the 13th of April 1996. I was tricked into going there by Jennifer O'Keeffe, Nicole Brady and Bethany Doyle. Megan McGrath was supposed to come but she had cramps and stayed in the dorm at the hostel. Jennifer told me that the boys from St Malachy's were having a midnight barbeque and were expecting us to be there. But when we got to the lake, there was no one there. The girls had drink. I didn't want any, but I took some anyway and threw some away when nobody was looking. Then Jennifer said we should all go for a swim until the boys came. She took off her clothes down to her underwear and all the others did the same. I said I didn't really feel like swimming, but Jennifer looked at me and said - did I not want to bury the hatchet? I did not want to cause trouble for anyone, so I took off my clothes and went swimming in my bra and pants. I had never been swimming by moonlight before and I liked it, even though the water was very cold. The girls were laughing and splashing and squealing, so I swam away from them and out into the middle of the lake where I just floated and looked at the stars. I didn't notice that the others had got out of the water until I started to swim back to the shore. I couldn't see them anywhere, but I saw a boy walking out from between the trees and toward the lake. I thought the St Malachy lads had arrived, so I swam faster because I didn't want them to see me in my underwear. I got to the shore before the boy, but my clothes were not where I had left them. The boy came nearer, and I recognised him, he was Lorcan O'Keeffe, Jennifer's brother. I heard someone laughing from the direction of the trees and I thought the girls were playing a trick on me and had hidden my clothes. I shouted at them to bring my clothes back, but nobody came. I began running toward the trees, but Lorcan grabbed my arm as I passed him and pulled me down onto the stones of the beach. I tried to get up, but he held me down. I screamed at the girls to help me and Lorcan slapped me across my face. He said, "Shut up, bitch or I'll fucking kill you." Then he raped me.

When it stopped, I tried to get up. He said "Where do you think you're going? I haven't finished with you yet, Foxy Anna."

I told him I wasn't Anna, that I was Claire. But he just laughed and said, "Nice try."

I screamed at him that I really was Claire, Anna's twin sister. I told him we had swapped places so Anna could go see her boyfriend's band. He stopped laughing and stared at me and then he let me go. I jumped up and ran into the trees. And then I ran until I got to the hostel. I climbed in through the broken window we had used to sneak out. I ran to the shower room, and I saw myself in the mirror. I thought I was somebody else. I wished I was too. My face was scratched, my pants were torn, and my bra was hanging off. I couldn't stop shivering. I pulled off my underwear and threw them in the bin and got under one of the showers. The water was only tepid, but I stayed there for a long time, then I wrapped myself in two towels and lay down on the bench against the wall and curled myself up into a ball. When it was light, I got up and crept back to the dorm. The air smelled of drink and everybody was asleep. I put on pyjamas and got into the bed, but I still could not stop shivering. I don't remember if I slept. When the others woke, I lay with my back to them and pretended I was asleep. A teacher came in and told Jennifer her father was on the phone. She said, "Come on Anna, let's be having you!"

I pretended to get up but kept my face to the wall and when she had gone, I lay down again. Someone said, "Are you OK, Anna?"

I knew it was Bethany. I didn't answer. When everyone went down to breakfast, I got up. I put on jeans and a jumper so all people could see were the scratches on my face, and not the bruises on my legs and arms. Someone said, "What do you think you're playing at Anna?"

It was Jennifer. I kept my back to her. She said, "Look at me, I'm talking to you, Anna Fox. Just what kind of dirty trick are you trying to pull on my brother?"

I knew she knew then, and I turned to face her. I said, "I'm not Anna, I'm Claire. Your brother raped me. Did he tell you that?"

She said, "You lying little slut."

I didn't wait for more, I ran past her and down the stairs and outside. I hid until the coach came. When the teachers wanted to know what had happened to my face, I said I slipped and fell. I had to go inside to get my stuff and I was packing it away when someone said my name. "Claire?" I spun round and Jennifer was there with Bethany and Nicole.

Bethany said, "It's true. She really is Claire."

Nicole said, "So what just what the hell do you think you're playing at?"

Jennifer said, "I don't give a toss which one you are, but you better listen to me. If you or your slut sister breathe so much as one bad word about my brother, your life is going to be one big crock of shit from now on. Do you understand me, you lying little bitch?"

A teacher came in then and told us off for keeping everyone waiting. I pushed past the girls and ran downstairs.

It was ten weeks before I did a pregnancy test. I already knew what the result would be. I carried on as normal after that, except that every night I went to bed and prayed that I would not wake up the next day. Then I began to think of ways to make it die. I thought of it as a thing, not a baby. I tried in all sorts of ways to make that happen. None of them worked. I wanted to tell someone, but there was no one. David was gone. I told him I didn't like him anymore. That was a lie. I could not tell my mother because my mother was dying. I could not tell my father because my mother was dying. I could not tell my sister, because I could not tell my sister. I don't know why I decided to tell Bethany, except that I remembered her asking me if I was OK that morning in the hostel dormitory. I waited until I caught her alone. She went white when I told her. She said, "Pregnant? I don't believe you. You can't be. And even if you were, why tell me? It's got nothing to do with me?"

I said, "You were there. You were one of them. You tricked me and you stole my clothes, and you left me there alone with him and he raped me. And I don't know what to do now. Please, will you help me, Bethany?"

Bethany said she had to go, but she'd meet me the next day after school, behind the PE Hall. But she brought Jennifer and Nicole. Jennifer called me a liar and a tramp. She said there was no baby. And if there was a baby it had nothing to do with Lorcan and I was wasting my time trying to trick him into giving me money. I said I didn't want money, I just needed someone to help me, because I didn't know what to do.

She said, "Don't make me laugh. You know exactly what you're doing, just like your lying tart of a sister. Everyone already knows she's a liar. Her name is dirt and so will yours be if you start spreading your lies."

I didn't know what she was talking about. I said I hadn't told my sister anything. They looked at one another and Jennifer said that if I had any sense, I would keep it that way. Then I knew that they would never help me, so I just walked away.

I thought about getting on a boat and going to England. But I didn't know what I was supposed to do when I got off at the other side. And I had no money. I met Bethany in the toilet at school and she stared at my stomach. She said, "So…?"

I told her I had made a mistake, there was no baby. She must have told the others because when I passed Jennifer and Nicole in the corridor, Jennifer called me a sick, twisted, lying little bitch. I was only just gone seven months pregnant, when I went into labour. It didn't matter, I already had a plan and the things I thought I would need packed in my gym bag at the back of the wardrobe. A torch, two candles with two saucers to stand them in, two big towels, old ones in case they were missed, my mother's sewing scissors and a plastic bag. I left it as long as possible after the pains began, to leave the house. It was after eight o'clock and it was November. It was very cold. There were no lights on the road, but I had the torch. The Old Mill was half a mile outside the town, I knew teenagers used it when they mitched off school and for drinking in on summer nights, but on a cold winter night I thought I would be safe. All the windows were boarded up, but I knew I could get in through the back door which was hanging off its hinges. I had already decided on the room I would use. It was the only one where the ceiling didn't look like it might cave in at any second. The floor was littered with cans, bottles, cigarette ends and food wrappers. I cleared a space and lit the candles. I spread my towel on the floor and that was where I gave birth to my baby. It was all over faster than I expected, but it hurt so much that I cried all the time, but I only screamed out loud once.

My baby, a tiny girl, gave one cry as she was born and another cry when I wrapped her in the second towel and put her in the plastic bag. I thought it would protect her from the cold ground. After that she was quiet, and I wondered if she were dead. I couldn't make up my mind whether it was better that she was or not. I was weak and feverish and just wanted it all to be over. I knew where I would leave her, in the porch of Mrs Farrell's house. She was the Parish Priest's housekeeper. I imagined she would know what to do. I walked to her house, and I thought my legs would go from under me. The baby made no sound at all. I laid her on the floor of the roofed porch, then I walked away and left her there. I was almost certain she was dead. Part of me wanted to stop and look in the bag to see for sure, but the biggest part of me just wanted to get rid of her, then go home and sleep or die. I really didn't care which. Afterwards, I really did believe that I was dying. My body was racked with pain and sweat poured from me in little streams. I stayed in bed all of the next day and the one after. I could hardly stand up, even to make my way to the bathroom. There was blood and stuff coming out of me and Anna heard me crying. I had to shout to her through the door that I was having a really bad period. On the third day I began to feel a little better and realised that I was not going to die after all. So, then I waited for them to come for me. I already knew from the TV in my bedroom that they had found her the morning after I left her. They said she had been born alive but had died of hypothermia. They said the police were anxious to trace the mother, who would be in need of medical assistance. They said she had nothing to fear in coming forward and would be treated with compassion. I did not believe that. I had committed murder and would spend my life in prison. I was terrified but at the same time a part of me wanted them to come for me, so I could get the waiting part over with. But they didn't come. I heard they buried her in a communal grave for unknown babies, with no name, but the one the police gave her. I couldn't stop thinking about her then. I wanted so badly to go and find the place where they buried her, but I was afraid they were waiting there and watching for me and so I never did go. All of this happened a long time ago, but I have thought about her every day since. I think about her dying in the dark and the cold and I wonder if anyone ever brings her flowers. I think that I have been dying every day since and that is long enough to die.

Signed: Claire Fox Dated: 10th June 2002

***

I understood so many things now. The changes in Claire, her breaking up with David, leaving school, London. I understood why Jennifer & Co behaved as they did toward me on my return to school, after the Wicklow trip. They knew what Lorcan had done to Claire and clearly expected her to have told me about it too. All of these things clicked together in my brain as I laid down my sister's testimony, but only in the way of a muted soundtrack to the real action, which was the agony, the guilt, the rage I was experiencing. Alongside all of this were the questions still to be answered – why had my father lied about my sister's death? Why had he chosen to withhold her final message to me? And having made the decision to withhold it from me, why hadn't he destroyed it? Had there also been a note to him? It seemed from Claire's letter that there had, and distraught as I was, I began feverishly searching among his papers. There was no note, instead I discovered an envelope containing an authorisation to remove Claire's body from the UK along with a copy of Claire's death certificate and, tucked in with it, a copy of the post-mortem result setting out in detail the manner of my sister's suicide.

*

I think it is fair to say that I was sick in mind and body in the weeks that followed my discovery. I cried off work citing flu and pushed as many of my patients as I could onto a locum. Then I shut myself up and gave myself over to suffering. I wanted to suffer, I wanted to punish myself in any way I could. I began obsessively googling the subject of suicide by hanging, reading and re-reading every horror-filled piece. I learned that hanging was often chosen in the erroneous belief that it promised a quick, almost painless death. That and the idea that it was easy – 'simple' was the word used, as well as 'clean' – meaning that people considering suicide believed that hanging themselves meant there would be little damage to the body and therefore no harrowing images for those discovering it. No harrowing images! I tormented myself repeatedly with imagining Claire hanging in that wardrobe. I forced myself to think about her last minutes - or had it been hours – from the moment the rope had tightened about her neck to the moment darkness closed over her. I relived that time in mind, over and over again, refusing to shy away from the questions my reading had raised. Did the tightening rope burn the skin of her neck? Did her diaphragm ache from the futile attempt to draw in oxygen? Did she change her mind after it was too late to do anything about it, and thrash about uselessly trying to take in air? I read graphic accounts of people who, having changed their minds at the last minute, had clawed at the cord cutting into their flesh, to no avail, I knew I was driving myself to the edge of sanity, but I knew too that I could not spare myself a single horror, so I read and re-read until thoughts and images of my sister's violent and lonely death possessed me and I almost collapsed beneath the weight of grief and rage and guilt. I wanted to howl out that grief and rage, but I would not allow myself the luxury or relief of tears. I think it was because, even then, on some level I knew I needed to keep all that rage and fury stored up inside of me. I think I knew I would need it. I think that even then, with no clear idea of how, I knew I would use it to avenge my sister.

*

Timing is everything – a cliché I know, but as someone said, clichés are clichés for a reason, and the fact is that if things had not happened exactly as and when they did, I might not be writing this now. As it was, I could almost argue that a confluence of events – a perfect storm indeed, made me a murderer. The first element was Lorcan O'Keeffe being acquitted of raping that girl, Orla Reid. That was back in July, and I did wonder if that red-haired detective would remember having seen me at the trial. I saw her. I sat through quite a lot of it, though I stayed well clear of what I thought of as Lorcan's entourage. I remember Rachel telling me once that she had spotted me there. I could tell she was surprised, then she told me it would mean a lot to Jennifer. The words were no sooner out of her mouth when I saw realisation dawn in Rachel's eyes – of course I wasn't there for Jennifer, and certainly not for Lorcan. I was there to see Orla Reid, that big-eyed, frail-seeming little girl get justice. Only of course she didn't.

The second element was Paul Dempsey walking into my surgery with an abscessed molar. He wasn't a patient but had rung earlier in the hope of an appointment. He was in pain, and I'd had a cancellation, so I fitted him in. He recognised me from the courtroom, he told me. He'd assumed I had been part of Lorcan's entourage. I put him right on that front and that was when he told me he was Orla Reid's uncle, her dead father's younger brother. Needless to say, he considered Lorcan O'Keeffe the scum of the earth - sentiments with which I fully agreed. I forgot all about the encounter, until three months later, when I found Claire's suicide note, that's when I had the idea of approaching Paul Dempsey and attempting to persuade him to help me. I believe that had he turned me down, I'd have found a way to do it all myself, but I could see that it would make things a lot easier if I had an accomplice, particular in regard to what I had in mind for Lorcan O'Keeffe. I also knew of course, that by involving another person, I ran some risk, the worst of which was that they could decide to turn me in to the guards. But as it turned out, I needn't have worried, the idea of helping to mete out a form of justice to his niece's rapist came as music to Paul's ears. I told him about Claire, of course, and the news that she had not been Lorcan's first victim only whetted Paul's appetite for the business. I have to admit that I was not entirely frank about the extent of my intentions, however. Paul did not know how Claire had died, nor did he know that anyone else was to die. As far as he was concerned, the plan was that Lorcan would be picked up, held somewhere for a couple of nights, ideally frightened out of his wits and ultimately coerced (Paul actually stipulated that a good kicking should come into the business) into confessing to his crimes, both against my sister and, more pertinently for Paul, against Orla, before being released.

*

When it came to the women, all Paul knew was that there were people I believed were implicated in what had happened to my sister, who, like Lorcan, were to be taught a lesson, to which end, I would be calling on him for help with some practicalities in making that happen. I provided him with a pre-paid SIM only phone for use when he needed to contact me, and I bought a second one for my own use. The third and final element of the storm, was seeing that Class of '98 photo on Facebook, a photo which included me, Jennifer, Nicole, Rachel, Bethany and Megan. Liz tagged me in the post, but I didn't see it until about a week after finding Claire's suicide note and testimonial. By then I was already contemplating how I might set about killing Lorcan, but seeing those three faces - Jennifer, Nicole, and Bethany - I had not yet made up my mind about the level of Megan's culpability – I knew with certainty that they too must die. I held all three responsible for Claire's suffering and eventual death. They had been complicit in her rape, as they would have been had it really been me on that lakeshore that night. They had let it happen, for all I knew, they had watched it happen. And afterward, they had turned their backs on her when she went to them, pregnant, terrified, and alone and asked for help. I did not believe that they had swallowed Claire's story of there never having been a baby. And at the very least, when an abandoned baby was found in our own town, they must have had some sort of suspicion that Claire might have been involved. If they had come forward, any one of them, even anonymously and so at no cost to themselves, then Claire could have been identified as the mother. And who could say that if she had gotten the care she needed, then things might have ended differently? And if I could not change the ending, I could at least try to balance the scales – all four must die. But let me be clear about one thing, the moment I made the decision to allow myself to play judge and jury with Lorcan and the others, I accepted that I too must be judged. My sister was a gentle child, and it was I who had put her in the way of monsters – if the others were to pay the ultimate price, then, once having meted out punishment to them, I would too. That was the deal I struck with myself. The idea of sending defaced copies of the school photo came to me, I will confess, when I was deeply under the influence of wine. I had printed off just one copy of the photo and found a sort of savage relief in scratching out their face one-by-one. First Jennifer, then Nicole, then Bethany, I hesitated over Megan, but in the end, I had a go at her image too. Looking at my handiwork I thought how gratifying it would be to send them each a copy, at which point I printed off six more copies, this time scratching out just one face in each. I was thinking ahead by now, considering such things as covering up my tracks – if I was going to post the photos, then I'd post them to all six of us, Rachel and I included. Killing four people, possibly five, would take some time, I imagined; I had no intention of having my work cut short by the police, before I had finished my task to my absolute satisfaction. For that reason, I already knew the deaths of the women would need to appear at least plausibly accidental.

*

I set to work finding addresses for the five women and posted the photos. I was careful to wear a pair of surgical gloves each time I handled both the photos and the envelopes. As I dropped them in a post-box, I remember thinking with satisfaction that things were now in motion. The photos, although they might well not realise it, were my way of saying to Jennifer, Nicole and Bethany that from here on out, they would do well to look over their shoulders. But the truth is when I thought about killing them - Jennifer, Nicole, Bethany, possibly Megan, I had no clear idea of how I would do it. I quite simply wanted their lives to be taken from them, as Claire's has been taken from her. With Lorcan it was quite different. I admit I thought about castrating him, of stabbing him through both eyes with the heel of my stiletto. But when I thought about him dying, there was only one scenario that came close to befitting his crime against my innocent, gentle sister. I had begun following him, I already knew where he worked, and it was easy to discover where he and Paula lived. It didn't take long to discover that he was playing around behind her back. I saw him with a stunning looking brunette, much younger than himself, as well as Paula. I followed him to a discreet little wine bar and watched from a distance as he plied her with drink and pawed her; I was not so far away that I could not hear his braying laugh ringing out like a mockery of my dead sister.

*

So, the plan was Nicole, Bethany, Jennifer, although not necessarily in that order. How they died was actually immaterial to me; I have no real taste for bloodletting. Forget that good twin/bad twin. That's the stuff of Hollywood; I am not actually a monster. No, the plan was to strike how and when it made most sense. But for that, I needed to learn something about their schedules, which was where Rachel came in. Unlike the rest of the A Team members, I had remained on friendly terms with Rachel, though I saw less and less of her over the years, especially after she got married and had three kids in quick succession. I needed to remedy that and began calling her more, suggested we meet and catch up properly. Through her I found out about something of the lives of the other women, as well as Lorcan. I knew for instance that Paula and Lorcan had no kids and were on their third cycle of fertility treatment. I knew that Jennifer was well on the way to turning into an alco, after her marriage break-up, that Nicole had been on the verge of getting married when the guy dumped her, and that Megan was still living at home with her mother. More importantly I learned something of their routines, which was how I ended up joining the yoga class Nicola attended on a weekly basis. The thought of cosying up to her made me want to vomit, and I was fairly sure she wouldn't be overjoyed to spend much time in my company either. Certainly, around the time of the school trip to Wicklow, Nicole had resented me, possibly even hated my guts, most on account of Lorcan O'Keeffe. But as it turned out, I was quite pleasantly surprised at how amenable she was to meeting up for coffee when I suggested it. But as I reminded myself, a lot of water had passed under the bridge and Nicole had always loved to be liked, expected to be adored, so why should my seeming desire to renew our long-abandoned friendship strike her as anything other than perfectly natural?

*

Killing Nicole was actually surprisingly easy. I knew she'd be running on the Hill of Howth that day. I knew the place she would stop to catch her breath. All I had to do was be there, waiting, then slip up behind her and.... sometimes I wonder whether, had she turned around at the psychological moment, so that we were face-to-face, it would have been so easy. But she didn't turn around, and with one single push, I had become a murderer. They say it is easier once you have done it once; murder, I mean. But actually, I did not find that to be the case. Firstly, I liked Bethany a lot more than I did Nicole. Secondly, I didn't have to use my own two hands to kill her. One might be forgiven for thinking that would have made it easier, but that wasn't the case either. The car did the hard work for me, but there was that sound as it hit her; sickening, then she was tossed into the air, and I half expected her to land on the roof. But she must have fallen to one side, because when I looked for her in the rear-view mirror, I could see a mound in the road. Driving away I kept wondering if she was dead or alive. I also found myself reflecting that, had she been an animal I had accidently struck, I'd have gone back to check, and, if necessary, put out of its misery. Except of course this hadn't been an accident; I wanted Bethany dead. And the truth is I never once wavered in my resolve to kill any one of them. If I found myself beginning to, all that was needed was to visualise my sister in that wardrobe in the throes of her final agony. I found that did the trick. I did have a bad moment all the same, when it turned out that poor Liz Wade had a car the same colour and model as the one I used to kill Bethany. Paul was a mechanic by trade, and it was through his contacts in the motor industry – by which I mean, some dodgy dealer he put me in touch with, that I got hold of the car. I would later drive it to a field, pour a can of petrol over it and set it alight. I had not foreseen that Liz would be a suspect, but fortunately she had an alibi for the times both Nicole and Bethany died. And I think I should point out that I did play fair, well as much as one can play fair when setting about killing a bunch of people. But I did try to ensure that the innocent would not be implicated in any of my crimes. Which is why I made sure to wait until I knew Nicole's boyfriend was away on business, that sort of thing. It was also Paul who scouted out the lock-up we would use to hold Lorcan. This was a barn in the middle of a farmyard, both yard and farmhouse had been vacant for years and were tucked away at the end of a laneway somewhere outside Garristown. The idea of making it appear an attempt had been made on my own life, only came about after that red-headed detective began making me nervous. I had not expected Rachel to pipe up about Claire like that, the focus was supposed to stay firmly on the A Team.

*

She's sharp, DS Bassett, I actually quite like her, under different circumstances I'd probably be happy to go for a drink with her. And if I did, one of the first things I'd do would be to tell her she's barking up the wrong tree with that partner of hers, the one that looks like Che Guevara. But as it was, I didn't want her making any links to Claire, and then I caught her studying the framed photograph of Claire that I'd stupidly left in plain view. And she saw me seeing her. That was when I cobbled together the idea of making it look like someone had tried to run my car off the road and into the sea. It needed to happen late at night when there was likely to be no one about, and as I'd signed up months earlier for the conference in Belfast, I had the perfect excuse for having been driving home in the small hours. In case they checked, I did actually drive up to Belfast, where I registered and showed my face at a drinks reception before driving back to Dublin again. And the weather played into my hands too. It was a filthy night, which made it even less likely we'd be seen staging the attack. It had been important to choose a stretch of road where there was no CCTV coverage, and where it would make it seem that the intention had really been to kill me. It was also important that nobody happened along at the crucial moment, nobody that is, but Ant Fitzpatrick.

*

That was a mistake of course, Paul's involving someone with a criminal record. And I should have known, I thought Ant looked like a thug the first time I set eyes on him. But Paul argued that he needed someone to help him with the actual abduction of Lorcan and saw Ant as the perfect fit for the job. Admittedly the guy did have a certain set of skills – it was Ant who identified the location of the blind spots in the car park Lorcan used, while he was at the gym. And I admit I quite warmed to him after Paul told me with what enthusiasm Ant 'coshed' Lorcan and manhandled him into the back of the van that day. Paul was already in the van of course, waiting with rope and duct tape. The van in question was Ant's payment for his part in the abduction. Paul wanted no reward for the satisfaction of seeing his niece vindicated, but Ant with no personal investment in the affair, needed actual remuneration. Owning his own van was, according to Paul, the pinnacle of Ant's aspirations in life and I was happy enough to cough up the price, in cash of course. How was I to know the idiot would drive it about untaxed and uninsured. Still, he came in useful in helping stage the attempt on my own life.

As I said, the weather was in our favour, meaning we had the road to ourselves long enough for Paul to do the necessary damage to my car. He said it needed to look authentic, so I had to get out and shelter beneath a golf umbrella while he rammed it from behind and on the driver's side, using a near written off car he'd chosen for the purpose. When he was satisfied, Paul climbed into the driver's seat of my car, and I watched as he sent it veering off the road and up onto the grass bank before disappearing out of sight. Afterwards, when they came to interview me, the red-haired detective and Che Guevara, I didn't have to fake my reluctance to relive the supposed events of the previous night. The truth was I had been genuinely afraid that the car would not stop where Paul so confidently predicted it would, safely shy of the edge, but plunge to the rocks and sea below, with Paul trapped inside. I had a bad moment as I climbed the bank afterwards and felt an enormous sense of relief when I saw that Paul had been right and the car had stopped pretty much where he had expected and that he was unharmed. All that was needed then was for us to switch places, Paul to double back the way he had come and for me to sit behind the wheel and wait until our 'witness' came along. Ant had driven toward us from the other direction, it was important that CCTV footage pick him up at a couple of spots along the road to make everything look authentic. Arrived at the staging point, he was to stop, get out and flag down the next car that came along. He would then lead whoever it was, to my car, telling them I was hysterical and refusing to open the door for him. As it turned out, the first car to stop held the perfect witnesses, a couple on their way back from a wedding, elderly, respectable, credible. Of course, I played it up for their benefit, putting on a show of hysteria when Ant appeared with them in his wake. I only shut up when he backed away and the woman, her name was Marie, took his place at the driver's window. I then allowed myself to be coaxed into getting out of the car, at which point Marie put her arms about me and held me, telling me that it was all alright and I was safe now. I can still remember the feel of her soft woollen coat, wet now from the rain, as well as a curious sense of comfort in the soft scented plumpness of her. It was only later that I realised she had been wearing the same perfume my mother wore, Estee Lauder's Youth Dew.

*

And so, to Jennifer. Somehow, I had been sure I would enjoy killing Jennifer, but it wasn't at all the way I had imagined. The idea for how to do it, came to me the day we went back to her place after our visit to Bethany's wife and I discovered that Jennifer was in the habit of drinking in the hot tub in her back garden late at night; the perfect scenario for another 'accident'. I did a practice run by taking Jennifer up on her invitation to come use the hot tub, that way I was able to suss out just how pissed Jennifer actually got. Very pissed as it turned out. So much so, I considered doing it there and then, but I resisted the temptation. But I did take the opportunity to check the door in the rear garden wall. It was bolted on the inside, but I soon changed that. There was always the risk Jennifer would discover it was unlocked, but I doubted it. It was clear from the stiffness of the bolts that they hadn't been opened in a long time, and somehow, I couldn't quite see Jennifer checking on them. I also made sure that Rachel knew I had been round to Jennifer's, that way, should any traces be found in or around the tub, they'd be accounted for. And once again, in the interests of playing fair, I made sure to choose a time for the actual killing, when Jennifer's kids and ex-husband were safely out of the country. It was important not to be seen approaching the house that night, so I'd scouted out the lane that ran behind it.

The night of 6th March was a bitterly cold one, but I was well wrapped against it. Over black running trousers, top and jacket, I was wearing a cheap padded and hooded parka, baggy tracksuit bottoms, a pair of gloves and a pair of black trainers. I made my way along the laneway behind Jennifer's home, and tried the door in the rear wall, it was unlocked. I let myself in and made my way through the garden toward the house. Jennifer was expecting me, I had left it until that afternoon to call and ask if I could come over. I impressed upon her that I needed to talk to her urgently and in confidence. I didn't expressly say it, but I implied that I was referring to what had happened to Nicole and Bethany. I was pleasantly surprised when she immediately agreed, then again let's face it, she was fast running out of friends, living ones at least. Anyway, she not only agreed, but suggested I bring a swimsuit so we could do our chatting in the hot tub. I passed it on the way to the house, the hot tub, it was bubbling and steaming in readiness for us. I continued to the patio, then made my way round to the front door. I rang the bell, pulling off my gloves and stuffing them into my pockets. Jennifer answered the door in a short white bathrobe and her sequinned flipflops. Her hair was loose about her shoulders, and her face was flushed; even without the glass in her hand, it would have been obvious she'd already been drinking. She looked me up and down, raised her eyebrows. "I just hope you have your bikini on underneath that lot?"

That was actually the most difficult part of the entire thing, resisting Jennifer's attempts to get me into the hot tub. I told her I was feeling a bit under the weather and thought I might be coming down with a flu bug or something, but I might get in later after I'd had a few drinks to warm me up. I sat down next to the tub and watched as she untied her robe and let it drop, revealing a white bikini. She slid her feet out of her flipflops and climbed into the frothing, steaming water, sinking down so that it covered her thin, tanned body all the way up to her chin. She stretched out a hand and picked up the glass of champagne she'd left on the edge of the tub.

"Cheers" she said, and we chinked glasses.

I sipped mine, while Jennifer drained her glass and reached out for the bottle which was resting along with a second unopened one in a bucket of ice, she'd left within reaching distance. While she was doing that, I discreetly tipped out my champagne and was ready with my empty glass when she pressed a refill on me. "I feel like getting hammered," she said.

It was obvious she was already halfway to hammered. She began singing along to the song blaring through the open conservatory doors - Ed Sheeran's Castle on the Hill, then stopped suddenly. "All men are shits!" she slurred. "All men, absolutely ALL men are shits. Am I right or am I wrong, Anna?"

I was thinking about her brother as I replied, "I think you might be right, Jennifer."

She laughed uproariously and there was another clinking of glasses. Once again, she drained her glass and had another shot at enticing me into the hot tub. I resisted but allowed her to refill my glass. Jennifer leaned back, resting her head against the padded edge of the tub. She closed her eyes and began humming to herself. If she remembered the reason I was supposed to be there, she was in no hurry to bring it up. In the end it was I who mentioned what had happened to Nicole and Bethany. Jennifer's eyes opened and suddenly she began to cry, tears trickling down her face. Weak, maudlin drunken tears. And in that moment, I was so enraged I had to resist the urge to grab her by her scrawny neck and strangle her to death. Instead, I drained my glass. In the time it took to do that, Jennifer's eyes had closed once more, her head lolled to one side and her chin was in the water; she was asleep. It was not the way I had imagined it would be. Somehow, with Jennifer, I had imagined that there would be a moment - a moment when I would speak my sister's name aloud. A moment when she would see in my eyes that I knew, and in that moment realisation would dawn. Jennifer would know what I had done, know what I was about to do. Instead, she had evaded me, slipped away into drunken sleep. And because time was against me now, I knew I would not get another opportunity. It was now or never. And it was all so easy then. I pulled the gloves from my pocket, put them on, went and knelt behind her, placed both hands lightly on her head and pushed. Jennifer slid under the warm water. She didn't even struggle as I held her there.

Afterwards, I picked up my glass and walked away. I left the way I had come, through the door in the rear garden wall. As I made my way to my car, I dropped the glass into a bin. Then piece by piece, I shed my outer garments in bins along the route. The trainers I disposed of last, in a clothes bank halfway between Jennifer's home and my own. Later, after I had showered and was lying on my bed, I wondered how it was that of all of them, killing Jennifer had left me feeling no better, had in fact left me feeling nothing at all.

***

CHAPTER 43

Saturday 11th March

"You don't really think she's gone back there?" said JP, as the car sped toward Anna Fox's apartment complex.

"Not a chance," Tina's tone was grim.

"But you obviously expect to find something there, else why would you have asked Coleman to have the Super declare it a crime scene?"

"If we do find something there, it will be because she wants us to. Let's face it, Anna Fox has been three steps ahead of us all along."

They had done what they could. A photo of Anna had been released to the media as a person being sought by the Gardai. An arrest warrant had also been issued for her arrest. But Tina could not shake the feeling that it was all too little too late.

*

Backup had got there minutes before them and had already gained access to the block that housed Anna's apartment and were awaiting further instructions. Expecting no response, Tina nevertheless rang the bell to Anna's apartment before calling out to identify herself and JP and stating their intention to gain entry. This was met with the expected silence and the door remained firmly shut. Tina gave the nod and she and JP stood to one side while the door was forced. Inside, all was as pristine as before.

While JP made a search of the apartment, Tina stood a moment in the doorway of the living room where they had twice interviewed Anna.

Her gaze fell on the dresser next to the French windows, the silver framed photograph was back in place. Tina walked across and picked it up, her gaze taking in the wide, smiling eyes of a young girl with her hair in plaits. She picked up the envelope on which the frame had been resting, and read her own name, which had been written in bold capitals. She replaced the photograph and carried the envelope across to the big cream sofa, where she settled herself. Sliding a finger beneath the flap, she ripped the envelope open and drew out two more envelopes. The larger of the two had written across it, again in bold capitals, the words - **TO BE READ FIRST**

Laying the smaller envelope on the sofa armrest, she tore the other open. JP appeared in the doorway. "Needless to say, she's not here," he told her.

Tina gestured to him silently and he came and sat down sit next to her. Tina drew out the contents of the envelope, some typed sheets of A4 paper stapled together at one corner. Unfolding the sheets, she began to read.

My name is Claire Sarah Fox, and I was raped by Lorcan O'Keeffe...

When she had finished, without a word, Tina passed the sheets to JP. While he read, she picked up the smaller envelope, opened it and drew out a single sheet. It was, she saw, a photocopy of a handwritten note, the letters large and rounded and curiously childlike. Once again, she began to read,

Dear Anna,

Knowing you the way I do, I am sure that right now you are probably feeling very angry with me. You won't understand what I have done or why, and you will probably find it hard to forgive me. That is one of the reasons I have written down everything that happened - in the hope that, knowing it all will mean that in time, you might be able to forgive me after all. But before I say more, all of this is for your eyes only, Anna. Dad can never know any of this, it would destroy him, I think. Already, the letter I have left for him will have caused him pain enough. But at least he can tell himself it was my depression that made me so unhappy I could not go on living in this world. And after all, that is really not such a lie. But for you Anna, I have written the whole truth, knowing as I did it, that the truth would hurt you greatly. But please don't think I did it for that reason - to hurt or to punish you. You have to believe me, Anna - I never blamed you. Never. But there is a reason why I have to tell you these things. It is a selfish reason, and if there was anyone else in the world, I could ask... but there is only you, Anna. So, the reason - there is a favour I need to ask of you. Please will you plant flowers on her grave for me? I never did, you see. First because I was too afraid, and then because I was too ashamed, and later because, well it was too late, and I knew I could never go back. So please will you do it for me, Anna? Yellow flowers, not white. I know people say white for innocence, but I have always thought that white is so cold. No, yellow flowers for her – warm, bright, beautiful yellow flowers. And when you have done that, will you talk to her for me? Tell her I never lived a day without thinking of her. Ask her to forgive me. As I hope you can too, my darling sister.

With all my love, Claire xx

Tina got up and without a word, dropped the letter into JP's lap. She crossed to the French windows, fumbled with the lock, then stepped outside. The deck was dotted with stone urns planted with daffodils, narcissi, and red tulips. The brazen colours of the petals, their natural sheen accentuated by the spring sunshine brought Tina's thoughts back to Glasnevin cemetery and the masses of freshly planted yellow flowers on the plot of ground where Claire's baby lay. Turning her back on the flowers and the memory, she watched through the open window as JP slowly laid down the typed sheets and picked up the suicide note. She saw the set of his jaw as he read and when he had finished, met his eyes, which had narrowed in pain.

"Jesus Christ," he said. "That poor little girl."

Tina said nothing. Lowering herself onto a wrought iron garden chair, she rested her forearms on her thighs and dropped her gaze to the stained wood of the deck. She glanced up as JP came out, the note still in his hand.

"So, it was Anna all along, then," he said. "But why...?"

"You just read why; she held them all responsible for what happened to Claire..."

"I didn't mean why did she do it, I meant why now? Why after all this time?"

"I don't think she knew until quite recently," said Tina. "You saw what Claire wrote - she left a separate suicide note for her father. I'm guessing he found both notes but kept the one intended for Anna from her. I suppose he thought he was sparing her, by letting her believe Claire died in an accident."

"You think so?" JP shook his head.

"I do," Tina met his gaze. "There's something I haven't told you. I visited the grave where the little girl was buried, the Roches Stores baby?"

"OK?"

"It's in the Angel's Plot in Glasnevin Cemetery. There are a lot of communal graves there, for babies, you know? "

JP nodded, "I've heard, but I've never seen them."

"Well anyway, there's about thirty or so babies buried in each grave. I found the one where they buried her – Grace – you remember that was the name the investigating guards gave her? Well, that one particular grave had a load of flowers, very obviously freshly planted flowers I mean. None of the other communal graves had anything like it. They were yellow flowers, heaps and heaps of yellow flowers."

JP's eyes went to the note in his hand. "That's what Claire asked Anna to do, plant yellow flowers on her baby's grave."

"I know. It had to have been Anna who planted them. Which must mean she'd only recently read Claire's suicide note. Don't you think so?"

"I suppose so," JP frowned. "But what I don't get is why their father didn't destroy the letter. I mean why keep it from Anna all these years, then leave it lying around where there was the risk that she might find it?"

Tina shook her head, "I don't know. But remember, Anna's father died from dementia. Rachel told us so."

"You think he just forgot about the note then, is that what you mean?"

"I think it's a possibility. Chances are he held onto it at first because he didn't like the idea of destroying it, and then well, dementia and all that. Look who knows, this is all just guess work."

JP was staring at the note in his hand again. "But why did Anna leave this for you? I mean it's as good as pointing the finger at herself."

Tina shrugged, "Maybe she just doesn't care that we know what she did."

"Then why not just hand herself in?"

"I don't know," Tina admitted. "Maybe that's not part of the plan. Or maybe she hasn't quite finished what she started."

JP stared. "You mean Lorcan O'Keeffe, don't you."

Tina didn't answer, they both knew it had not been intended as a question.

*

***

I played no part in the abduction of Lorcan O'Keeffe. I left that to Paul and Ant.

But I won't pretend I didn't take pleasure in the thought of him under lock and key in that big old barn. Paul assured me it was soundproofed and securely padlocked from the outside. He also paid Lorcan a visit every evening to check that all was well, masked of course and wearing gloves so as to leave no traces of himself. Afterwards he would call me with an update. At first, he reported, our captive had displayed only outrage, fury even, but that changed quickly enough when he laid eyes on the set-up, Paul, acting under my instructions, had prepared at the barn. After his first night alone there, Lorcan began to beg. It pleased me to hear that. I also liked the thought of him all alone in that place, gazing in dread at what was suspended above his head, at the contraption to which it was attached. I liked to imagine him fretting and sweating and fearing what might be to come. I amused myself by doing a little research on the psychology of imprisonment. Like most psychological traumas, this moves in stages – disbelief, emotional alienation through to acceptance. There would be an attempt to rationalise - to impose routine in an attempt to create some version of normality. Good luck with that in a space lit by one single naked bulb, with bare brick walls and stone floors, no heating and boarded up windows! Nowhere to go, even if you weren't bound to a chair. Nobody to talk to, even if your mouth wasn't gagged with masking tape. Paul was under strict instructions from me, never to utter a word during his daily visits, other than to make a single demand of Lorcan. Did Lorcan despair? I liked to think so, but I also like to think there was still some flicker of hope in his heart, yet to be damped. And most of all, I liked to think of him as some big trapped and terrified bird shitting itself in the anxiety to be free.

*

Three nights was all we had in the end, to let Lorcan suffer in his head before he suffered in deed. I wanted it to be longer, but once we found out that Ant had been picked up trying to board a ferry to leave the country, we realised we had to move sooner than planned. At least he had the wits to call Paul as soon as he spotted the guards heading his way. As with Paul and me, Ant had been working off a separate phone and had time to lose it before he was picked up for questioning. Paul rang me as soon as he heard from Ant, he was as certain as he could be that Ant would not lead the guards to Lorcan, but it was clear he wanted to bring things forward to be on the safe side. The suddenness of it took me by surprise. I had been working up to this day for what seemed liked forever, and now it had come, I felt unprepared, reluctant almost. I suppose that should have told me something about myself, something about the way my thoughts, at least on a subconscious level, were tending. Because it certainly wasn't on Lorcan O'Keeffe's account that I felt myself hesitating, and still I was thrown. I think that accounts for what I did in going to see Megan that day, instead of proceeding straight to the place where Lorcan was being held. It was taking a risk in going anywhere near one of the other women, and I knew it. But with my final confrontation with Lorcan now suddenly imminent, it was time to decide Megan's fate once and for all.

And so, I went and confronted Megan; Megan with her big vacant eyes and her seeming inability to make head or tail of what I was asking her. Does she, I still wonder, even understand the meaning of the word culpable? In any event, even as I was yelling at her to tell me exactly how much she knew of what had happened to Claire, I already knew I would not harm her. What was the point? Three people had died already, and it had done little if anything to appease the emptiness inside of me. There was only one way to fix that and that was by keeping my appointment with Lorcan O'Keeffe, then it really would be endgame. As I said before, I am not actually a monster. I mean, the day I planted the daffodils and yellow tulips on the grave of Claire's baby girl, I actually cried.

*

So, was I in any way moved at the sight of Lorcan's plight? I admit I was taken aback at the condition he was in. His hair was matted and slick from sweat, and his face showed two days' worth of beard growth. He was tied to the chair, bound about his waist; his hands and feet were also bound, and he was shoeless and sockless. He was dressed in the suit trousers and shirt he had been wearing when Paul and Ant picked him up, after the gym. If there had been a jacket and tie, these were gone now and everything else was rumpled and stained with dust and dirt. There was blood on his shirt too, his face was bruised, and he had one black eye. When he first saw me, I actually think he believed I was there to help him. Being gagged, he could not actually call out to me, but his eyes lit up and he began making muffled, guttural sounds. He writhed about on the chair and the muscles of his face twitched while his shoulders and legs jerked as though he were in spasm. I approached him, glancing back at Paul who was leaning against the barn door, arms folded, eyes on Lorcan. This, he knew, was the time for me to play my part. Paul had initially been taken aback when I first told him what I wanted him to arrange for me in that barn. But again, he had no idea of my true intentions and quickly warmed to the idea. "If that doesn't make the bastard confess, nothing will," he agreed, grimly.

He hadn't quite understood my insistence on the amount of equipment I had demanded.

"It's not like you're actually going to go through with it," he had argued. "So, all you really need is the..."

"I need it all, Paul," I had insisted. "It has to look like we mean it, otherwise it just won't work. He has to be scared out of his wits, that's the whole point, otherwise he won't do what we need him to do."

And Paul had seen the sense of what I was saying and all the equipment I had specified was here now and in place. Up closer the stink emanating from Lorcan disgusted me, and I was close enough to reach out and touch him. Instead, I glanced back at Paul.

"Has he agreed to sign it yet?" In fact, I knew that Lorcan had agreed two days ago to sign whatever confession Paul asked him to.

"So, he says," Paul replied tersely. Lorcan began nodding his head madly in a show of acquiescence.

"Good, then let's get this over with." I reached out a hand, took a hold of the tape that had been used to gag Lorcan and tugged. It came away with a ripping sound and Lorcan let out a sort of yelp, then began gasping as though he might never get enough air into his lungs again. When he finally did speak, it was to say my name, pleadingly.

"Anna, Anna please! Get me out of here!"

"You're going nowhere until you write down what I tell you to, word for word, then sign it." I told him. "Do you understand that?"

"Yes, I understand, yes, yes!" Lorcan's tone was frantic. "Anything. Just tell me what to write. Anything, anything!"

I nodded to Paul, who unfolded his arms and came and stood next to me, his eyes through the mask, fixed on Lorcan. "You sure you trust this bastard to do as he says?" he asked me.

"Jesus Christ, Anna, I swear I will," Lorcan bleated. "I swear on my life. I'll do it right now, this minute. Just tell me what and I'll do it."

"Untie his hands so he can write, please" I told Paul, and he reached into the pocket of his jacket and pulled out a Stanley knife. When he went to stand behind him, Lorcan began straining to see what Paul was doing back there. His hands free, he brought them down stiffly onto his knees, grimaced with pain as tried to work the fingers. Back at my side, Paul warned him, "One false move mate!"

I pulled out the pen and pad I'd brought with me in my bag. "Can you hold the pen, or do you need a minute?" I asked Lorcan.

"I think I'm OK." He took the pen, and I placed the open pad on his knees.

"Write exactly what I say. Do you understand?"

Lorcan nodded, "I understand."

"And I don't want any questions or excuses, do you understand that too? You just write what I tell you to, OK?"

"Yes, I understand, I'll write it exactly as you say."

"OK, then let's begin." I began dictating. "This is the sworn confession of Lorcan O'Keeffe…"

*

It took him forever to write, his hands had clearly cramped from being bound so tightly. And twice the pen paused and hovered over the paper at the words I was putting on the page in his name. But he didn't protest and at last it was done. I took the paper and pad from him and returned them to my bag.

"Please may I go now," said Lorcan, sounding for all the world like a polite, but tired little boy.

By way of reply, I motioned to Paul, who slipped back behind the chair, grabbed Lorcan by the elbows, pulled his hands behind his back once more and rebound them. Lorcan let out a howl of protest.

"No! No! This isn't right," he yelled, as he tried and failed to escape Paul's grip. "You promised you'd let me go if I wrote what you said. I wrote it, I fucking wrote it! You can't do this to me, it isn't fair. You promised, you promised..."

"Shut up!" Paul commanded, and as Lorcan continued to wrestle, hit him a blow across the back of the head. The yells became whimpers. "But you promised, you promised you'd set me free. I did what you said, and you promised..."

"You'll be set free when we've left," I said. "Someone will come and release you."

Turning to Paul, I said, "You can go now, thanks. I need five minutes alone with him."

Paul looked at me and frowned, "You sure you want to do that?"

"I'm positive. Five minutes and I'll be out of here too."

It was clear Paul was very reluctant to leave me there alone with Lorcan, but I brooked no arguments and minutes later we heard the sound of a car driving away. Instantly I saw a change in Lorcan. His body visibly relaxed and some of the tension drained from his face.

"Jesus Christ Anna, I thought he was going to...."

"Shut your mouth," I ordered.

Lorcan obeyed instantly and his eyes followed me as I crossed to the double doors and opened them wide. "Where are you going?" he called after me as I went outside.

I didn't answer. I crossed the yard to where I had left the range rover, on loan from Paul. Once inside the car, I took the notepad from my bag, tore off the page on which Lorcan had written, folded it in half and shoved it in my pocket. Then started the engine and drove it up to the open barn doorway and eased it carefully inside, stopping when I was satisfied, I had reached the perfect spot. I got out and began doing the necessary.

Lorcan watched my every move and I saw puzzlement replaced by dawning suspicion and, finally, terror as the penny finally dropped. But it wasn't until I came close once more, and reached for the noose dangling above his head, that he began to tremble and wail.

"Anna, for God's sake, what are you doing?! Anna no! Jesus Christ no. I didn't do it, I swear I didn't do it. You got this all wrong. I swear to ..."

My hand still on the rope, I paused and met his terrified eyes. "What?" I faked surprise. "Did you just tell me I got this wrong?"

"You did. I swear on my life you did. I swear..."

"No, but hang on a second," I interrupted his grovelling. I pulled the sheet of notepaper from my pocket, unfolded it and pretended to read it, then shook my head regretfully. "Nope. I'm afraid that just won't wash. Because look here."

I turned the sheet round so he could see his own handwriting. "Can you see what it reads? Here let me help you – it reads - I Lorcan O'Keeffe..."

"I know, but you made me write it, you made me," Lorcan was sobbing now. "But I didn't know, I didn't know..."

"You didn't know it was what?" I cut across him. "You didn't know it was Claire, is that what you're trying to say? You raped my twin sister, but only because you thought it was me? So that's alright, is it? You piece of filth!"

I told him then, above the blubbering and the sobbing and the begging. I told him how Claire had suffered. I told him how she had given birth, all alone in a dark and filthy ruin in the middle of the night. I told him how his child had died, and what that had done to Claire.

"You've wanted a child, haven't you Lorcan," I ended. "You and the lovely Paula? I know all about it, all that effort, the money, all that hope, only to have it crushed over and over again. And all the time your child was lying in a grave for unwanted babies".

I told him then how Claire had judged herself, found herself guilty and about the penalty she had demanded of herself. And finally, I told him about her awful, lonely death.

"And now it's only fitting," I finished. "It's only fitting that you should pay the same penalty. Don't you think that's only fair, Lorcan?"

He was still wailing and begging and pleading as I slipped the noose over his head.

*

I have been writing this on the train to Belfast. Well, I didn't have time to grab a book and I always like something interesting to read when I travel. In spite of knowing they are possibly looking for me by now, it is good to be out and about again. I have not been back to my apartment since the day Lorcan was abducted and the guest house where I've been staying was comfortable enough but a bit pokey. I left my car behind too, it seemed safer to take the train, so it feels as though all the things that make me who I am, are no longer mine. Even my appearance. Every now and then I look up from my new laptop and catch my reflection in the window of the train. I quite like my jet-black bob. It's just a wig, but it makes me think I might cut my own hair, ring the changes a bit now that I am in this new unchartered phase of my life. When they go to my home, they will find the envelope containing copies of Claire's letter and testimonial. These will of course link me to the four deaths. That should be immaterial now. When I made up my mind to do this, see it through to the very end, I accepted, or at least I thought I had accepted that in signing the death warrants of Nicole, Bethany, Jennifer and Lorcan, I was also signing my own. It seemed only fair and fitting and at the time I imagined the sacrifice would cost me little.

After all, with what I was about to do, and the reason I was doing it, what was there for me to live for? And yet, now it comes to it, I find it is not such a little thing after all, to give up willingly on life. I don't regret any of what I did, and the truth is, it has not dulled my taste for life. Besides, if I had really intended to take my own life, why would I have moved money about as I have recently, as well as loading it on a series of pre-paid credit cards?

The thing is, I keep thinking about that prayer Claire and I used to say at bedtime. And how Claire so anxiously demanded reassurance that, were she to die in the night, I would die with her. And I realise that nothing has really changed. Yes, Claire died, and I wish that were not so. But why should that mean that I must die too? And would Claire want that – anymore than she would have wanted me to take revenge, even on Lorcan? And even if I could convince myself otherwise, I am not one of those people who believe the dead know or care what is done in their name. No, the dead have no address and no expectations. Then again, who is to say what Claire would or would not have wanted? When she sat down to write that testimonial, which clearly, she intended for my eyes alone, was her motive really so pure and simple as flowers for her baby's grave? Isn't it conceivable, that on some level, conscious or unconscious, she wanted, needed even, for me to know how absolutely I had, however unintentionally, destroyed her life? But perhaps I am simply incapable of understanding such purity, such simplicity of motive. Perhaps I actually have always been a bitch after all.

***

CHAPTER 44

Friday 24th March

The desk sergeant took the call and as requested, passed on the message to Tina. She was off duty and at home at the time, sipping coffee and thinking about Anna Fox, wondering as she did at least ten times every day, where the woman was. They were fairly certain Anna had travelled to Scotland on the Larne/Stranraer ferry. After that – nothing so far. Immediately she got the call, Tina gave instructions that SOCO, the State Pathologist's office and Coleman, in that order, be informed. As soon as she hung up, she called JP, the call went to voicemail and Tina left a message.

"JP. I think we've found him. I'm on my way. Meet me at this address."

She gave him the details and rang off. The location was a barn, part of an old and abandoned farmstead in rural Garristown. They found the body seated in a metal chair suspended from a rope which was still swinging slightly. The state of the body combined with the smell of excrement and sweat and the reek of terror that still hung about the place, almost made Tina retch. She did not need the State Pathologist to tell her that Lorcan O'Keeffe had not died by his own hand. He had been bound to the chair, the noose put about his neck, then strung up with aid of a winch and pulley. With the aid of a vehicle, by the look of the track marks leading to the barn door and discernible in the dust covered barn floor. The note was in his trouser pocket. It was short and to the point.

This is the confession of Lorcan O'Keeffe of The Lodge, Woodview Crescent, Killiney, County Dublin. I, Lorcan O'Keeffe confess to the attempted rape of Anna Fox, on a date in January 1996. I, Lorcan O'Keeffe confess to raping Claire Fox at a lake near Roundwood, County Wicklow on the 13th of April 1996. I, Lorcan O'Keeffe confess to raping Orla Reid at her home in Santry, County Dublin, on 7th August 2013. I make this confession freely and by my own will.

Signed this 11th day of March 2017 Lorcan O'Keeffe

Freely and by my own will, thought Tina grimly, but a small part of her could not help but be glad for Orla. When her phone rang, she assumed it was JP, instead it was the Gannett.

"Tina?"

"Yeah, what's up? I'm out here at the scene of the…"

He cut across her. "I know Tina, but I thought you should know. It's JP. He's been in an accident, on the bike. I'm sorry, he's in critical care."

*

"His family want to be alone with him for now," the nurse with the blackcurrant eyes was kind but firm.

"Of course," said Tina, "I understand."

She had driven to the hospital, siren screaming and blue light flashing. Her hands on the steering wheel trembled. She had not even considered the possibility that she would not be permitted to see him. The nurse's words took the adrenalin fuelled wind from her sails and she walked away slowly, unsure what to do with herself.

Outside on the hospital steps, she stood for a moment and drew in a deep breath. It was, she thought, one of those diamond spring days she loved best, brilliant and bright and so sharp it seemed it might cut you in half. A perfect day too, for passing off the glitter of tears as nothing more than the sun in your eyes. She thought about going back to the office, but how to face the normality of it all, the hum of the computers, the whirr of the printers, phones ringing, the clack of keyboards, people being kind to her? She dug about in her jacket pocket in the vain hope of finding a hanky there. Her fingers closed on something soft. She pulled it out and stared at the cotton square. It was scrunched up and stained and Tina suddenly remembered where it had come from.

It was the handkerchief JP had given her to clean her muddy boots the day they had gone to inspect Anna Fox's car. She brought it to her face, not to dry her eyes with, but because it had been his and perhaps something of the scent of him might still be on it. She had told the nurse that she understood, and she did. She understood that she had no place at JP's bedside right now, while he fought for his life. She understood that the fact they had drank lukewarm, muddy coffee from the same Thermos on countless cold nights of fruitless surveillance, meant damn all now. Nor did the fact that he had entrusted her with the spare key to his home.

And suddenly realisation struck – the cat – the damn cat. She remembered the promise she had made. They had been called to what might have been a suspicious death but turned out to be accidental. An elderly man living alone with his dog, had fallen down the stairs and broken his neck. His dog had been found next to the body, emaciated from near starvation, in such a state that it was clear the unfortunate creature would have to be put down and out its suffering. JP had said afterwards, as they drove away, "If anything were ever to happen to me, I want you to have Mrs C."

Tina had laughed out loud, "What? No bleedin' chance. Give her to your mother."

"I can't. My mother is allergic to cats."

"Well give her to someone else, then. I hate cats,"

"No, you don't hate them…"

"Well, maybe I don't actually hate them. But I don't want one."

JP had turned to her then, no trace of humour in his face or voice. “But for me, you’d make an exception for Mrs C, right? It will make me feel easier if you’d promise. You know just in case anything ever happened to me.”

And looking at him, she had known that he was absolutely in earnest. So, she’d pulled a face, as she agreed lightly, “OK, fine, I’d make an exception for Mrs C.”

“You promise? If anything happens to me, you go get her from my place, I’m giving you my spare key.”

And Tina, never for a single moment thinking it would ever come to that, had agreed. “Yes, I promise! But you’re going nowhere, so shut up now, you morbid big girl’s blouse.”

And now there was no getting away from that promise. Back in her car, Tina punched the steering wheel so hard it hurt her fists and yelled at the windscreen.

"Me and my damn promises."

*

Mrs C was asleep in an armchair. She opened one eye as Tina approached, stretched out a paw and yawned, showing impressive fangs, then got to her feet, turned in a circle, curled up once more and went back to sleep. Tina left her and went to the kitchen. The food and water bowls were on the floor next to the fridge. She picked them up, tipped the remaining food into the waste bin, rinsed them at the sink, found a Tesco bag-for-life in a drawer and put the bowls inside. The paper sack of dried cat food was in the utility room, as was the cat-carrier, exactly where JP had said they would be. Tina put the food in with the bowls, picked up the cat carrier and went back to the living room.

“Come on Mrs C,” she told the still sleeping cat. “Time to go on your holliers to sunny Raheny. Bit of a step down I know, but you’ll see, it won’t be for long.”

Even as she said it, she wondered who she was trying to reassure, herself or the cat. It took her almost twenty minutes to get Mrs C into the carrier and she came out of the exercise with an angry red scratch on the back of one hand. By the time cat and cat accoutrements were safely in the car, she was sweating like a menopausal hog. Mrs C wailed loudly all the way to Tina's apartment and once released from bondage, leapt onto the windowsill of the tiny living room, sat with her back to Tina, swishing her bushy tail furiously and proceeded yowling once again. Tina had just made the decision to ignore it for a while in the hope that the creature would settle when her mobile rang. She pounced on it, heard the fearful tone of her own voice as she breathed hello.

"Hello," the woman's voice was softly spoken, a little shaky.

"Am I speaking to Detective Sergeant Martina Bassett?"

"You are, who is this?"

"This is Helen O'Rourke."

"Helen O'Rourke...?"

"Yes. I'm JP's mother. I thought I should call you to let you know what's happening. One of the nurses said you'd been to the hospital, I'm so sorry we missed you, Tina. You don't mind if I call you Tina, do you? It's how JP always refers to you."

"No, no, of course. It's Tina, I'm Tina, I mean...," She knew she was babbling. It was the surprise, the surprise and fear.

"JP - is he...please tell me he's.... please tell me how he is?"

*

When she had rang off, Tina turned and addressed herself to the cat's back.

"Listen here, you fat moggy, I don't speak Cat, but I understand you're not happy about the present arrangement."

As though in agreement, the cat on the windowsill, let out a yowl.

"Exactly," said Tina. "You don't want me, you want JP, which for your information, is about the only thing we're agreed on. But it is what it is, and right now we're stuck with one another. So how about we make things easier for both of us and try to get along? What do you say? Let's just try to get along together until JP comes home. Because he will. He's not out of the woods yet, not by a long stretch, but he'll get there, and he'll come home. So, what do you say to that, Mrs C?"

But Mrs C had nothing to say. And in the end, Tina took out her laptop, searched YouTube and, in the hope that it might in some small way comfort them both, played Rory Gallagher's *A Million Miles Away*

*

EPILOGUE

Anna steps out of the water, drives her brown toes into the sliders she has left at the pool's edge. She pads across to the shower, where she lets the cool water trickle over her body. Stepping out again, she runs her hands over her face, through her short, dyed red hair, squeezing gently. Crossing the deck, she makes her way to where the loungers are set back from the water beneath waving palm trees and parasols. In the time it takes to walk that far, the water has dried on her skin. She puts on her sunglasses, a wide-brimmed straw hat, adjusts the lounger to the desired angle. As soon as she stretches out, a waiter appears at her side, the pre-ordered cocktail balanced on a silver tray. She reaches for the glass, feels the chill of its stem against her fingers. She murmurs her thanks, he smiles showing dazzling teeth, his dark-eyed gaze slides toward her breasts. She turns her head, looks straight ahead, raises the sugared rim to her lips, all she can taste is the cold.

Suddenly everything meshes, blurs – the white of the retreating waiter's shirt, the impossible blue of the sky, the mirrored dazzle of the ocean, the distant purple mountains. She feels a sensation of hollowness at her core. And in spite of the warm soft air on her skin; Anna shivers in the sun.

***

ABOUT THE AUTHOR

Maria Hoey, a poet and author, from Dublin, Ireland, has been writing since she was eight years old. Her debut novel, The Last Lost Girl, was published by Poolbeg Press, and shortlisted for the Kate O'Brien Debut Award 2018. Maria's second novel, On Bone Bridge was also published by Poolbeg Press.

Maria, who has one daughter, Rebecca, now lives in the beautiful lakeside village of Keshcarrigan, County Leitrim, with her husband, Garrett, their moustachioed cat, Tatty, and their dog, Jack.

Printed in Great Britain
by Amazon